D0800815

GENEALOGY

A NOVEL

MAE WOOD

ATACAMA BOOKS

This is a work of fiction. Any names or characters, businesses or places, events or incidents, are fictitious or used fictitiously.

ISBN (paperback) 978-0-9862886-9-2

Copyright © 2018 by Mae Wood
All rights reserved. This book or any portion thereof
may not be reproduced or used in any manner whatsoever
without the express written permission of the publisher
except for the use of brief quotations in a book review.
Contact Mae@MaeWood.com

Edited by Julia Ganis
Proofread by Proofing with Style/ Marla Esposito
Cover design by RBA Designs/ Letitia Hasser

DEDICATION

To my own Alice and her daughters

ONE

ALI

P*resent day - August*

SHE DIDN'T WANT to move, and I didn't want her to move either. But we were doing it, together. Sifting and sorting. Shredding and donating. Culling a lifetime into piles to be packed and placed into boxes. The lucky things would end up in my grandmother's new six-hundred-twenty-three square foot assisted-living apartment. The not-so-lucky would end up on a curb.

"These linens," she said, pointing to the bottom drawer of the sideboard in her formal dining room. "You need them."

"Grammie, I don't even have a dining room table," I said, trucking along in our project to conquer the contents of at least one room this weekend.

"You had one before and you'll have one again. And these are Irish linen."

I thought of my tiny kitchen table, covered in discarded mail and unread magazines, not draped in substantial creamy white. She knew I didn't have the space. I *made* space for the vintage black satin peep-toe pumps of hers from the fifties and had placed those in the "Ali" pile with a smile, but linens were a different story. The tablecloths were huge. For a table big enough to seat a dozen guests.

"They were Alice's," she said.

The trump card played, I bent and pulled them from the low drawer. I was Alice's namesake, but I'd always gone by Ali because Alice felt formal and traditional, two words that didn't fit me. She was the great-grandmother who I'd never met, who died a decade before I was born, but whose existence was never far from my mind. "Ali. A-L-I," I'd explained a million times over my life. "It's short for Alice. I'm named for my great-grandmother."

"Well, one good thing is that your monograms match."

I fingered the tiny beverage napkins, trimmed in hand-tatted lace and embroidered with *ALW*.

ALW—I smiled. Alice Lenore Wertheimer. Alice Lenora Waller. I was flirting with becoming Alice Waller Sayer, but I was solidly myself at the moment.

"Did she embroider these?" I asked, the old fabric stiff and smooth to the touch.

"I don't know. I don't remember my mother doing any needlework, but I suppose all women did back then."

"True," I said, flattening out the material with my palm and tugging out a crease. I dragged yet another plastic bin over and began piling the linens in, amazed that they had survived the years.

"The story on one of those tablecloths is that it was a wedding present from some member of the Denny family."

Ah, an old Seattle story. I knew it wasn't going to be long before I got one. My ancestors were early settlers of the city and my grandmother carried the banner of native Seattleite proudly, looking down her pioneer nose at the Microsofties and the Californians who had invaded her precious land. And though she'd moved to Kansas City with my grandfather nearly fifty years ago, the city was in her DNA.

I half-listened to her prattle on about some trip to Japan to obtain plants and animals for the Woodland Park Zoo as I examined the linens and placed them in the plastic storage tub.

"Okay," I said, looking around the room, the sideboard now empty. Something accomplished today, and it made me feel good to have one of the many small tasks that it would take to empty her house of nearly fifty years. I looked at my watch. "I have to leave at three to head back to the hospital, so what can we get done in an hour?"

"One drawer to go," she said from the dining chair where she'd settled in while I'd knelt in front of the sideboard. "The bottom one."

Her words made my chest ache but also soothed them. I hated that she was getting confused more often. It reminded me that one day Grammie would be gone, but it also convinced me that we were making the right decision to move her. No more worry about her alone in this big house.

"All done," I said, pointing to my tub of linens.

"The bottom-bottom one, Ali. The apron is a drawer."

"I didn't know that," I said, feeling sheepish that I'd thought she had been confused. "A secret drawer?"

"That's the point," she said. The sideboard had been in this house my entire life and I'd never known that. I tilted my head to look at the piece, not quite believing her. "It's where your grandpa kept his favorite pistol."

"Still there?" I said with a smile, reaching down under the lip of the cabinet.

"Well, maybe. It's been a long time since I dug around in that thing."

"I'm going to change your name to Mrs. Basil E. Frankweiler," I said, giving the concealed drawer a tug. It didn't budge. Maybe she was confused after all. "Or Mrs. Piggle-Wiggle. But only if we find a Degas or pirate gold."

"It was a statue of an angel. Leonardo da Vinci," she corrected me. In and out. Touch and go. Here and there. I was never sure where a conversation would lead us, and based upon the swelling in her extremities, I wasn't sure today was going to be a good day for coherent conversation. It wasn't her head so much as her heart that was slowly killing her by refusing to pump. She needed access to round the clock medical care now, not just sitters and family at the house, and we were making that happen although no one was happy about it.

"Oh, that's right," I replied, the memories flooding back of the story of a headstrong girl and her younger brother running away to the Met. "What I really remember about that book was them taking a bath in the fountain." My grandmother and I were very close. The afternoons of my childhood had been spent at her house with my brother and sister. And while my parents were at work, Grammie showered us with troves of books. She was a children's librarian. Or she had been until she'd gotten married. Because, as she'd explained a million times to me over the years, in those days nice women didn't work outside the home after they were married, and so she'd retreated to a life of children and tennis and dinner parties.

I gave the drawer another tug and it budged a few inches, but it didn't slide open.

"Oh, and the sideboard is yours too. No argument. It was—"

"Alice's?" I guessed as I wiggled the drawer open to find not pieces of eight or a sketch of a ballerina, but more table linens.

"No, her mother's. You'll be the fifth generation of women in our family to own it."

I looked at the dark, heavy Victorian behemoth with new eyes, knowing it was going home with me. And knowing I had nowhere in my tiny, Ikea-furnished apartment to put it, but I spoke the truth: "Thank you. I'll be a good caretaker."

"I know you will, sweet pea."

I looked down at the linens, focusing on the task rather than the meaning of the work I was doing, filling the plastic bin with more ancient fabric than I'd ever begin to use. Under the last tablecloth, I found a small, flat box. The pistol? I recognized the foil-stamped logo. Frederick & Nelson, the grand Seattle department store that now only existed on Grammie's bad days when she'd ask me or someone else to take her there for lunch.

"Grandpa's gun?" I asked, setting the box into my lap

as I sat on the floor. I lifted the lid. "Papers," I said, a little weary at the prospect of spending the last bit of time before I had to leave focused on her reading each paper carefully before deciding whether she could part with it.

My grandmother was a pack rat. I'd recently dropped off two decades of yellow-spined *National Geographic*s at the recycling center and her garage was still stuffed to the gills with boxes of papers. I'd had visions of a huge bonfire while she was at a doctor's appointment just to speed up the process.

The box resting in my cross-legged lap, I riffled through the contents. "Letters," I said, pulling one out. At least it wasn't receipts from the nineteen sixties, though the hospital bill from my mom's tonsillectomy at age eight had been a gem. The total bill was a few hundred dollars and Mom had spent three days in a children's ward. Most of my patients were sent home by the end of the day with a bill in the thousands.

The cream envelope was golden at the seams, the clean, cursive writing enchanting. I couldn't remember the last time I'd seen graceful, purposeful handwriting with a fountain pen and not just a hasty scrawl of ballpoint on a scratch pad.

Alice Hirshhorn, the letter's front proclaimed.

"Letters to Alice," I told Grammie, now curious. I examined the faded postmark and noticed the stamps were strange. "From the Philippines?" I guessed.

"I have those?" my grandmother said, her voice full of excitement and disbelief.

In answer I turned the envelope in my palm, slid the pages out and carefully unfolded the letter. *September 20,*

1915. My dearest Alice, the script greeted me. A love letter. A hundred-year-old love letter.

"Great-Grandpa was in the Philippines?" I asked, my eyes and brain straining to decipher the tight calligraphy.

"Oh no. Not your great-grandfather," Grammie said, her eyes sparkling with her mother's secrets. "Elliott."

"Who's Elliott?" I asked, my eyes scanning through the pages, trying to make sense of the fancy script. When was the last time I'd seen a handwritten letter? Something more than the note that my sister tucked in with her kid's drawings for me to put on my fridge. A six-page letter. With no scratched-out sections, even. Was this like a final draft? Did people do that back then? Write drafts of letters, work to get their words just right, and then write it out nicely on fancy stationery? Or did they think before they wrote? Either way, the whole concept of handwritten letters was foreign to me.

"Some man Alice knew. He wanted her to move to the Philippines with him, but that's all I know."

"What do you mean, that's all you know?"

"That's really all I know. I found the letters once when I was a girl. I started reading them and my mother found me, took the letters, and I don't remember seeing them again. I guess I kept them when she died, but that was so long ago that I don't quite remember."

"Forty-ish years ago," I said looking up at her. "I'm going to take them."

"Fine with me. But the dining room table goes with them."

There were seconds when I was thankful her memory was going and then I would spend hours, if not days, feeling awful for those moments. As I did the math on

7

how much a storage unit would cost me for the year or so we could hope she'd be with us floated through my brain, this was one of those times.

I set the letters with the linens and began straightening up before I made us a simple late lunch of sandwiches, and left. "Next time we'll dive into the china cabinet," I said as I grabbed my purse and work tote. "Mom will be back from Austin tomorrow. She's been down with Jess and her family. I'll be MIA all week with work, but we'll have dinner together."

"Sounds lovely, sweet pea," she said as we exchanged kisses to cheeks. "I'm so glad you moved home, Ali. I truly am."

"Me too," I said, but I didn't mean it.

ugust

ROUNDS at the hospital were about getting into the zone where I, Alice Lenora Waller, didn't exist, and some fictional Dr. Waller strode through the halls. I knew doctors had a bad rap when it came to ego and attitude. I was no different. And I definitely could have the attitude, but the ego that people claimed I had, that had fallen away six months ago.

After three months back in Kansas City, I was still getting the feel of the place even though I knew the hospital, with its surgical suites, cafeterias, and my clinic, like the back of my hand. But the parts of the city that hadn't been there when I was in high school? The parts that had changed in the years since I'd left for college? So many restaurants, faces, and names that were all new to me.

Except for a smattering of high school friends, only a few who I'd kept in close contact with over the years, the city was entirely familiar yet new to me.

I was a blue-scrubbed, white-coated doctor who lived just south of the downtown medical district among the other blue-scrubbed, white-coated doctors, the blue-scrubbed, short-coated medical students, not to mention the brightly scrubbed nurses and other medical staff. It was a far cry from the lily-white suburb I'd grown up in, but still felt provincial after my time in DC and Boston.

Most mornings I walked to work. It was hot and humid and I nearly regretted it, but it was less than a mile and I liked the time to clear my head.

Because as much as I refused to admit it, sometimes I still woke up in Boston with Scott warm in the bed next to me, skin to skin but for the slip of a silk gown I liked to sleep in. And it took me rolling over to smack my phone's alarm or my pager and finding myself alone to remember that he wasn't here. That he wasn't on call. That he was in California, where I was supposed to have been.

Home again, home again, jiggity jig.

My hair in a tight braid, the tail end pinned under, I slung my black messenger bag across my body. I trudged to the hospital, nabbing a to-go box of random breakfast items that would go cold as I picked at my meal but devoured the files in front of me.

I had two surgery days a week. Clinics three days a week and an erratic on-call schedule that was grueling. Lowest man—or woman—on the group's totem pole meant that I covered holidays and got exactly one three-day weekend a month completely off the calendar. I wouldn't change a thing about it except the location.

The practice itself was what I'd wanted, and I shunted the thoughts of sunny beaches and a sexy orthopod off to the side of my thoughts as best as I could. Because when I began thinking about that life that I didn't have, that life I'd anticipated, I could only catalogue my faults and failings. The first being every minutia that distinguished me from Thad Graves, the guy from Chicago who had landed the spot—*my* spot—as the cochlear implant specialist at UC Irvine.

I didn't get the job, and the life that I'd planned around it disappeared. Having life's first big failure at thirty-three wasn't the worst thing that could happen to a person, but I wasn't used to any failure and it made me feel awful.

I'd decided to lick my wounds at home while I decided on my next move. Now I was stuck in limbo, filling in for a surgeon in Kansas City who was taking a sabbatical, and spending my free time looking for a permanent position.

Home again, home again, jiggety jog.

At my desk, I washed down a bite of gummy oatmeal with cold coffee and scrolled through the file on my laptop. Seventeen-month-old male. Bilateral profound deafness since birth. Two weeks post-op. And today was the payoff.

I was a computer science major in college, and during medical school I'd developed an interest in cochlear implants because the technology fascinated me. But when, during my internship, I was in the room when a baby turned his head at his mother's voice for the first time in his life, and I saw his eyes light up in excitement and his parents break down in sobbing joy, I was hooked.

The capacity to change lives. The ability to give someone the perception of sound. No other medicine did that—offered something so fundamental to the human condition. No one created vision. No one transplanted the olfactory system or supplemented the sense of taste. No one could make a patient feel again. But we could make a patient hear. And I knew the detractors, the people who thought I was personally involved in some sort of attack on the deaf community. And I didn't buy what they were selling. Because today Jackson Ursini's life was going to change. That I was sure of.

I dumped the remains of my breakfast into the trash bin and went to greet him and his parents. I didn't regularly go to mappings, but Jackson was special. He was my first patient—from consult through procedure—that I'd cared for at this hospital. I wanted to be there for him, for his parents, but mostly for myself. Because this was going to go right. I was determined it was.

When I entered the room, Jackson was perched in his mom's lap with a pacifier in his mouth, connected by a lead to the computer that Stacey, the audiologist, controlled.

"Jackson," his mom said, her voice quavering, looking from her son to me with worry on her face.

"You're not going to break him. Call to him," I encouraged her.

"Back on now," said Stacey.

Stronger, Mrs. Ursini spoke. "Jackson?"

Jackson kept sucking on his pacifier.

"Again," Stacey instructed.

"Jack, Jack." A big, hopeful smile spread on her face, not quite reaching her eyes, which were filling with worry. "Jackson?"

Still no response. My anxiety was beginning to rise.

Because this was all a gamble. A gamble by the parents to put their baby through surgery, taking the risk that he'd make it through the procedure and that this contraption that we installed and calibrated would work. There were no guarantees. No promises. Only science, and chance, and guts.

Stacey tinkered on the computer and I walked over to stand behind her shoulder to look at what was happening. "Yeah," I said softly, agreeing with her as she increased the threshold.

"Again," said Stacey.

"Jackson. Jackson." Mrs. Ursini jostled him on her knees. "Jackson, Jackson, Jackson," she kept calling.

Jackson's eyes grew big and his head began to swivel. Seventeen months of silence broken by his mother's voice.

There was no need for Stacey's encouragement anymore.

"Jackson, oh. Jackson, I love you, I love you, Jackson. I love you." The words rushed out of his mother's smiling mouth as tears streamed down her cheeks.

Jackson's confusion intensified and that was normal. He was plunged into a world of sound, a world he didn't know existed. And as much as I'd like to say it was like a schmaltzy movie and he would look at his mom and smile sweetly and coo at her, the odds were that wasn't going to happen. In fact, some would cry. Some would become agitated and scared. But it was all magic. Getting his brain to process sound was my gig. And we'd done that. Now it was up to the engineers and audiologist and therapists to get him to understand sound and language. I quietly slipped out of the room, wanting to let Stacey do her thing and the Ursini family to have this time.

The rest of the afternoon was filled with two pediatric consults, reams of reporting to complete, and after yet another dinner at my favorite of the hospital's cafeterias, I walked home through the darkness to my apartment.

∼

I WOKE up the next day not to my pager or the alarm on my cell, but to an actual phone call. Only a half dozen people could get through my do not disturb setting and I'd answer every one of those calls in a heartbeat.

"Good morning, Grammie," I said, rolling to my back and holding the phone to my ear in the darkness.

"Ali. I've sent the men with the dining room table, the chairs, and the sideboard to your apartment."

"Grammie," I began, wanting to tell her that she hadn't told me about a delivery, but knowing that she didn't need the grief. No harm had been done, except my interrupted sleep. And interrupted sleep? I made it through a residency and a fellowship. I didn't know what uninterrupted sleep was.

"They say you won't answer your door."

I wrenched my phone away from my ear and looked at the screen. Sure enough. Four missed calls. *Perhaps I should also set my door buzzer to ring through.* I smirked.

"Thanks, Grammie. I'll let them in."

I buzzed in the delivery guys and looked around my apartment, trying to figure out where to put the sideboard. Shoving around a few unopened boxes from my move, whose contents were a complete mystery to me, I made some space in the living room. I could put my TV on top of it, I decided.

Soon enough two well-built men left with my Ikea TV stand and kitchen table as a part of their tip, and I was the proud owner of a sideboard and a long mahogany dining table. For all of my formal dinner party needs.

A text from Scott beeped through on my phone, pulling me from my daydream of a table full of friends laughing over cartons of Chinese delivery. He was asking if I was around. And for once, the stars aligned. I didn't even bother texting back. I called him.

"Hey," he exhaled. Even in a single word, I felt his exhaustion.

"Long day?" I asked, giving him the opening to dump his troubles on me.

"And an awful one. Three hours into a total hip and the patient coded."

And the specter that haunts every surgeon raised its head. No one wants a patient to die on the table. Early in my residency, I'd been pulling a gallbladder and the patient went into cardiac arrest. We'd stabilized her, but it remained the scariest moment of my life. Far scarier even than the ER rotation when you never knew what was coming, because in the ER, the patient arrived in distress that you hadn't caused and your goal was to stabilize. That moment with the gallbladder patient? I'd had a hand in that.

"That sucks."

"Yeah. It does. Just got done talking with the family. So, tell me something good. Anything good."

"Well, I'm now the proud owner of an antique dining

15

room suite. Grammie forced it on me and now it's taking up about half of my apartment. It's huge."

"Furniture? That's the best you can do?"

"I've got a long weekend coming up," I said, rushing to make him happy and soothe him. "So three days together in SoCal?"

"That sounds cool, if we can swing three days. Send me the dates and I'll run it against my schedule."

If we can swing it? I could definitely swing it. Even if he was on call and got stuck at the hospital, there wasn't a reason that I couldn't get in a few days of sunshine, we could enjoy a few meals together, even if just someplace quick, and I could sleep in a bed that smelled like him.

"Okay," I said, not wanting to fight with him right now. "I'll send you the dates. Let me know and I'll book flights."

"Cool. I'm being paged. Talk to you later. Love you."

"Love you," I replied, echoing his words and trying not to let his brusqueness bother me. He'd had one of the worst days a doctor can have and I shouldn't read anything into his distance. It'd been a hard few months on our relationship as we sorted out the long distance thing and I kept looking for a permanent position near him.

I sat down at my new-to-me dining room table, an antique chair creaking under my weight, and surveyed the delivery. I decided I should pack away the linens back into their home. Turning on a news podcast to keep me company, I started my task, unfolding and refolding the tablecloths, and embroidered napkins of all sizes, and there, on the bottom of the bin was the box of love letters. I set them aside until all the ancient linens were back in their sideboard home.

Switching off the podcast and warming up my coffee, I opened the Frederick & Nelson box of Alice's letters and wished I knew anything about archiving. I didn't want to ruin them, but I supposed they were now mine to ruin. I counted. Over three dozen letters. The postmarks and stamps were mainly from the Philippines, but some were from Japan and one was from Hong Kong. I organized them based upon postmark date as best I could. September 1915 through May 1918.

Nearly three years, and what was the story? Three years ago, my life looked very different. Scott and I met three years ago. Had moved in together about two years ago. Less than a year ago, we'd talked about getting married. Six months ago, we were California-bound. And now here I was in a one-bedroom apartment, five miles away from the house I'd grown up in, and alone except for my family and my high school best friend.

I opened the first letter and, struggling with the cursive, began to read.

Dear Alice,

North America is behind me, but you are at the forefront of my thoughts. We've just bid farewell to North America, as the Canadian coast slipped away. It's unseasonably cool and the water is rough. I was expecting bright blue skies and smooth seas, but that is not the case. Tea, regular small meals, and walks around the deck help keep the nausea away, but I ache nonetheless.

As much as regret gnaws at me, it won't hold me back. I move forward now with purpose. My purpose is to build a life for us. A life that I can eagerly and honestly ask you to join. I'd have asked if you'd be willing to join your life with mine as we wandered like lost sheep through the Seattle streets on my last night with you, and the idea was always on my mind, but I have little to offer but hope and hard work. That will not always be the case. I will write the vision and make it plain to you, dear Alice...

THREE

ELLIOTT

September 1915

THE SEA IS rough and the sky is gray, a proper metaphor for his state. He turns up the collar on his topcoat and crosses his arms, leaning back on the deck chair as Canada melts into the low clouds. It's too late to change this path. Not even his death would stop this steamer's passage to Japan. Body, it will carry him away from her. And his soul? Even if it is bound for some damnation, it is with her.

He is alone on the deck. The few other passengers who stood to bid farewell to dry land have departed indoors for tea or coffee or a bit of warmth. He knows he won't find any warmth for himself. The sun he left behind in Seattle, and the world is a horizon of endless sea.

How he should have said "come with me" or "marry

me" or any other combination of sounds that would have procured her presence on this steamer beside him.

But he didn't. Because five days isn't enough to be certain enough for a lifetime, is it? A mere week ago he walked into the observation end of a train, somewhere just west of Sandpoint, Idaho. He'd missed his planned train due to a washout on his way up from Utah, and after a delay of two days, had bought a ticket for the first available Pullman berth bound for Seattle. From Seattle, to Vancouver, and from Vancouver back to his home in the Philippine Islands. Well, his home for the past five years, and one that would surely have changed during his nine-month vacation back to the States. There was no doubt in his mind that even if the place hadn't changed, if his uncle's house stood with his bedroom intact, even if his social circle remained the same and he still spent his nights at the club, playing bridge, that he was changed. And he'd forever be different.

He'd caught her profile at first. She was lit from behind by afternoon sun streaming in from the plate-glass window. Her soft, dark hair folded gently into a knot at the base of her neck. The high collar of her long-sleeved white blouse tall against her graceful neck. And a pair of perfectly plump lips that curved in delight as she pulled a magazine down from the rack. He was transfixed, his own collar growing tight and his mouth growing dry. He watched her for a moment, his hands still clasped behind his back, as she settled into a club chair near another woman and devoted herself to her reading.

It would be rude to interrupt her. Even if he did, what possibly would be appropriate, what possibly could be proper for him to say? They were strangers. There was no one to make an introduction. So he waited and watched her out of the corner of his eye from his own club chair across the car while reading four-day-old news from a Chicago paper.

Did she have a companion? A chaperone? A husband? A friend? The world was wide and wild, that he knew, and the idea of her floating alone through it unsettled him. She looked comfortable and confident and completely at ease in the car that was filled with people reading, playing cards, and chatting as the train chugged westward.

He'd come home with the notion that he'd be bringing a wife with him on his return, but if that was ever truly a mission for his vacation, he had failed. Introductions had been made. Addresses exchanged and letters promised. But in this moment, he thanked Providence that his notion had been folly.

Her blue skirt flitted at her ankles as she resettled in a chair at a table, pulling out a journal and pencil. She immersed herself in sketching and he took the opportunity to fully examine her. She wasn't tall or short. Or memorably thin or thick. There was a languidness about her posture. She was in her head, in her drawing, and no longer in this observation car and no longer even in this world. He knew that place. It was the place he visited so regularly that he didn't need a map.

He watched her work, her hand fluidly moving about the page. There was no band on any finger. No signifier that she belonged to anyone. He almost would have preferred to see a narrow ring of gold. To know that she had a husband watching out for her, protecting her.

An itch to see what she was sketching crept upon him, nearly overtaking all propriety. A vase of flowers? A

Western landscape? Perhaps something like Remington, cowfolk in action? Or something stylized and modern like the cover of the magazine that sat on the table next to her? What did those hands feel like? Were they as soft as silk? Did the sides of her fingers have small calluses, developed from hours of drawing? Were the focused eyes brown or green?

He was too distracted to even pretend to continue reading the days-old news. He set his unfinished paper to the side and walked toward the outdoor observation platform, slowing his gait to a near standstill when he passed her. But no luck. She hadn't looked up and silently invited him to say hello. The train lumbered into a turn and he wobbled, his arms flinging wide to stay himself. His right palm landed on a tabletop with a smack. He looked down and found his hand only a few inches from hers. Her arm was outstretched and one of her pencils was clutched in her fist. His eyes shot to her face and startled blue eyes landed on his. Blue. One mystery solved.

"Pardon me," he said to her, righting himself. He forced himself to step away from her. Two more steps and he wrenched the door to the platform open. That breath of fresh air was sorely needed.

When he returned from the observation platform, she was gone. Through his evening meal, he chatted pleasantly with his assigned tablemates in the dining car, but she never materialized. Perhaps his mind created her. She was a vision, after all.

Following a game of bridge in the parlor car with his dinner companions, he trundled down the length of the train a bit tipsy. When he located the number of his Pullman berth, he drew back the heavy curtain. And there she was. Wrapped in a white nightgown with wisps of frothy lace cupping her chin. An open book clutched in her hands, the electric reading light shining down over her shoulder. Once again, the big blue eyes.

"Oh, excuse me," he said, snapping the curtain closed. He examined his ticket. *46*. He looked at the placard by the berth into which he'd just intruded, concerned that the gin may have dulled his faculties. But no, it still read *46*. Rather than linger on the other side of his—no, her berth—no, it *was* his berth, one he'd waited two days in Idaho to procure—he returned to the parlor car and located a porter, who located the Pullman conductor, who inspected his ticket as he explained the situation.

After being set straight that the gin had in fact impeded his ability to distinguish a six from an eight, he was directed to a neighboring berth numbered forty-eight. With the aid of the porter holding the curtain to his berth into the aisle to provide him room, he changed out of his suit and into his pajamas. Bidding the porter goodnight, he switched on his own electric light with the idea of sinking into the biography in his valise, but found his mind filled with thoughts of that moment that didn't happen. Of his stuttered apology and quick snap of the drape. Of the woman who was a stranger to him, resting in her own narrow bed just feet away. He removed his glasses, placing them safely on the window ledge, switched off the light, curled onto his side, and waited for sleep to take him.

Now on the deck of the ship, Elliott recrosses his arms against the cold. Pacing, as the ship continues to carry him away from her, he accepts that he cannot change the decisions he has made. The decisions that brought him to this moment, being ferried away from Alice. He steps inside, locates a porter, hands over his topcoat, and requests a cup of hot tea and stationery. Settling in at a table, he withdraws his black lacquered fountain pen from his interior jacket pocket and rolls it through his fingers. Words opened the world to him before, and now they will tether him to her across the vast Pacific.

The porter deposits a teapot in front of him, locking it to the table with a small brass arm. The teacup and saucer appear. In deference to him and the other first class passengers, the teacup sports a delicate handle. Soon a sheaf of letterhead arrives on the tabletop.

Nippon Yusen Kaisha, S.S. Sado Maru proclaims the top of each page. The creamy, empty vastness humbles him. His eagerness of a few moments ago, his confidence that his words would bind him to Alice and Alice to him, falters as the reality of their situation intrudes.

It will be two weeks until he can post these letters to Alice. And then two weeks at best until she receives them. It will be nearly November by then. She will be teaching her students each day and reading and painting and drawing each evening. He does the math in reverse. Even if she writes to him, it may be six weeks until her first letter could possibly make it to Iloilo. It could be as long as two months. And what of the five days they spent together? How real was any of it?

He continues to roll the pen between his fingers, formulating a new plan because the plan has now changed. He's certain of that. The plan was for him to vacation, potentially return with a wife, and assume operations of the family business so that his uncle could take his own trip back to America. His uncle is set to depart after the New Year and will be gone for over a year, seeing family and lobbying for investments to expand their business. Accounting for the incalculable variances of life, including those strange happenings that resulted in his path crossing hers, of the unknowns of travel and of time transitioning the business back to his uncle's purview, he figures for another few months. May 1917. That's the earliest he can return to Seattle. Almost twenty months. By the time he reaches his uncle's house, it will only be eighteen months.

And he will chip away at that time. Word by word.

He uncaps his pen and writes.

DEAR ALICE,

North America is behind me, but you are at the forefront of my thoughts. We've just bid farewell to North America, as the Canadian coast slipped away. It's unseasonably cool and the water is rough. I was expecting bright blue skies and smooth seas, but that is not the case. Tea, regular small meals, and walks around the deck help keep the nausea at bay, but I ache nonetheless.

I was awake much of the night, thinking over all that I said our last evening together. I haven't changed my mind regarding any of it.

As much as regret gnaws at me, it won't hold me back. I move forward now with purpose. My purpose is to build a life for us. A life that I can eagerly and honestly ask you to join. I'd have asked if you'd be willing to join your life with mine as we wandered like lost sheep through the Seattle streets on my last night with you, and the idea was always on my mind, but I have little to offer but hope and hard work. That will not always be the case. I will write the vision and make it plain, dear Alice.

We've learned much about each other already, but I will tell you the whole story about me so that you can see that if all I have are bootstraps, I will pull myself up by them. I was born in Burr Oak, Michigan in 1890. My father was a pastor in the Lutheran Church and died when I was ten. After his death we moved from Michigan to Indiana, and lived with my mother's sister and her family. My education was always a priority. I was schooled by the Church and spent a year in seminary before I withdrew, upsetting my family, but it wasn't the path for me. I couldn't continue on and lead a congregation. It was not my calling. I promised I would pay back every cent that the Church spent on my education and I have made good on my word, which is why I do not have much to my name. But I am free and clear now, Alice. Free to start from scratch and build an empire. I have found my calling—to build a life of adventures with you.

After leaving seminary, I enrolled at the University of Michigan and was able to teach German classes as a way of supporting myself. I took extra classes, graduated a bit early with a degree in economics, and was fortunate to be offered a position teaching at the high school in Goshen, Indiana.

It was there that I read about the United States government sending teachers to the Philippine Islands. One of my mother's brothers had ventured there several years earlier. So I wrote to him, applied for the position, and was offered a job. I had to find a replacement to complete the rest of the term with the high school, and I even paid my replacement some of my own money in order to ensure that he would take the position and work out the term. When I give my word, I mean it, Alice.

I taught out my three-year contract with the government

and then began work at my uncle's store. He is a pharmacist by training, but we began brokering small loans and we are focused on turning our venture into a bona fide bank. There is much opportunity in Iloilo. In fact, that was the purpose of my first vacation home in five years—to rejuvenate myself before we begin work on building the bank in earnest.

My vacation home also had a secondary purpose, one advanced by my mother and aunts. Indiana, Michigan, and Utah were my main stops, and they were filled with many introductions to so many young women. All coordinated by our families. And no one, I give you my word on this, holds a candle to you. I'm not an odd-looking fellow. I'm not quiet or shy. I'm not slow or dimwitted. But I am particular and that makes me peculiar in a way. If I wanted a wife, as my family wants me to find one, then I could have taken one years ago. I don't want a wife. I want a companion in this life. I want someone with whom to conspire, to travel, to go on adventures large and small.

I think you understand me. And I think I understand you. I cannot explain it and every day of this long voyage home I have marveled at its reality, wondered at your reality, and at times, questioned my sanity at finding you and then saying good-bye. If you were not real, I would wish you so. I spent a large part of the past few days thinking over what I said on our last night together. I haven't changed my mind regarding any of it.

As soon as I arrive home, I will set plans with my uncle for our future and my fastest path back to you. Please, wait for me, Alice. Please write and keep me in your mind, and if you find space, in your heart as well. For you have taken up residence in mine and I deeply desire that you will make a home of it.

Yours,

Elliott

FOUR

ELLIOTT

O*ctober 1915*

AS THE SHIP moors in Japan, he hands a dozen letters to the purser with assurances they will be immediately posted. All tightly sealed, with seven addressed to Miss Alice Hirshhorn, Astoria Hotel, Seattle, Washington. The others are to his mother in Indiana and his brother in Michigan. Writing his uncle would be a waste, as he would likely arrive in Iloilo ahead of any letter. And he needs to be face-to-face to sell this plan. To sell his uncle on letting him return to the States again so shortly.

He paces the deck, eager to disembark, eager to book passage to the Philippine Islands. He is ready for more now. Ready to expand his small pawn operation into more formal loans and land mortgages, and if that fails, perhaps he will persuade the Bank of the Philippine

Islands to open a branch in Iloilo. Right now the Indo-chine banks' branches are the only option for substantial credit. Men far away are becoming wealthy off of deals he has access to. He could speculate in sugar cane or rice or coconut as well as they could. As could all of his vagabond friends who call the Philippines home.

His fingers clutch the metal railing and he looks down on the vast chaos of the port below, determined to best all obstacles in his course because he now has a purpose greater than building a bank. That was a vision of lucre, not of a life. He knows fully what he wants and he will get it—capital and a delightful woman with an easy laugh and clear blue eyes.

His feet are once again on the earth, and other than purchasing a few fresh persimmons in a paper bag from a wooden cart, he doesn't pause, and hires a carriage to take him to the business district.

"Monsieur," greets the officious bank manager, the leather soles of his polished black shoes ticking on the marble floor of the branch office, his dark hair combed back from his face and his hand outstretched to welcome Elliott. It is men like these who Elliott seeks to supplant in the Philippines. "We confirmed your letter of credit," he says in French, requiring Elliott to engage all of his faculties to follow the words. "Unfortunately, we are unable to fulfill it. Due to the war, we are unable to provide funds to Germans."

"I am not German," Elliott responds, mindful of using his best French pronunciation. That he had never ventured to Europe, and his accent in all languages was marked by his American tongue and the German of his childhood—those were concerns he normally had. The words from the banker are far more pressing and outweigh all else. Elliott has less than forty dollars in his pocket, and he doubts that is sufficient to secure decent passage to Manila, much less all the way to Iloilo.

"Sir," the man continues, waving his hand up and down Elliott's body to indicate that there is no doubt of Elliott's nationality. Elliott's tall stature, his pale skin, his ruddy blond hair, his square jaw and his blue eyes—when combined with his last name of Keller, Elliott cannot deny his ancestry. And since leaving the States, he always finds it funny when a stranger first greets him in German. But he is American by birth, and at this moment he finds the banker's insistence anything but humorous.

"I am American," announces Elliott.

The manager eyes him, disbelieving him. "Your passport, please, sir," says the manager, extending a hand, palm up, confident that he has called a bluff.

Elliott extracts his passport from his pocket and passes the book to the man who examines it carefully before handing it back.

"*C'est bon*," the manager continues with a reluctant nod. "We will have your requested funds forthwith."

Elliott steps out onto the street, the equivalent of a hundred dollars in his pocket. By foot he makes his way through the streets of Yokohama to the agency where he books his passage to the Philippines. The next steamer to Manila is in three days' time. Three days in Japan and no plans. No calls to fulfill. No introductions to attain or greetings to pass forward.

Seated at a table in a café next door to the bank that is designed for men like him, he borrows a map. He drinks his tea and enjoys the sweet bite of the persimmons, peeled and sliced with his pocket knife while he looks at the map. Nikko catches his eye. At a dinner party before he left for the States, a couple regaled other guests about their recent trip to the ancient city with its three-hundred-year-old shrines and hot springs dotted through the mountains. If five days is enough time to fall in love, he reasons, then three days is enough time to explore Nikko.

The next day, he steps off the northbound train, winds through the streets of Nikko, and having spent the train ride studying a map he purchased, sets off to explore the city.

His accommodations arranged, he takes his time strolling among the paths and temples amid the dense greenery, pausing to sketch the sites in his pocket journal and jotting a note to send a postcard of the ancient royal bridge to Alice. Nikko is lovely. He has been to Japan before, but Nikko is the Japan of his dreams. As the evening falls, he remembers that a few weeks ago he was also aimlessly roaming the coast on the other side of this vast ocean. Weeks and a lifetime ago and just yesterday. Then, Alice was at his side, and she is with him now in his head.

The morning following his gin-soaked card game on the train, he saw her breakfasting alone in the dining car, the soft spine of her closed sketch book bent around a pencil.

"Excuse me, once more," he said, standing at her table, but avoiding setting his eyes on hers to give her space from him. "I want to apologize for my intrusion last night."

"Oh, never mind that," she said, taking a sip from a

31

coffee cup. "Bound to happen at some point on the journey. Have you breakfasted?"

"No," he said, fighting with himself about saying more. About asking anything from her, before taking a leap. "May I join you?"

She nodded in response, her eyes on his. Clear blue eyes set above rosy cheeks and framed by brown curls once again tied up at the nape of her graceful neck.

He sat opposite her and ordered his eggs, toast, and coffee from the porter. "My name is Elliott Keller."

"Nice to meet you, Mr. Keller. I'm Alice Hirshhorn."

"Miss Hirshhorn, it is a pleasure to formally make your acquaintance."

"As it is to meet you, Mr. Keller. Will your wife be joining us?"

She might already be seated before me, he thought, but he said, "No, I'm not married."

It didn't escape his notice when her eyes widened slightly at his words, and hope flared in his chest, making his breath hitch. He did not trust his words and she did not speak, so they sat in quiet contemplation, looking across the table draped with white linen at each other, until the porter returned and offered her more coffee.

"Mrs. Hirshhorn," he began, hopeful that in his eagerness he had not misheard her unmarried title.

"It's miss," she corrected him in a snap accompanied by a warm smile, as she added lumps of sugar to her fresh coffee.

And that winged thing that moved in his chest took flight.

"Miss Hirshhorn—" And the words stuck again. He wasn't sure what to say next. How to carry the conversation. She sipped her coffee and her eyes wandered to the window. He had to call her back to him, but was lost as to how. A hot cup of coffee landed in front of him and he found words. "Are you headed to Seattle?"

"Yes. There isn't much in between here and there," she said, facing him again while gesturing with her hand toward the grassland stretching into the distance that trundled by the window. "Is Seattle your destination as well?"

"No. I'm headed back to the Philippine Islands."

"The Philippine Islands!" she exclaimed, leaning in a few degrees, her shoulders rolling toward the table, to speak with him more personably. "And I thought Seattle was the frontier. What takes you to the ends of the earth?"

"It's not quite the ends of the earth. We have electricity and a golf club."

"Manila, then?"

"Iloilo."

"Il… What's the name of the place again?"

"Iloilo. It's on an island south of the one where Manila is located. If you can visualize the Islands, Iloilo is in the middle."

A knowing nod is her response.

"I'm surprised you know the Philippine Islands."

"I'm a school teacher. The names of all of the major rivers in the world, the life cycles of frogs and butterflies, and long division are some of my specialties."

"Ah, I taught for a few years myself. Working for the United States government and teaching English to the native children. Now, my uncle and I run a drug store and we have a small loan business that we're going to be expanding." And he wished it were more. That he could lay claim to several drug stores. That the loan business was a full-fledged banking operation. But it would get there. He would get there.

"Were you a Thomasite?"

He shook his head to focus on this curious, beautiful woman in front of him. "No, I wasn't one of the original group of teachers. I came to the Philippines five years ago."

"I was finishing my teaching degree and read about the opportunity teaching native children, but it seemed so dreadfully far."

"Far from Seattle?"

"Oh, no. Far from Indiana. Seattle may be the frontier, but at least it's in the country. Compromise with my father," she said with a shrug.

Elliott had met lots of women before, but none who were unmarried and had fled to the newest corner of the nation to teach as a compromise with their fathers, and, since leaving for the Islands five years ago, few from Indiana. "My family is from Ft. Wayne," he said, not quite sure how to address the adventurous spirit he recognized within her.

"Are you joshing? I'm from Portland," she said. Her eyes widened and he fell into their blue depths.

"I'm not joking in the least. And, might I ask about Hirshhorn? I'm assuming you're German?"

"Yes, my grandparents immigrated."

"As did mine. I'm sure we have people in common. Hardy sons and daughters of the homeland turned American. Do you speak any German?"

"A few words, but not often these days."

Elliott nodded in understanding. "I haven't spoken it

in years." He hasn't spoken it outside of teaching lessons, he realizes, but he dreams in it. His first language, the one that rarely passes his lips, is the one that comes to him in his slumber.

Elliott's eyes had drifted to a couple newly seated opposite them, the woman finished with a hat, a droopy red ribbon trimming the brim, her companion in a brown suit. Elliott took them in, imagining their story.

"Runaways from the circus," Miss Hirshhorn whispered.

Elliott's eyes traveled to her blue ones, finding them filled with mirth and mischief.

"Runaways *from* the circus?" he asked.

"Well, not everyone can run away *to* the circus. Some people clearly have to run away *from* the circus."

She had held his fascination before that moment. But with her joke, he was hers.

"I was thinking he's a painter. European of some sort. Minor country. Dane. Or Lichtenberger. Pushed out because of the war. Traveling from place to place with his sister." The man's fingers reached across the table to pet the woman's. "Or his wife," Elliott amended.

"And him," she challenged, tilting her head toward a rumpled man reading a rumpled newspaper.

"Canadian shipbuilder. Just back from Chicago. You?"

"His suit looks like he slept in it, so he doesn't have a berth, I'd say. Hopping on and off the train at various stops, perhaps in the dead of night. Salesman of some sort. Barbed wire fencing, perhaps? Furs? Timber?"

He has played this game a million times in his life. He is an observer. Taking in everything and putting out into the world what is required. To have a companion, he'd like that immensely and he'd like to know the woman across the table from him much better.

～

AT THE LARGEST red gate he pauses, marveling. Could it really be true that this was created, that this has stood for centuries, without a single metal nail? Alice would marvel at it too. The urge to be with her overcomes him, so he reaches for her in the way he can.

Dear Alice,

I am in Nikko, having this little paper chat with you under a huge ancient gate. They say that these are built without a single metal nail. Only wood, painstakingly fitted together so that it stands the test of time. The passion to build something that lasts not from stone but from life—that I understand deeply.

The sea crossing was fine and tiresome. Mainly monotonous. I made a friendship with a British woman a few years older than us and her son. They were destined for Hong Kong. The son, Rhys, was eight and we played many rounds of Old Maid, and by the time our crossing was through, he was becoming quite the student of Hearts. Only a bit of time more, and he will make a fine bridge partner.

I enjoy cards, Alice. I hope you do, too. Now, before you worry, I don't play poker or whist if there is serious gambling. I have had to work too hard for money to find risking it at chance to be any fun. If you are not a card player, I trust that I can convert you into quite the fine bridge partner. Bridge takes patience and a quick mind, but it also takes a willingness to bluff and silent communication with your partner who sits across the table. We will be famous for that, because I see the delight in your blue eyes at the idea of some bald-faced bluffing and our having secret, wordless communications right in the middle of a busy room.

Back in Iloilo, I expect that I'll rejoin my friends at the club on many nights, laughing, having a few drinks with a few hands of cards and, if the evening demands it, some dancing. My friend Lewis Twombly is always good as a partner. He came over to teach shortly before I did, and has parlayed his talents into a sales position with an oil company. Lewis is a good friend to me. I tell you this now, so that you don't think I'm playing you for a fool: there are women in our set, including Penny Powell. She's quite sharp, but utterly spoiled and not a match for me, though I hope that perhaps one day her eyes will open to Lewis.

The others in our set are a variety of expatriates, mainly Americans and Brits. We have a Swiss who is also part of our set. His origin excludes him from formal membership at the club, but he's quite the excellent golfer, so no one cries too much about his inclusion. The Spanish have their own club, which is grand. Even though the Islands now belong to us, the Spanish roots run deep and many of the buildings have a certain Iberian style and the families are intermixed quite thoroughly with the native population. An American Gibraltar, I suppose. Keeping with their tradition, the Spanish club hosts a few balls a year. One even includes masks in a riot of colors. I look forward to escorting you.

That is in the future. For now, I am in Nikko and you are in Seattle. The dense trees here remind me of Seattle and of the walk we took around Alki Point with Mount Rainer in the distance.

It will be the perfect place for a honeymoon, and a good place to get the feel of dry land under our legs before completing the long journey to Iloilo.

I have already scouted out a few places for picnics. There is a long red bridge, much like you'd see over a koi pond in a botanic garden. This one has recently been replaced, and its low profile stretches long across a gorge. Upon my return to town I will look for a postcard to place in this envelope for you so that you can see it. There is also a shrine from the 1600s that is a marvel. Like gargoyles on a castle, this shrine is decorated with carved dragons, monkeys, and even a sleeping cat! Time has gnawed on it, but does not diminish its grandeur.

I've enjoyed this little chat with you, Alice, in a place that I hope will become special to us both. Now, I must see as much of this place as I can, take notes and commit it to memory so that I may be a suitable guide for you. I will write again soon.

Yours,

Elliott

FIVE

ELLIOTT

N *ovember 1915*

HOME, as it is. Elliott disembarks down a rough wooden gangplank onto the docks, valise clutched in one hand, letters to Alice in the other. He barks at a young man and orders his trunk to be delivered to his uncle's house. The post office is a short walk from the docks. After the few final days at sea, including being holed up in a bay just outside town, waiting for a storm to break so that they could safely enter the city's harbor, the steady earth beneath his feet feels alien. This place that has been his home for five years, new and fresh and utterly odd.

Like ants, men stream up planks and back down them, hefting crates and trunks, two mail sacks slung over the shoulders of a stooped man. Elliott renews his grasp on

39

his letters in his hand and sets off toward where the post office was, hoping it is still in the same place.

At the post office, three letters embark on their journey to her, retracing his course across the Pacific.

The steamer voyaged from Japan to Manila and then from Manila to Iloilo. He could have filled a ship with words to her, but restraint proved his ally and enemy. Too many would seem rambling and overwhelming, and although he feels lovesick, he has no desire to show that to her. His nature bends that way, toward the florid and maudlin and poetic. Nurture bent him the other—to facts and figures and a God who takes accounts.

And the result? A man who spends time in his head, who dreams with passion and fervor, but who cloaks those dreams in firm plans.

Now at his uncle's house, his aunt greets him with a glass of ice water, and after a bath, Elliott settles in on the veranda.

"Some lemonade, Elliott?" his aunt asks and he accepts, taking the kindness and wishing it had some gin in it.

She sits across from him on a teak bench, her green day dress covering all of her save her hands and face. "Any news?"

He knows what his aunt wants to hear and he knows that he's going to disappoint her. "I'm alone."

"I could tell that much myself. Did you meet the Murdoch daughter?" The lightness in her eyes tells him that she already knows. Already knows that he made no promises, but implied them. That Margaret Murdoch of Ft. Wayne, Indiana should join him next year, when his fortunes are more stable, when he has made plans for them, for a house of his own, for a carriage that isn't borrowed, for a life suitable for a wife.

"I did."

"Are you going to make me drag this out of you? I don't want to wait until Otto returns this evening. You must tell me now."

"Aunt Martha." He sighs. "Margaret won't be coming." Her face falls. "I plan to return to Seattle in 1917 and, if all goes to plan, become permanently fixed to Miss Alice Hirshhorn."

Her face is frozen in surprise.

"We shall see what Uncle Otto thinks, and perhaps I can return to her sooner," he continues. "She's a school teacher. From Portland, Indiana. I leave you to write letters to determine precisely if, or more likely how, our families know each other, but I intend to return to her, to marry her, and then return with her here after a suitable honeymoon in Japan." He had not said it aloud before. The words were plain on his lips, an easy paragraph of a plan. If only words could make plans come true. Before Martha can gather her thoughts, he announces his intent to go to find his uncle.

The walk to the center of town from his uncle's home is short, and the rains of the wet season have given way to blue skies. The city has changed in his absence, he thinks, noting his barbershop is now home to a tobacconist and the stationers is now a haberdashery. Nine months and everything has changed.

The bell perched over the door announces his arrival. Carl, the assistant who worked in his stead, greets him hello. He smiles and shakes hands with the man, glad to see him and even happier to see the pharmacy bustling with customers. His uncle stands behind the counter, white coat signifying his role as pharmacist to the expatriates, mainly Americans, who have sought a chance at a fortune in the Philippine Islands.

"Uncle!" he calls. He and Otto greet one another in the middle of the shop floor and assist a few customers before retiring to the back office for a chat, letting Carl handle the store. It is nearly siesta, when the shop will close for midday.

"Come to collect me for siesta? I don't know how much rest either of us will get as I have no doubt that Martha will want to hear about everything," Otto says, leaning back in his chair and rolling his ankles to relieve the pressure of standing all morning.

"I need to speak about business before telling Aunt Martha anything more," Elliott says.

"What did you already tell her?" Otto leans forward, his head tilted in excitement.

"There is a woman I intend to marry. Provided that all goes to plan, once you return from your travels, I will return to Seattle, marry her, and then happily settle into the bosom of marital life that Aunt Martha has been pushing me into."

"Confident, as always, Elliott," his uncle notes wryly, leaning back in his chair and crossing his outstretched legs at the ankles. Because men like Elliott are confident. Confident enough to leave homes and family and friends behind. Confident enough to board trains and ships to arrive at a place they have only read about. Confident enough to know that by their wits and work they will thrive. These are not men who are seeking refuge, forced out of their lives. No, these are men who arrive to claim, to dominate, to create a world for themselves in their own image.

"There is a confidence that comes from knowledge," Elliott says, his voice deep, steady, and certain.

"This next year will be good for you, then," says Otto, ignoring Elliott's announcement. "Test your mettle. The store is yours to run, as you know. Your aunt and I depart in a month, shortly before Christmas, so there is time to talk in detail once you've rested. We've already sold the house, but you have occupancy until the new year. The contents stay with the home, but the carriage and horse are yours."

Elliott starts, his confidence ever so slightly paling in the face of reality. "You do plan to return, don't you?"

"Of course. I've already made contact with friends back home and have introductions with their more important friends in San Francisco and Chicago. Even one potential meeting in New York, as far-fetched as that seems. The world is at war, but marches on nonetheless, and I fear that eventually we will be sucked into the war as well. And even if not the war, modernity will creep to all corners, including this small one that we occupy. Fertile land, an abundance of labor, the United States staying neutral—sugar fuels the world. Sometimes it feels like Spaniards have turned every bit of arable land into sugarcane fields. I don't want to join them in that endeavor, but farmers need capital to expand and we're going to be the men to do just that."

∼

ELLIOTT's first month back is filled with dinner parties,

where Elliott sings for his supper by sharing news and updates from his trip back to the States, and his aunt and uncle are bid Godspeed.

At the club one lazy afternoon, over a game of bridge, Elliott chats with his friend Lewis while his bridge partner Penny makes eyes at them both from behind her hand of cards.

"My uncle has sold his house, so I have to find a new place to lay my head," Elliott tells the table.

Penny's eyes shoot to his and for a fraction of a second are fixed on his before she requests another cocktail from the waiter. The invitation still stands, Elliott notices. But Princess Penny Powell isn't for him. She might have been. And, had he caught another train and not met Alice, she might be for him right now in this instant, but she's not. Alice is for him, and he thinks back to her laugh, her quietness, and her soft beauty and sharp wit.

"Your bid, Elliott," Lewis prompts, and Elliott snaps back into the game and places a bid of one spade without much thought. "Dreaming of the States still?"

"Two clubs," bids Joseph Carlisle, a relatively new arrival to Iloilo, and a man who, from what Elliott has gathered, filled Elliott's empty place in their social set.

"No," says Elliott, not wanting to share the truth of his thoughts. "Wondering if I could find a house to rent with good sea views and breezes."

"Well, let's ask around then for a house with a good sea view and breezes," says Lewis. "You are playing against the newest vice president of the Standard Vacuum Oil Company," he announces to the table.

A chorus of congratulations fills the air, and Lewis

accepts them all with a proud smile that is tempered by his polished manners.

"The company will pay the rent for a house for me, on the assumption that I have a wife and family, and I can't imagine bumping around a house alone. I've already asked Joseph to join me and there is no reason that you can't join us as well. A proper bachelor existence. The two of you would split the salary for the houseboy, and we'd all go in together for a cook."

"Sounds grand to me," says Joseph. "I've been in the hotel for five months, so it's probably time to do something."

A little smile creeps across Elliott's face at the remark. Because that is his problem with Joseph—the man doesn't seem to do anything. Joseph is jovial enough, and quite the pianist, which has proved very handy to have around at parties. From Elliott's discreet inquiries, he's learned that Joseph is from Washington, DC, does not claim relation to any famous politician, and has no visible means of support, but lives well and pays his bills. Joseph also has no aim. And that is what unsettles Elliott about the man. They are all expatriates, far from their home countries, here to make their fortunes, but Joseph seems to already have a fortune and seems satisfied to spend his days golfing and his evenings gadding about Iloilo. It's not that Elliott doesn't like him, for Elliott would love to be like him, but Elliott doesn't quite trust him, just as he hadn't quite trusted the men like Joseph he'd met at the University of Michigan.

Elliott had little to risk other than his own future when he'd quit the seminary, and studied in Ann Arbor. He'd had little to risk other than a very modest salary when he resigned his position teaching back in Indiana to teach in the Philippine Islands. Yet those risks were big to him. The gambles had consequences and Elliott had won. For Joseph, gambles were meaningless because whoever his father turned out to be, Joseph had a different confidence than the men Elliott now golfed and drank with. Joseph's confidence was born out of a life knowing that he would not fail. Elliott's was born out of knowing that he must not fail.

"Elliott? What say you?" Joseph asks.

A house with three bachelors is not Elliott's plan. A small cottage near the sea where he could carve out a home for himself—a home he could give Alice—that is his plan. But the temptation to put away or even invest a few more pesos a month is too great, and eighteen months is too long to excuse such excess of running a home for a single man. He makes quick work of the math, and even if he lived with Lewis and Joseph for six months, that savings would allow him to afford a full-time cook for Alice as well as more than comfortable passage from Seattle for two. There isn't a decision to make.

"Count me in," he replies.

Dear Alice,

Things are settled as they can be and plans are underway. My uncle has agreed to return no later than May, and if all goes well, early April 1917. If I can find someone suitable and utterly trustworthy to mind our business while I am gone, and on the theory that nothing drastic can happen in a month or so's time, I am free to leave for Seattle in March. I am looking forward to April, but working toward a March voyage. That will put me knocking outside your door, my arms full of roses, in May or April 1917. We can spend a week or so together before becoming permanently fixed. There is a question that I want to ask you, and I want to ask in person, not through a letter. I suspect that you know what it is. And I hope I am correctly anticipating your happy reply.

If you are feeling bold, sweet Alice, I have a more adventurous proposal for you. Meet me in Japan in July of this coming year. That part of the voyage is easy. Seattle to Vancouver to Yokohama. I will send you money so that you can travel comfortably. And if we are as suited as I believe us to be, we can continue to travel home to Iloilo. And if I am wrong, and we are not suited, then I will place you on a ship back to Seattle and you can tell your students of your grand summer adventure to the Orient. Much more exciting than another summer on the shores of Lake Michigan, I assure you.

On my side of the Pacific, the plans for the bank are moving forward. My uncle has several introductions set up on his travels to solicit prospective investments and I've begun politicking locally for men like my friend Penny's father to organize a national bank that is not tied to the French or Spanish. I am confident that we will be successful and that we will be able to establish a branch, if not a full office, in Iloilo. There was much groundwork laid while I was in the States. I am working daily to prepare a life for us, but in the meantime, Alice, write me and tell me when in July I shall meet you in Japan.

Yours,

Elliott

SIX

ELLIOTT

*S*ummer 1916

A PARCEL HAS ARRIVED from her. Claimed at the post office, a slip in his postal box, the package was lost, the postal clerk explains, but it was found a few days later, as it had been hidden on a shelf, buried with all of the letters and parcels from around the world that flooded into this outpost of a post office.

He recognizes his name by her hand immediately. The large first letters. Mr. Elliott Keller. He imagines an *s* following the title, squeezed in between the *r* and the period, wondering what it will look like to see that in her hand.

Elliott is desperate to open it, but he wants to be alone with this thing from her. If it is what he thinks, then the months of damn near begging in his letters have paid off.

He walks beside the sea wall, the roar of the waves crashing on the turbulent sea as the rainy season takes hold with its first storm. A fine mist splashes up in his path, anointing him with the sea's blessing. The afternoon clouds loom heavy and promise a downpour. Up the steps to the stucco home he shares with Lewis and Joseph. The houseboy takes his jacket and umbrella, and Elliott settles down on the veranda with the brown paper package on his lap.

His fingers glide over his name written in her hand. The last letter he received marked a milestone in his life. They were now as caught up as they would be. When he first arrived home, he was surprised to find letters from her arriving in his post office box almost daily, and then, after a few weeks the numbers thinned. Not from negligence on her part, or feinting of love on his, but because they were now in a back and forth conversation by the mail.

What gripped him in the last letter, dated April, was not her discussion of returning to Indiana and the shores of Lake Michigan for the summer with her family, but the way she closed it. Her "fondly" transitioning to "love." And how he wished he could hear that word from her lips. How he wished he could have spoken that word to her. Because it felt right, but he didn't want to scare her with the intensity of his feelings. A half a world away, he kicked himself, cursed himself for not telling her what was in his heart.

Wiggling his fingers under the bindings, he unfolds the paper, folding it neatly to keep. The lid comes off and inside is what he hoped. A photograph of her. Three-quarters profile, looking over her shoulder. The quiet smile he'd adored, her eyes bright with happiness, and those eyes told him what he needed to know. That she felt it, too. That she knew, too. That this picture was taken for him alone and no other. It is as close to a boudoir picture as he's ever seen. She is more beautiful than he dared remember. The empty veranda is suddenly much too public. He tucks the photograph under the papers in the box and shuffles off to his bedroom.

Latching the door behind him, he pushes back the mosquito netting and sits on his bed, the box next to him. He pulls the photograph out, careful to hold it by the edges, ghosting his fingers across her soft skin, skin that he touched but a few times and dreams of touching at night.

The letter! He unfolds it, to find it illuminated, the margins painted and inked with swirls and glyphs and stylized grapes and foxes in the most magical way.

DEAR ELLIOTT,

I've finally taken a photograph that looks like me. I know you probably think I was avoiding your request, but I was not. For three months, I've sat for photographs, but they all looked too dour, far too serious to send you. Because when I think of you, I think of laughter and warmth and that is what you deserve from me as well.

Do you want to know the trick of it? I was thinking about our little canoe excursion and how I was determined to show you how capable I was, only to discover that you are quite the boatman who didn't need assistance from this lady. I do appreciate you humoring me, because it was a great laugh at the time and I think of the day often.

This is my last letter to you from Seattle until the fall. In a few days, I'll be back on the train, heading across our great country, and I cannot wait to see what surprises are in store for me. Hopefully no men invading my berth this time.

A year, please say that it is only a year until you are on your way back to see me. Though your offer to meet in Japan sounds lovely, I'm not quite that brave, but flattered you think me so. Going across the States takes only a little courage—and I am fluent in English.

I hope you like the accents I've painted on the pages. I've recently finished painting flowers on a ceramic water pitcher and think it turned out nicely. I'm looking forward to showing it to you someday. In the meantime, these little doo-dads and what-nots are inspired in part by the covers of this magazine my roommate subscribes to, and some gorgeous paper in a stationer's shop window. I decided to try my hand in creating a similar border. I hope it does not disappoint.

My teaching contract has been renewed for the upcoming school year, and, after that we shall see, won't we?

Love,

Your Alice

ELLIOTT READS the short letter again. And a third time. It's more than he could imagine. *Love.* She wrote love. She'd never said it. Neither of them had, but there was no doubt now. *Love, Your Alice.*

The letter in his right hand and her photograph in his left, he paces his bedroom. He looks out the window and envisions standing in this room with her. With her in the nightgown he'd seen her in on the train. With her flushed from his kisses as she'd been that evening after the theater, where they'd sat for an hour in the darkness, hand in hand.

He needs to be near her again, to see her, to hear her. *A year. A year. A year.*

He props her picture up on his writing desk and smooths the letter with the flats of his palms. He reads it once more. He sets out writing paper and fills his fountain pen. He dates the first sheet and the words rush out of him onto the paper.

DEAREST ALICE,

I could kiss you on your very kissable lips! Thank you, my darling, for your photograph. It does more than resemble you, but captures and reflects the joy you bring me. Even when you are serious, such as instructing me on how far to dip my oar under water on our canoeing adventure, there is a light in you. For that I am incomparably thankful.

A year from now we shall be together, God willing, and after a few days to ensure this all isn't a fever dream—and I am sure it is not—our future will be fixed. We will be fixed. Together we shall go on any adventure you wish, more canoeing and picnics and movies and long rambling walks in the evening, now taken hand in hand with confidence. The hundreds of humdrum aspects of life will be richer with you beside me. With us together.

And who knows what characters we may meet along the way? Spies from the Ottoman Empire, sent to the Philippine Islands all the way from Constantinople? A one-legged opera star with vaudeville dreams? Or even two strangers on a train unaware of the stars' plans for them?

It is more than the stars who have brought you to me, dear

Alice. I do not believe in fate. I believe in hard work. Yet I also know the heavy role of chance in our lives. A thousand tiny missteps and our paths would not have crossed. And missteps is what they would be. There is no destiny. Our destiny is what we ourselves create. Yet you feel like destiny to me. Like you and I were written even before there were stars in the sky. The stars did not bring you to me. We are beyond time. We are beyond the twelve months and the ocean between us.

Even the parcel with your photograph and beautifully rendered illuminated letter—you are quite the talent and I look forward to your painted pitcher gracing our breakfast table. I do wonder what you're trying to tell me, though, with the fox and the grapes. Surely not that I will call you sour. Because, dear Alice, know this. There is nothing but sweetness in me now. Nothing but hope for the future.

You know that I have long struggled with my decision to leave the seminary and depart from my appointed path toward the Church. I knew it was the right decision when I made it and I didn't regret it, but I couldn't justify it. There was nothing I could point to and say "There. That was why." Despite my adventures in the Islands, at times my choice seemed like an Easter chocolate. It looks good and tasty from the outside, but the inside is hollow. Was the agony I'd put my family through worth anything in the end? Was my work to repay my debt to the Church for my education truly worth anything? When I met you, I had less than one hundred dollars to my name. I was returning to Iloilo still a shell.

You filled me up, Alice.

I am in my bedroom, behind a locked door so that I can carve out this time with you. Before Joseph and Lewis return with whomever they are dragging to sup at our house this evening. This time is sacred. You are sacred to me. Tomorrow I will write to you of all of those humdrum things that fill my day-to-day, but right now, I need you to know this—I am yours.

Love,

Your Elliott

THE NEXT MORNING Elliott mails the letter on his way into the store where he spends his day managing the pharmacy as one handles a wind-up toy and digging into his lending accounts. He speculates in sugar, makes a loan to a local fisherman for another boat, and drafts a letter to his lawyer to request a foreclosure on an unpaid mortgage. It's a rough plot of land, and likely better suited for a coconut grove than the failed sugar crop the borrower put in the ground, but Elliott will take the toehold in building his future.

Before siesta, he looks at the sky and determines that the rain may hold off long enough for a short round of golf on the club's nine holes. His next chance to golf may come months from now because he needs the rare combination of a slow day in the store and dry weather. He goes home to pick up his clubs and knee breeches and finds Joseph packing a swimming outfit and towels.

"We're off to Guimaras, if you want to join us. Penny Powell's parents are in Manila and she's having a bit of a do at the family beach house. Lewis is even taking the afternoon off. He's down at the docks arranging for some paraws or pump boats to get us there while Cook wrangles some picnic treats for us."

Elliott doesn't hesitate to change his plans. A small bag to carry his swimming outfit, a towel, and a bottle of gin.

What more could a man truly need for an afternoon at the Powell beach house?

With a wicker hamper between them, Joseph and Elliott skirt the sea wall all the way to the docks where they meet up with the rest of their set. Lewis is taking the lead, motioning to the dozen of their friends which boat they should sit on, making sure that the ice is packed and plenty for the day, and whatever arrangements he deems need to be made are made. Elliott settles in on the bench of his assigned paraw and Penny sits next to him, chatting about how fun this little impromptu outing will be, how pleasant the weather is, and how thankful she is that her parents are in Manila.

Soon the sails are hoisted and the three boats are underway, crashing through the surf and then sliding along the surface of the sea. Guimaras is a short ride away. He and Lewis had paddled across the strait once, merely to prove to themselves it could be done. But the present company is much more pleasant and pretty. Penny and Edith and Whitney and Pru and some woman who always lurks around the edges, and Elliott isn't sure if he's ever even been formally introduced to her. Rachel, he thinks. Something Old Testament and pretty. He should ask someone before they arrive and he inevitably lands in conversation with her. Rebecca is another pretty biblical name, he muses, the name softly slipping out his mouth and immediately consumed by the wind and waves as he wonders what Alice would think of that name for a daughter.

"She likes you," Penny says to him, leaning in toward him, one hand clutching the wide brim of her smart straw hat against the sea breeze.

Elliott turns toward her in confusion, wondering how Penny knows Alice and then realizing that they don't know each other. "Who?" he asks.

"Leah," Penny says.

Not Rachel, but Leah, he thinks. Leah, the unloved one. "Well, she can go on liking me all she wants, but it's not going further than that. And at the risk of being impolitic, I could say the same about Joseph. He's fond of you."

"Truly?"

"Yes. And I tell you this in confidence, Penny. Truly in confidence. He likes you very much. Told me as much one evening at our house when he berated me about being too tired to go to the club in hopes of playing bridge with you."

"He also can go on liking me, for all he wants. He can like me for as long as he wants as well, for that matter," she replies with a wink.

"Really?" Elliott answers with curiosity. He hadn't noticed Penny being more friendly than her usual self to Joseph when the gang spent long evenings together at the club since his return, and he thought Joseph's interest was one-sided, but he always found it difficult to determine whether Penny was ever being earnest.

"We shall see," she replies, echoing Elliott's noncommittal phrase, and Elliott chuckles in response.

"Do you want to tell Miss Leah Whoever She Is or shall I need to be aloof all day?"

"Oh! Don't do that! I was counting on your dancing some, and as much as I'm fond of Joseph, I've never seen him dance. Maxixe, foxtrot, he's always on the sides, which is funny, don't you think? Otherwise he's always quite the center of attention." Elliott shrugs because no response is needed to Penny's prattle. "Perhaps he has two left feet," she muses.

"Cruel isn't becoming on you," Elliott tuts, a playful note in his deep voice.

"Me? I'm only bemoaning that the man can't dance. Nothing cruel there. And I think it's by choice, not by reason of his birth."

"Well, if the esteemed Penelope Powell cannot move the man to dance, he is intractable."

"And are you more amenable to my wishes?" she says with a smile that teeters between angelic and wicked.

"I am nearly fixed, sweet Penny, but of course I'll dance with you."

"Especially if it helps ward off Leah, I suppose."

"Am I that transparent?"

"As a plate-glass window. And anyone would know you're hung up on your Alice."

"Alice again?" moans Lewis with a roll of his eyes. "Listen, friend," he says, beckoning with his forefinger for Elliott's attention. "Can you do all of us lonely singles a favor and not gnash your teeth too loudly while we all have a good time? That would be superb."

Elliott turns his head away from Lewis and the gang, gazing out across the water. Because as much as he doesn't want to be, he is still in fact single. The happy chatter of his friends dissolves into the background as he remembers being with Alice on a boat and wishing she were next to him on this boat, headed to this party. He thinks of their picnic, the day before he left, the day that stretched into evening and through the night and into the small hours of the morning. He'd planned a visit to the zoo and lunch on the banks of Green Lake. He'd waited in the sitting room of the hotel, his hat in hand.

"Good morning." She'd greeted him with a smile, wearing a white blouse, tied with a blue ribbon that matched her eyes, and a long dark skirt that hid her from the world, but try as it might, could not hide her from him.

"Good morning," he'd said, resisting the urge to greet her with a kiss and instead settling for the warmth of her smile. "I was thinking we'd go up to the zoo," he said and she agreed.

"Yes! They even have some camels, from what I read in the paper. I'd like to go to Egypt one day, see the pyramids. But today I'll settle for a camel."

"Europe and Egypt. And anywhere else you want to explore," he'd promised.

And off they'd set on a northbound trolley. Through the metal cages of the zoo, they'd thrown peanuts to bears, who'd stood on their back legs and begged for the small treat. The sun had warmed them as he'd promenaded her to the lake, feeling proud that such a beautiful creature graced his arm and enjoying how her sweet laughter filled his ears. He'd noticed her gaze longingly at the boats dancing on the water.

"Shall I see about renting one?" he'd asked, pointing to a small wooden shack with boats stacked beside it.

"Could we?" No hemming or hawing or demurring. A simple welcomeness to explore with him. That was what he enjoyed about her the most.

"Of course," he answered, happy to be able to bring her joy.

"Have you paddled a boat before?" she'd asked as the

boat had wobbled more than a little bit before he took his place on the caned seat behind her.

"Never," he said.

"Well, then, let me give you a few pointers," she'd said over her shoulder before launching into detailed instructions on how to hold the paddle, how to move it through the water, how to drag it to slow or twist it to steer.

"Alice," he'd said, barely able to tamp down his laughter at her zealous helpfulness. "I live on an island."

"Oh," she'd said, dipping her head. The large brim of her hat obscured her face, but not the flush of color that crept up her cheeks. "So, you're probably better than I am. My family goes to a camp on Lake Michigan in the summer." She turned her body away, facing forward and paddling.

"I'd like to go with you," he'd called to her, digging his paddle into the water to propel them away from the small pier and along the quiet banks, the tall evergreens towering over them, casting long reflections on the sun-dappled afternoon.

"I'd like that, too," she'd said, looking over her shoulder at him. "Every August."

"Mark it down."

The sunlight bounces back at him, reflected by the water, but it's not Lake Michigan as he'd hoped a year ago, but the strait. Even if he left tomorrow, setting aside everything in haste to meet her, he wouldn't make it in time. But next August. Next August he will.

Once ashore, the party climbs the steep path to the gingerbread confection of the Powell home that is perched on a cliff above the beach. Elliott's eyes take in the sweeping lawn and impressive view across the strait to their home.

"Sugar," Joseph calls to Penny, the name a play not on her sweetness but the basis of her family's wealth, "lawn bowling or croquet?"

"Croquet," answers Penny over her shoulder as she directs the help to set up a tent for shade. Of course, it's croquet for Penny, thinks Elliott. Lawn bowling isn't secretly savage enough for her tastes, the reigning princess of Iloilo.

A houseboy brings out the equipment and the men pace the lawn, sticking wickets into the neatly trimmed grass. Another boatful of their set arrives on the dock, and the men in lightweight suits and women shaded by brightly painted parasols parade to the Powell house.

Cocktails and talk of walking down to the beach to swim gives way to more cocktails and less talk of swimming. The phonograph emerges from the house and jaunty ragtime sounds fill the humid tropical air. The sky begins to deepen as afternoon slides into evening.

"I'm holding you to dancing soon," calls Penny, who is flanked by Pru and Joseph. "Until then, let's make a foursome for one final game before we lose the light entirely. Girls versus boys."

Elliott washes down the last of his gin and tonic, then crunches the melting ice in his teeth. "Joseph, do you think we can manage?"

"Not without reinforcements. Saunders!" Joseph calls across the lawn to a group lounging in chairs, waving his hands above his head. "Grab a girl and join us!"

The sky is deep blue and riotous lavender, streaked with orange. Penny roquets Elliott's ball, knocking her red one into his green one and sending his well out of position and not far from the cliff's edge. "You may need more backup than simply Georgie to manage us," crows Penny as Pru and Abigail smile.

"We shall see," says Elliott. He steps up to his ball, weighing his mallet in his palms, and surveys the course. A solid *whack* and his ball sails through a wicket. Elliott raises his mallet above his head in triumph. The game is far from over, but the men are still in it.

He takes a spin on the grass, providing the women with a preview of his fancy footwork to come. The soft ground gives way under his feet. His heart is in his throat, his stomach in his shoes, all of him plummeting to the sea below.

By Providence, fate or pure luck, Elliott lands on a rocky ledge, his fall broken by a clump of shrubs.

The sounds from the clamoring sea below and his friends shrieking above wash over him as he lies on his hard bed of smashed plants. He turns his ankles, then his wrists, then kicks his legs, and pulls his arms into his body and finally shifts his head upward to the heavens, thanking God for this moment, for his breath refilling his burning lungs, for his life.

"Elliott!" The cries above coalesce into frantic calls of his name.

"Ladies, back, please stand back," barks Joseph above the fray.

"Here! I'm down here," Elliott answers when he has finished his prayers and his breath has fully returned to him.

"Hold on!" shouts Joseph. "I'm coming down! Fetch rope! Saunders, Petry! Run to the house and fetch rope and have the servants bring out something to act as a stretcher in case he's badly injured."

"I can move!" calls Elliott to his would-be rescuers. "I'm just over the edge a bit. No need for anyone to come down. Just throw a rope over. I could probably climb up, but I'm afraid the ground will give way again."

"Ladies, back. Please. Back!" Joseph's voice again. "A dozen feet from the edge at least and I'd prefer it if you were at the house. Penny, I mean you."

"I'm sure we'd both prefer a lot of things," she retorts, and even in his precious predicament Elliott smiles at Penny's sass.

Presently a rope is thrown over, and with the last rays of daylight fading, Elliott hoists himself up a few feet before he is hauled up by his friends.

~

By ELECTRIC LIGHT AND TORCHES, the party crosses the strait and returns to the city. Joseph, Lewis, and Elliott arrive at home as the church bells toll eleven, all of them drunk. Elliott especially so. After his fall, the first drink was to steady himself. The second drink, to celebrate. And every drink afterward was in sorrow. How wrong he'd been just yesterday, when he thought he and Alice were eternal. They were mortal and he'd walked away from her.

Once alone in his bedroom, he crawls under the mosquito netting that drapes over his bed and turns on his electric reading light. But tonight is not for reading. Even if his brain were not swimming and eyes were not crossing from drink, there is only one thing he wants. So he spends time with her the only way he can.

ALICE, my love,

I was so wrong. So perfectly, irrevocably wrong. I should have not gotten on that steamer without you by my side. Have I ruined it all?

We are not timeless. We are temporary and I've ruined this gift of you, and I, by not taking what was offered and clinging to it and clutching it tight with all of my being, I am now on the brink of losing everything. I've been circumspect before, but it's nearing midnight and I'm drunk and I no longer care for what is proper. I only want what is right and that's you.

We were at Penny Powell's today and playing croquet and I stepped too close to the edge of a cliff and the ground gave way under my feet and I fell. By some miracle, I landed on a small ledge about a dozen feet down rather than a hundred feet into the waves. Four feet to the right and five feet to the left and I would be in the belly of the sea now instead of writing you this letter. I wouldn't have the chance to right my great wrong.

Come with me, Alice. Stay with me, explore with me, journey with me. Marry me. Because when the ground gives way under my feet again, I don't want to have been the man who sent you pink roses, too afraid to buy the red ones that I wanted to give you. I don't want to be the man who worked so long to prepare the perfect place for you that he spent all of his life waiting. I'm sick of waiting. Beyond full of it. Without you I am hollow.

I want to be the man with you, who gets to hold you in his arms, who receives your smiles and laughter and companionship and love.

Have I scared you off with my honesty? I don't give a whit for propriety. I don't have time for it. I am here. So are you. And in this little brief and wild existence, we should be together.

Mark the days, Alice. Count them. Because in April I will come to you and this time I shall never say good-bye. I remain, forever as I have breath, your loving,

Elliott

SEVEN

⚜

ELLIOTT

January 1917

AT HOME, summer would have turned into fall, fall into winter, and winter into spring. But in the tropics the seasons are marked by rain. Elliott longs for the rainy season to begin, but it won't for months. This year's dry season brought the relief of cooler temperatures, and hopefully the rains will bring relief from the outbreak of cholera that haunts the city's outskirts before it intrudes on their lives.

Elliott and Joseph promenade Penny and Leah around the city one evening, chatting and laughing on their way to enjoy drinks on the men's veranda by the shore.

"And the acting! It's so, well—it's enthusiastic," Penny gushes as they stroll.

"You're being kind, Penny," chides Elliott, marveling that she's chosen this otherwise unremarkable moment to bite her sharp tongue.

"Pah!" she replies, clutching her hand around the crook of Joseph's elbow.

"Tomorrow begins three nights of *La Bohème*. Sugar, I think we should go. Front row. Honor their enthusiasm with our own," says Joseph to her.

"*La Bohème!*" exclaims Leah. "That's something I'd like to see."

"That's something I'd like to see performed by another company," says Penny.

Elliott chuckles under his breath.

"I've only heard it in recordings," says Leah. "Have you seen it, Elliott?" she asks, her happy brown eyes dancing for him as they wander from Penny and Joseph's embrace to Elliott's face, her real question never asked.

He should offer her his arm, as it is polite, but he keeps his distance from her. This outing was only undertaken after begging from Joseph about how Penny wouldn't be allowed out to the theater if it were just the two of them, that he needed another couple to appease her parents, and that Elliott could work on his Italian. Of course Elliott objected that Italian sung by a traveling troupe of middling Portuguese performers was probably not the most authentic of accents, but he relented when Joseph promised to buy dinner before the show. There may be only one Penny who mattered to Joseph, but every penny mattered to Elliott. Every penny got him that much closer to being able to provide for Alice. Twenty pesos ill-spent were twenty pesos that would not buy her art supplies, food for her table, or a roof under which she could paint and breathe and laugh with him.

"No, I haven't." His answer does not welcome further inquiry from her and also does not confess the truth. Elliott has only heard Puccini performed once—the traveling production of *Tosca* that they just watched. And even with his provincial background, he agrees with Penny's assessment. To see it some day with Alice, performed in Paris or Milan or Prague or even San Francisco? That would be worth every penny. Because while Alice might agree with Penny's assessment, her criticism would not be so cutting.

They approach the men's house, expecting to find it empty, as Lewis is traveling in the more southerly islands for business, but the houseboy remains on duty, far after his expected hours.

"Excuse me, sirs," he says, handing Elliott an envelope as he quickly greets them before hurrying away. "I am leaving."

Elliott tears open the envelope, quickly reads the letter, and looks to Joseph, knowing that whatever fun his housemate had planned with Penny is now entirely ruined.

"Lewis has contracted cholera," Elliott tells the group. The women gasp, hands over their round, open mouths, their eyes wide in a world lit by a few electric lamps. "He's in the hospital. Struck down while on his way back from Cebu." He repeats the letter's facts, trying to force the worry from his mind because he knows there is nothing he can do for his friend.

Cholera has lurked on the edges of their consciousness for months. It has been mostly confined to the poorer parts of the city, those filled with natives and not those traveled by expatriates. But their houseboy? The men who transport them on boats and bullock carts as they go about their lives? The women who cook their food? They are invited into their lives and houses every day. A few weeks ago an older Irish woman succumbed, and the club mourned her passing with a wake. But to their set, it was a novelty. Drinks and songs and tales through the long night. Cholera and death were things that happened to others. Not something that would happen to them.

"We will walk you both home," says Joseph. His competence that often is so well hidden by his jokes and leisure rises to the surface. "Come now, girls." He places Penny's hand on his arm and with a surefooted stride that Elliott tries to match, they return Penny and Leah to their families.

"Should we learn to cook and clean and care for ourselves?" Elliott asks Joseph on the walk home. "Because I did most all of my own chores while in Ann Arbor. I'm not scared of hard work, and as long as we coordinate, we can probably eliminate much of the contamination risk from encountering others."

"And go to the market ourselves? Draw our own water? Shutter your business? No. We will go on as normal and pray for a happy outcome."

∾

As FEBRUARY ROLLS IN, a gaunt Lewis returns to the house. Propped up in a teak chair on the veranda, he greets his friends with a bright smile and with a porter at his side. Lewis wastes no words. "I'm leaving."

Elliott and Joseph begin to chatter in response and Lewis silences them with a raised hand. "Now, look. It's been in the works for a bit, but with this cholera business and the situation with the war, the company is moving up the timeframe. I'm being moved to Tokyo and will be number two for the entire Oriental division."

Elliott examines his friend, sunken and tired from the travails, not believing a bit of it. That this shell of a man could even travel to Japan, much less run a division of a company as large as Standard Vacuum. "Really?" he asks.

"Yes, that's the plan. But first I will head back to the States for a bit. Not only to fully recover, but to meet with the San Francisco office and perhaps head to New York, but for now it's San Francisco."

"That's a long journey," Elliott says, again swallowing his concern.

"It is. And I'll be recovering here, and I hope—" He pauses and a lightness enters his eyes. "Joseph, would you mind excusing yourself?"

"That's rather forward of you, don't you think?" Joseph teases as he taps the arm of his chair, rises, and leaves them alone.

"Now that we don't have the government's eyes and ears on us, I have a proposition for you."

"The government?"

"Well, did you honestly think he was a wealthy gadabout who decided to land in Iloilo? Iloilo," Lewis repeats with slight disdain.

Elliott feels gullible because he'd believed just that. "He's a spy?"

"I think that's too strong of a word. I think he's part of

69

an advance team of sorts, sent to shore us up just in case the Germans and their U-boats show up in the Islands."

"Fooled me," Elliott admits. Because if he's going to admit anything, confess anything, it's to Lewis and no one else. "What about this proposition?"

"I want to offer you a job."

"A job?"

"Yes, well, specifically my job. You've got a way with people and figures. It's mainly papers, and the travel is simply to maintain relationships with our customers. No serious sales are done. Especially since right now with the war, we're pretty much the only game in Asia. You'd keep the house, have a nice salary with plenty of pocket money. Might even be enough for you to comfortably buy my Rambler when I leave. I'll sell it to you whether you take the position or not."

"I don't need a car," says Elliott, tempted by the idea, but knowing that even a simple used car would be hundreds, if not thousands of pesos.

"An oilman can't be seen with a horse and buggy, or even worse in a bullock cart. It's that simple. And you're smart enough to know that."

"I'm heading back to the States in a few months," Elliott says, the real reason for his objection on the tip of his tongue.

"To collect a bride, no doubt," says Lewis, cutting him off with a knowing smile. "But I won't be leaving until I'm strong enough for the journey, and it doesn't look like I'll be leaving tomorrow," he says, gesturing up and down his thin frame with a lazy hand. "Doctors say I'll need a month at least. That puts us at March or the beginning of April, and if memory serves," Lewis's voice takes on a teasing tone, "that's your timetable to leave for Seattle regardless of this offer. To be frank with you, Elliott, Standard Vacuum is an amazing opportunity to show your stuff. I know you dream of opening a local bank here, but that will tie you here forever. And what if the Islands do gain their independence? How likely will they be to show you and all of us the door? Standard Oil will open doors for you. Let's say that your Alice doesn't much like the tropics? You can move to a position in Siberia or Iowa or even in the same building as Rockefeller and Archbold themselves. No one can say no to New York City."

Maybe he's right, thinks Elliott. New York always has been a dream of his, to one day see it, but not at the expense of missing Alice a second time. "As tempting as that is—" He begins to explain how it won't matter where he can take Alice in the future if he cannot first get to Alice this spring and make her his wife.

"And here's what I can do to sweeten the deal," Lewis continues, ignoring Elliott's interruption. "I told Robert, my boss, about you and your Alice, and since he knows about my current situation, you'll accompany me to San Francisco as my not-quite-a-nursemaid, and meet some folks, and then be free to collect your Alice from Seattle on your way back to Iloilo."

"The store—" Elliott begins.

"We have plenty of time for you to find a buyer."

"It isn't mine to sell," Elliott admits.

"You're wearing me out, old friend," Lewis says, rolling his shoulders to find a more comfortable position in his chair. "I was at least expecting your usual 'We will see,' but I'm not even getting that."

"We *will* see," says Elliott, giving in to Lewis because he sees the exhaustion in his friend's face, but not the deathly pallor that was once there.

"That's all I'm asking."

That evening Elliott writes his uncle, seeking guidance, seeking permission, and seeking prayers for Lewis's recovery. He isn't sure what to do and for the first time since meeting Alice, he feels adrift. Should he sell his family's business? Hire someone to run it for him? He owes his uncle so much and the thought of selling the pharmacy brings Judas Iscariot to his mind. Elliott betrayed his family once by leaving seminary. They forgave him that, but would they forgive him this? He can only ask and await a response in his post office box.

In March, Lewis is strong enough to take slow walks around downtown, their houseboy on his heels in case he needs assistance. And with Lewis's improvement, Elliott's time to decide whether he will take the position with Standard Vacuum or continue to chart his own course is coming to a close.

Cholera still rages in the poorer quarters of the city, but Lewis's brush is the only impact Elliott feels and, as he waits a response from his uncle, his thoughts are taken with concerns far from the Islands. The tall letters on the tops of newspapers that shout the daily death toll give way to tall letters screaming about war. About how the Germans are declaring open season on all vessels sailing under the United States flag. About how Germany is luring Mexico to bring war to the Americas. The days slowly build to an announcement of the inevitable declaration.

Dear Alice,

It's happened. The nightmare at the edges of our dreams, threatening to swallow us whole, has become real. We are at war. And here I was, already packing my trunk to return to you. Now we wait to find out what our future holds.

If I could come back to you, I would leave today. And I will as soon as I can make arrangements.

I received word today from my uncle Otto that he and my aunt are staying stateside and not returning. She doesn't want to be on the next Lusitania, and the comforts of home and family are sticky webs from which they do not long to escape. And with that, the store is mine. To run it, to sell it. Half of the proceeds from any outcome are to go to them, now back in Indiana. Until I can make up my mind which path to take, and then follow it, I'm here. And you are there.

There is an opportunity that I want to discuss with you, so I'll do it on paper and hope you agree with whatever conclusion I come to in this little chat of ours.

My friend Lewis has offered me his position with Standard Vacuum. It's the Asian arm of Standard Oil. Lewis is being promoted and will be moving to Japan. I'd be taking his place and running the Philippine division. It's not the bank. But it's Standard Oil. The world would be our oyster, Alice. I could take different positions and move through the company while we explore the world. But most importantly, it would bring me back to you.

If I take the position, the plan is that I will accompany Lewis to San Francisco for some meetings, after which I will be free to come to you in Seattle, and when you are ready, we can leave for Iloilo. And if Iloilo isn't to your taste, then we can live in Manila. If you want a taste of British life, we can live in Brunei. If you'd like to learn French, we can be based out of somewhere in Indochina within a few years. The world at our fingertips.

If I don't take the position, I will continue to work to expand the business here. I am close to being able to sell off the pharmacy portion and focus on the other aspects of the business, and I have confidence that I will be offered a position with the newly opened bank branch here, if I only ask after the opportunity. I'm doing well. We're doing well, Alice. I'm seeing good returns and expect the growth will continue, even with the war. In fact, with the war expanding I expect other sources of capital may be harder to come by and our own position may improve.

Regardless of what path I take, what path I pick alone because you are not here to decide with me, Lewis has offered to sell me his Rambler. He's got some story about how an oilman can't be seen riding around on the back of a cart, but I am not tempted for me. I am tempted for you. A driver and an automobile to give you freedom. And on Sundays after church, we'd drive up to the club for luncheon, and the lazy afternoon would be our own. We can tie a canoe to the Rambler and you can pretend to teach me how to paddle. This time, instead of along a lake lined with dense evergreen, it will be along the sea, in bays governed by tall outcroppings of rock and gentled by soft sands.

Then one day, glaciers and fjords and even the Nile. We'll explore them together, Alice, on our grand adventure. And this war, and this separation, will be a footnote.

So it is decided. A Standard Oil man I will be. I am heartened to hear that you are trying to learn Spanish. Though English is the official language of the place, Spanish is unavoidable and you will be more comfortable if you can navigate with other languages. Not only for life in Iloilo, but for whatever the future holds.

In the meantime, sweet Alice, be safe and happy and try to find joy even in our further delayed separation. There are things we cannot change. This war is one of them. We cannot, and will not, let it change us. I will remain steadfast in my devotion.

Love,

Elliott

EIGHT

ELLIOTT

 *pril 1918*

MY DEAREST ALICE,

A year at war and it feels like a lifetime. April 1918. I try not to think of the time that has been taken away from us, and rather, I focus on keeping my own head above water.

The shop continues to tick along under the manager I've hired. Revenues and profits are down, but business is steady and having it open continues to serve the community. My own work for Standard Vacuum has me traveling around the countryside, and on Sundays and one day every other week, I am on part of the city patrol. It's far from being enlisted, but I am doing my duty with pride. We keep watchful eyes so that if we see any signs of German activity, we will send for help to Ft. McKinley. Joseph is in charge of the civil patrol, as part of his duties. Or shall I call him Corporal Carlisle? The sneaky dog was indeed here to keep us safe from things far more dangerous than soft ground at the edge of a lawn.

In the meantime, he has become engaged to our friend Penny Powell, the sugar heiress. The wedding will be bittersweet for me. I am happy for my friends and will be happy to celebrate with them, but I will be sad that it isn't us they are celebrating. I will wear a happy smile at all times and raise my glass in toast to them. They need all the luck in the world.

Sometime soon Joseph's battalion is being sent to France. Whether to Penny or to this ceaseless, hungry war, either way I'm losing my last roommate and I have half a mind to give up the house by the sea. While the company will continue to pay for it, it seems a little too large without anyone else. I live in hope that the war will end, and that we will find ourselves together, and then we will enjoy lazy afternoons on the veranda, sketching and chatting and reading, with the song of the sea as the score. I hear it crash against the sea wall now. The tide is high. It is a new moon. The stars are so bright that even the glow from the city's electric lights cannot diminish God's glorious world.

That you exist at all, and continue in your faithful correspondence, is yet another sign of God's grace. Now, before I get overly sentimental, I will make a confession to you so that you know how truly cherished you are. Your photograph accompanies me to bed, dear Alice. I keep you tucked away between the pages of whatever book I am reading, so that I may pull you out for a few moments before I fall asleep. Presently I'm reading some book on oil production. It's as dry as it seems, but I do recognize that I need to learn more deeply about my business venture, so that I can more greatly ensure our success.

This war cannot last forever. It simply cannot. And when it ends, I will be by your side. We will spend a week in Seattle,

*becoming reacquainted, and then fix our course together for a
lifetime of grand adventures.*

    Yours,
    Elliott

THE NEXT MORNING after a breakfast of bread and honey
and tea, Elliott mails the letter at the post office. The
letter should arrive in Seattle before Alice leaves on her
summer vacation. Worst case, it will be waiting for her
when she returns for the new school year. And the best
case? That this damn war ends and he will join her on the
shores of Lake Michigan this summer.

On his way out the door, he checks his post box. No
ships with mail have arrived since he last checked two
days ago, but it is his habit to check. He turns his key in
the tiny lock and opens the door to reveal a letter. The
handwriting he knows as well as his own. *Mr. Elliott Keller,
Post Office Box 327, Iloilo, Philippine Islands.* Postmark of
January third. He turns the envelope over and sees her
name on the back. *A. Hirshhorn, Astoria Hotel, Seattle, Washington, United States.* He curses the world at war.

His need for her is so great that he walks to his house
rather than going to his office. Whatever letters and
telegrams await him there are not as important as these
words from her that have been withheld from him. And
written months ago? His heart tightens as the illusion of
their proximity shimmers and breaks. They are so far
apart, both in space and time. The thousands of miles he
swore to bridge with his letters, but how many of those
never made it to her? How many of her letters never
made it to him? Cursing the world again, he shoves the

letter in his jacket pocket and tromps home, his foul mood gathering.

At the house, he asks for a glass of ice water from the houseboy and, with the cool glass in hand, retreats to his bedroom. Sitting on the edge of his bed, he slips his thumb under the seam and wiggles the contents free.

Dear Elliott,

This is the dozenth time I've begun this letter to you and I'm determined I won't write it again. If there are mistakes, they are mine. All mistakes are mine. I said I would always write to you until you asked me to stop. You haven't asked me to stop, but it is time that I stop writing.

I'm engaged and will marry when the school term ends. There is no gentle or kind way to put that. I tried. Oh, Elliott, how I tried. The stack of ink-smeared and crumpled paper in my wastebasket attests to that.

All I can say is this—I am sorry, Elliott. I wish there was something I could write that would explain this, that would make this make sense. There isn't, though. I've tried for weeks and I can't try any more.

You are beyond dear to me. You are a dream that I never expected to live. Grace when I most needed it. I hope I was the same to you.

The world moved on from those five days we had, now nearly three years ago. We have both moved on even as we have fought to stay put. If only the world were different. If only I were different.

I've wrestled with myself for months, holding on to hope that the world would right itself and we'd find each other again. As much as a dreamer and adventurer I am, Elliott, I am also a pragmatist at heart. I was old when we met and I am older now. I know that I didn't share my age and once I realized that I was two years older than you, I didn't dare. I'm thirty. I said there is no good way to explain this and so I will stop trying—and failing—yet again. Please know that I want nothing for you but happiness and fulfillment. For you to see Europe. For you to build your bank or ascend to the top of Standard Oil.

But for me, I know what I want. I want a family. And I am seizing this opportunity, as it may be my last. Frederick is a good man and he makes me happy.

Do not feel like you have to write me in reply. If I never cross your mind again, I accept that. I will treasure our few days together and your letters as a dragon hoards gold—close to my heart, always on my mind, and buried beneath the surface as I carry on my life. Please, dear Elliott, please carry on with your life and know that I am

Forever yours,
Alice

HE DOESN'T KNOW how long he sits there, stupefied, before he opens his door and calls out to his houseboy for gin, tonic, a fresh glass, and lots of ice. Elliott reaches for the box under his bed where he has stashed her letters, intending to destroy them in his rage and hurt. Yet before he can locate matches, the houseboy knocks and presents him with a tray heavy with his request. Elliott takes the tray from him, sets it on his desk, and makes quick work. The first drink is mostly gin, a splash of tonic to fight off malaria, he reasons. A smirk forms on his lips. He feels so crazed that he doesn't need any more madness. He paces in his quiet room, the crashing waves accompanying the beat his feet strike on the wooden floor.

Drawing the shutters against the sun, Elliott makes another gin and tonic. He reclines against the side of his bed, seated on the floor with his legs stretched before him and Alice's letters scattered around him. Sixty-seven of them. And he reads them all again, looking for clues and finding none. His thoughts vacillate between saying to hell with the world and getting back to Seattle as quick as he can, and trying to force his heart to harden against her.

He knows neither will happen.

If he left today, there are no assurances that he'll make it before her wedding. And if he does, what can he offer her that he hasn't already offered? His heart, his fidelity, his work. They were all for her. They all belonged to her. Heat sears through him that even the cool of the drink can't beat back. His knuckles whiten as he squeezes his glass. He flings it into the wall, the glass bursting into shards and the smell of gin wafting through the salt air. Shame now joins the anger and hurt.

He stands and slips on his shoes. At the door to the house, he grabs his hat and he calls to the houseboy to clean up the mess in his room, and he begins an aimless walk along the edge of the sea.

NINE

ALI

ugust

I FOLDED up the last letter and placed it back in its envelope. It was from May 1918 and while Elliott's resignation at Alice's decision to marry someone else and his tepid wishes that she have a happy life made me sad, it was his closing that broke me. He asked her to keep him advised of her address always, so that he could write her, that they didn't know what the gods had in store for them.

She'd broken up with him and he still sent his love and clung to hope. My thoughts swirled, loud and heartbroken.

The war was nearing its end, wasn't it? A quick Google search on my phone gives me the answer: November 11, 1918. He'd written her the month before and nothing seemed amiss in that letter. Surely after so long she could have held out for a few more months? But of course I guess they had no way of knowing when the war would end. And she was engaged to someone else? To my great-grandfather? For how long before she told Elliott? Does that count as cheating? Because it feels like cheating to me.

And poor Elliott! All the way in the Philippines, working away to build a life for her, stuck there by family duty, and then by war? Loving her for so long and writing these heartfelt letters. To be loved like that! What was she thinking?

The bottle of wine that I'd opened while reading the second letter was nearly empty. The frozen French bread pizza was down to a scattering of tough, tomato-sauced crust. I took off my glasses and rubbed my eyes, urging them to focus on something more than two feet in front of me. The clock on my microwave came into view.

Eight o'clock. My dry eyes wandered to the wall of windows in the living area. I'd just blown six hours and my day off with piles of old letters. I couldn't remember the last time I'd sat so still for so long with something that wasn't medical.

As I halfheartedly cleaned away my plate and wine-glass, I shoved the cork back into the bottle. The idea of finishing the last glass crossed my mind, but I was exhausted. My mind was with Elliott. Who was this man? He loved her. Three years. And it wasn't his damn fault there was a world war. Only a few months more and the war would have been over.

In comparison, Scott and California now didn't seem so far away. A phone call. A video chat. A direct flight. I texted him to say hey. After a few minutes of willing a trail of dots to appear in response—a sign of life—I was still staring at a static screen. Nothing.

Maybe he was in surgery. Maybe he was busy. Maybe he was sleeping. And as silly as it seemed, I knew that if Elliott had gotten Alice's text, he would have texted back. If he'd been in surgery, he'd have texted to let her know he was going in and for how long. He was hungry for her. I looked back at the date of our last phone call exchange. Two days. I'd initiated it. I couldn't remember when he last called me. Was he hungry for me?

Before I let my heart sink too far in holding Scott in comparison to some love letters, I called one of my favorite people.

"Hello," my mom answered.

"Mom," I exhaled. "You're home?"

"Yes, we got in a few hours ago and we're still unpacking. Your dad's out with the dogs, letting them run off some steam after being kenneled for so long."

"I'm sorry I couldn't keep them." I apologized for the millionth time, wishing the dogs could have stayed with me.

"Ali, sweetie, you couldn't keep a goldfish from floating belly up right now. It will get better soon. I promise. It's easier to board them anyway."

There were people who rolled their eyes at the thought of the crazy life of a two-doctor couple. Friends of mine had parents who not-so-subtly suggested they might want to take a different path in life once they'd met their doctor spouse, but my mom the pediatrician was not one of them. And neither was my dad the ophthalmologist. Add in my older brother Patrick the oncologist and my sister Jessica, who had smartly gone to physical therapy school and lived in Texas, and their spouses and children. We were one happy family held together by string, tape, and an army of paid help.

"Grammie is looking forward to you being home," I said.

"I talked with her every day and also talked with her sitters. There was one time that she didn't remember that I was in Texas and was upset that I'd missed some dinner forty years ago, but it sounds like she's doing well. Her blood pressure was good and her weight remained pretty steady."

"Yeah, I'd say she's good. I spent some time over there while you were gone. Sorted through some more stuff. Got some awesome vintage shoes, and other than random old Seattle talk, she was alert and oriented. Her heart worries me more than anything. I noticed some edema in her ankles, but otherwise she looked good. But dear God, Mom. When you start to fall apart, we're just going to set a torch to the house, okay? Because I'm not doing it again."

"Is that why you sent me that *Times* article on Swedish death cleaning?"

"You know it. I'm not doing it again. Did you know that I found the receipt from your tonsillectomy? She kept that."

"So now isn't the time to tell you that I've got the busted piñata from your seventh birthday in the basement somewhere, but when I hold it, it fills me with joy, so I keep it?"

"Death cleaning or torch. Take your pick, but I'm not doing this again."

"I'm kidding, sweetie. Death cleaning, here we come.

But let's get Grammie settled before we find the matches, okay?"

"Deal. Also, if you want her sideboard and dining room table, you are more than welcome to them, but you'd better come fast. She fobbed them off on me and they are on the curb."

"Those are heirlooms," my mom said, the joy falling from her voice.

"Kidding, kidding. I'm sitting at the table now. The moving guys are probably posting my Ikea specials on Craigslist. It's all at my place, but if you want it at yours, just say the word."

"Were we not just talking about death cleaning?"

"Fine," I said, my gaze settling on the imposing sideboard, and thoughts of Elliott's tucked-away letters filled my heart, causing it to ache. "Was Alice happy?"

"Alice? My grandmother? Happy?" The words were out of her mouth in an array of confusion.

"Yes, Alice, was she happy? With Great-Grandpa Frederick," I said.

"Fred," she supplied. "He went by Fred. She seemed happy to me. Why do you ask?"

I wasn't sure I wanted to talk about the letters I'd read. I wasn't sure Mom knew and I didn't want to ruin any visions she had of her grandparents. My mind spun for an excuse, but the wine kept me from finding anything that made sense. I forced the truth out. "Because helping Grammie clean out stuff, I found a bunch of her love letters."

"From Fred?"

"No, that's the thing. It's some guy named Elliott who lived in the Philippines."

"I have no clue what you're talking about."

"We found this box of love letters to Alice from this guy she met before she got married. It's years, Mom. Years of him being in the Philippines for work and her being in Seattle teaching school. You've got to read them."

"You're serious about this? I mean, I knew there was some old boyfriend she carried a torch for because Grandpa, your great-grandpa, would tease her from time to time about someone else and she'd laugh and kiss him in response."

"Do you think she was happy with Fred?"

"I remember her being really easy with laughter and I remember sitting on her back porch in Seattle and shelling peas with her when I was little. I loved her a lot."

"Um, hi, you named your daughter after her," I teased. "So I gathered that much."

"And she was a beautiful painter. Very talented. That platter with the holly and ivy on it that I use at the holidays? She painted that."

I knew exactly what platter my mom was talking about. In my mind, it was "the ham platter." My mother always served the Christmas ham on it. I had never given the origin of the cream platter with the watercolor-like greenery painted on it a thought.

"What else?" I asked. I was greedy to learn about the woman whose name I carried.

"She was teaching school in Seattle when she met Fred. You need to ask Grammie more when she's having a good day, because I can't tell you much. Isn't that sad?" A beat of silence passed between us. "I loved her so much, and I can tell you that she liked cherry vanilla ice cream, sketched these funny cartoon things that she'd tape to the fridge, and visited New York during the Great Depression. But why she became a teacher? Why she moved to Seattle from Indiana? Whoever this guy in the Philippines was? The old boyfriend she was teased about? I don't know what to say about any of that."

"But she seemed happy, right?" I asked, begging for assurances that Alice's decision to walk away from Elliott wasn't a disaster.

"She seemed happy to me. You can never truly know about those things, and I was a child for most of the time I spent with her, but yes, she seemed very happy. She had the happiest smile. Lit up her eyes. You're going to say it's a chicken and egg thing. But you really do remind me of her."

After getting off the call with Mom, I realized that Scott still hadn't texted me back, so I texted him that I was off to bed, but not before I texted my high school best friend Caroline who had stayed in Kansas City, asking her to call me tomorrow.

I gave in to my foul mood, crawled into old flannel pajamas, and let my heart break for a man a hundred years ago.

TEN

ALI

ugust

THE NEXT AFTERNOON, I went for a long walk. I hated sweating or being hot. But I knew that I needed something for my body and an outlet for my brain. Maybe if I'd gotten Alice's artistic skills in addition to her blue eyes and dark hair and name, I'd paint or draw. Instead, I walked the places I lived. No headphones. No music. No distractions. Just me and my feet and an hour of not being needed. I stomped through all three miles.

Rationally, I knew relationships didn't work out. Scott hadn't been my first serious boyfriend. I'd given living together a halfhearted go during my last year in college. And it had cratered when I went to DC and he went to California. Always California. Land of boyfriends past and present. But Scott and I looked good together. And I didn't mean just in photographs. Our goals matched. Our drive matched. Our dreams matched.

I shoved my hand into my shorts pocket and pulled out my phone. He still hadn't texted back, but I didn't let that stop me from texting him again. *Phone date? I'm on call today but around. Call anytime you've got ten minutes. Let me know about the dates I sent you.*

As I unlocked the door to my apartment, my phone buzzed in my pocket and my heart fluttered at the thought of talking with Scott. But instead of a picture of his handsome sleeping profile, the screen filled with a silly face with a tongue stuck out. Caroline. Snapped by me while we were debriefing after our fifteen-year high school reunion. Blitzed didn't begin to describe her that night. We were fine and dandy at the event, but the trash talk at her house afterward resulted in the two of us both being supremely hungover the next day.

"Hey." I smiled into the phone. Ever since our paths crossed freshman year of high school, we'd been tight. And even though relationships grow and change over the years, and some disappear, our friendship had continued.

"Wanna go get drinks?" she asked.

"I'm on call, so if by 'drinks' you mean coffee, yes. But how about you come over here? I've got a glass of wine with your name on it and plenty of coffee for me. Bess is welcome as always."

We made plans and, as promised, when she showed up at my place that night without a baby but with a bag of carry-out Thai in hand, I had a glass of sweet white wine poured for her and a giant mug of decaf coffee with two heaping spoonfuls of sugar for myself.

"I'll never get your coffee addiction, especially when

it's brown hot water without the buzz," she complained, setting the thin plastic bag on the kitchen island.

"Gotta ration my caffeine intake. And I'm on call. So no booze for me tonight."

"I'm such a lightweight with this nursing thing, so it's just this one for me. Hey, new table!" she said, taking the wineglass.

"New to me, but old," I explained. "My grandma forced me to take it. Also, check out the sideboard."

"Totally goes with your style," she said with a smirk, gesturing from the intricately carved wood to the simple lines of the rest of my sleek, modern furniture in my open loft-style apartment. She turned and reached into the kitchen cabinets to grab plates while I opened the boxes of food.

"My style may have to change," I shrugged. "Because this is mine forever. The great-grandmother I'm named after? It was originally her mom's."

"That's super old. I think the oldest thing I'll have to pass down to Bess will be some forgotten cheese at the back of the fridge."

I snorted. Caroline was fastidious and there was no way she would have cheese molding in her fridge. "Yeah, this is pretty old. Around the Civil War maybe? I don't know for sure. But that does mean that it's survived being moved from Indiana to Seattle to Missouri."

"And one day back west to California. Any new leads on openings?"

We'll see, I thought, but I nodded in response to her remark. I'd been in touch with a recruiter about a possibility in Bakersfield, and while Bakersfield might technically be in California, it wasn't near Scott. And a life composed of strung-together weekend visits wasn't my vision. "Booked tickets for a long weekend next month."

"That'll be fun."

"Should be," I said honestly, pushing aside my concerns over Scott's less than enthusiastic reply about the dates I'd emailed him—*Sounds good. If you fly into Long Beach, I'll pick you up if I can. If you take the direct to LAX, book a car or a shuttle.*

"So," she said, sipping her wine. "Are we going to eat at the table? You've got a lot of work out on it."

"Let's eat in the kitchen or on the sofa. That," I said, gesturing to the letters on the table, "is our dessert."

"Is this a new fad diet, because I'm not buying into it."

"Even better. Alice, my great-grandma? Table owner number two? Those are hundred-year-old love letters written to her," I crowed, sharing my excitement with her.

"No way! For real?" Caroline shot over to the table and started looking at the letters and envelopes.

"Yeah, like right before and then during the First World War."

As we ate, I dove in and gave her the story. Of Elliott and Alice's made-for-a-movie meet-cute on a train. Of their five-day whirlwind romance. Of his years of faithful letters, professing his love and telling her of his hard work in trying to make a life for them. Of the war that interrupted their plans. And of Alice's betrayal by marrying someone else. That someone else being my great-grandfather.

"This is nuts," she said, hands on her hips, staring at the yellowed envelopes I'd meticulously organized and spread out across the table.

"So, so nuts," I agreed.

"I mean, from what you said, they had this epic love affair that got screwed up because of the war, but if it hadn't, you wouldn't be here."

"Exactly. I feel really bad for Elliott. I truly believe that he loved her deeply. And then she dumped him and married Fred. But if she hadn't dumped Elliott and married Fred, I wouldn't be here to feel sorry for him."

"I can't believe she kept these letters."

"I can," I said. "I think they really loved each other. I thought it was maybe scandalous when I learned about it. Something secret. But I asked my mom about Alice and she said that Fred used to tease her about some other man."

"You think he knew she loved someone else?"

"I don't know. I hope she loved them both, you know? Because the idea of her gutting Elliott and then being unhappy herself and making Fred unhappy too? That's—"

"Way too much to think through. Can I read them?"

"Of course! They are the best thing in the world. Better than chocolate. I wasn't kidding when I called them dessert. That one," I said, pointing to the one Elliott had written after falling off the cliff, "is my favorite, but you have to read up to it. I don't think you can start with it."

Me with a sparkling water and her with a touch more wine in her glass, we sat down and read through the letters together.

"You weren't lying. I love these." She exhaled, gently folding up Elliott's drunken letter and tucking it back into the envelope. "How many are there?"

"They're magical, aren't they? Thirty-seven. And I don't think I have them all. There are some months without a letter and some months that have two."

"Can I read more? I'll be careful."

"Of course."

Caroline placed her wineglass on the sideboard and picked up another letter, holding it carefully between her fingertips. "I'm still surprised any of them survived. Makes me sad, and not only for them, but for us in a way. Email and text aren't the same, you know?" I nodded my head in agreement. "No way anyone is going to want to read Stu's texts to me. Even though he did send me an emoticon heart this week. Or is it an emoji? What's the difference?"

I snapped up my phone to run down that little mystery of the universe and she batted her hand toward me.

"Oh, never mind that. I truly don't care what the difference is. Any clue what happened to Elliott?"

"None at all," I said, setting my phone back on the table. "The last one is actually dated a month before Alice got married. By the way, you've heard of a family bible? Not only are those real things, but I'm now the proud owner of one." I pointed to a worn, dark green book on top of the sideboard, next to Caroline's abandoned glass of wine. "The front couple of pages and back couple of pages have important dates. Alice married Frederick in June 1918. The last letter from Elliott was written in May, which means she probably got it around the time of her wedding, if not right afterward. It's him claiming that she hasn't ruined him, that he sensed her being distant in her letters, that he'll always care for her, and that he wishes her well. But it's not like the others. He's very formal in it."

"I guess that makes sense. I mean, she did tell him that she was breaking up with him to marry some other guy. He's a better person than I'd be."

"I'm not sure about that. By then, he probably had months to stew over it and lick his wounds. I wonder if he had someone else in his life. I hate the idea of him being alone."

"I'm sure he wasn't. No man who could write letters like this would end up alone. What's his last name?" she asked, flipping through the envelopes.

"I'm not quite sure. Isn't that funny? All of the letters are only signed 'Elliott' and his return address on the back flap is a post office box in the Philippine Islands. There are a couple with his first initials and last name written above the return address, but I can't quite make it out."

I found an example and passed it to Caroline.

"Heller?" she said, squinting as she tried to read the tight script.

"That's my guess."

Caroline grabbed her phone. "I'm snapping a picture of his name, and maybe I can figure it out."

"Okay, Sherlock Holmes. Have at it."

∾

A WEEK LATER, after a full day of inserting tubes in preschoolers' ears, I tossed on clean scrubs and sat down at my desk. Bright and early the next morning, I had a stapedectomy. I was pulling out a tiny bone in an eleven-year-old's ear and replacing it with a prosthesis. It was an important surgery, and one that I didn't do regularly, so it was critical that I get my head in the game, but I couldn't focus on his chart. My patients deserved better. They deserved the best I could offer. I needed to stretch my legs and give my brain a break.

I walked out of the hospital and around the giant headquarters of the world's biggest greeting card company. The temperature was just under boiling and the sun wasn't brutal, but I was confident I was the only one outside for fun. On the back side of the corporate campus, the tower in the park caught my eye and I headed toward it.

Everyone has some favorite random trivia about their hometown. Some source of local pride. Like how Paris, Kentucky was the hometown of one of my college roommates and also the inventor of the traffic light. Or how some place in West Virginia celebrated the first Mother's Day.

Kansas City is known for its barbecue, but remembering the First World War was important to us as a city. And so I headed toward the park and up the hill to the Liberty Memorial Tower. I'd visited as a child on field trips, but by the time I was a teenager, it, and much of the city around it, were crumbling and closed. I vaguely knew it reopened and was now fancy, but who plays tourist in their hometown?

But maybe someone there would be able to help me scratch my Elliott itch. Right era. Maybe he'd enlisted. Maybe he'd been drafted? He'd mentioned his friend Joseph being sent to France. Surely he would have told Alice if he was being sent too? Because when you love someone, you tell them the important things, right?

At the top of the hill, with the city's skyline spread out at my feet, I was surprised to find the memorial wasn't only the tower I'd remembered, but that the tower stood on top of a large pedestal that housed a museum about World War I. After some poking around, I found my way to the library and learned that by filling out some paper-work and promising to pay a whopping fifty cents a page in copying costs and a fee that was less than a decent dinner out, someone would run a computer search in the archives for records of Elliott, provided I could figure out his last name.

I left with a researcher's contact information tucked in my pocket and a promise to email her a picture of his indecipherable scrawl of a last name so we could begin the hunt.

That night I called Caroline and told her that I'd found someone to help me look for Elliott at the World War I memorial.

"Why'd you do that?"

"Why wouldn't I?"

"I googled him."

"I did too, but I didn't find anything."

"I did. Elliott Keller is his name. Not Heller. It's kinda heartbreaking," she confessed.

I braced for whatever was going to come, not liking the idea of bad things happening to Elliott. At that moment, I realized how desperately I wanted happiness for him. For a long life full of happiness.

"Well, I don't know it's him," she continued, her voice soft. "But I think the odds have to be good. There was an Elliott Keller who was a prisoner of war, held by the Japanese in China for like all of the Second World War. And when I ran down Kellers on the POW search, there were some Kellers who were POWs and held in the Philippines."

My chest constricted. "Did he survive?" I asked.

"I don't know. The website says that he was released,

but there are no details. Here's the crazy thing. The records say he was one of the longest-held Americans during the war. He was held for nearly four years. Four years."

"And his family?"

"Same story. Reports indicate that they were released at the end of the war. Upside is that they were only held for two years. Yeah, Elliott G. Keller. I'm looking at the website now. There's a Martha Keller, a Eugene Keller, and a Theodore Keller who were held in Manila."

"Martha was his aunt who he lived with," I whispered as the reality sunk in and a lump formed in my throat. There was no way it wasn't my Elliott.

"It says she survived, so that's good," she said.

I did the math. Elliott would have been in his fifties then and that meant his aunt was probably in her sixties at the youngest. Sixty years old and in a POW camp in Manila in the nineteen forties. The cholera epidemic that Elliott wrote about rushed into my mind. I didn't know anything about POW camps, but common sense told me they'd be ripe for cholera and a host of other awful tropical diseases that I hoped never to meet in my lifetime.

"Ready for some good news?"

"Absolutely?" I said, closing my eyes in hope.

"I think I may have found Theodore's daughter. I found an obituary for a Theodore Keller in Santa Fe and it listed survivors. One is named Gail Keller Copley. And through the magic of the computer—"

"You're kidding me," I exclaimed. "I mean, I'd like to meet his family, in the abstract, but what do I do?"

"I've found a Facebook account for a Gail Keller Copley. Her profile is pretty private, but she's checked into a few places in Albuquerque. That's so close to Santa Fe that it can't be a coincidence."

"B-but," I stammered. "How?"

"Tot story time at the library was super boring on Tuesday. At least to Bess. She was in her baby carrier and totally passed out. I wasn't going to wake her, so I was kind of stuck there and decided to chat up a librarian. Do it, Ali. Send her a Facebook message. You know you want to."

ELEVEN

❦

ALI

S eptember

STRAIGHT from a short day of clinic, I took the direct flight to LAX. Even with the drive to Scott's place—what I hoped would be our place very soon—it was quicker than taking a connection into Long Beach. But now that the flight out had been delayed, I realized my mistake. Six o'clock on a Friday. I sat in the back of the car and absent-mindedly chatted with the driver while we were stuck in the gridlock. *Kansas City. Half Kansas, half Missouri, actually. Yeah, the Chiefs have a lot of potential this season. Great barbecue. No, not for vacation. Boyfriend. Three years. I'm a doctor. Ear, nose, and throat. I specialize in ear surgeries. Looking to move my practice here.* And all the while, I surveyed the sun setting on my soon to be home and texted with Scott.

Me: *Still stuck on the 405.*

Scott: *That's the worst.*

Me: *The worst.*

Scott: *I just looked it up. See if the guy will go through Long Beach on PCH.*

Me: *The cars aren't going anywhere. We're literally stuck.*

Scott: *I made reservations at that Italian place for eight. Think we can make it?*

I glanced at the time, and sighed. By the looks of things, even if the road magically cleared, at best I'd be at his place at eight.

Me: *That's not happening.*

Scott: *Meet me there?*

Me: *I got on the plane straight from clinic. I'm in yoga pants and an old sweatshirt.*

Scott: *I never complain about you in yoga pants. Or out of them. You'll be fine.*

Yeah, okay, so we both knew what this weekend was about. Connecting. Remembering why we were together while we were apart. I needed that connection. I missed him. The abandoned, half-finished mugs of coffee that he left in his wake and all.

Me: *Nope. Not going out like this.*

Scott: *Fine. We'll order in. Text when you're close.*

I settled back into the seat, and wondered what Elliott and Alice's reunion would have been like. I had visions of her in her prettiest dress—blue to go with her eyes. Of her waiting at the waterfront for him, of him in a smart suit and derby hat, of him crowding the railing to look for her below and descending the stairs from the steamer, of him pushing through the crush of passengers in a determined quest to find her. Their eyes meet and the breath leaves them both. Smiles fill their faces. A tentative hello escapes both of their lips as they stand two feet apart among the bustling crowd before he takes her in his arms and kisses her.

And here I was, in the back of a ten-year-old Volkswagen, wearing yoga pants, and now, per my phone, only a mere forty minutes from my guy. I'd like to say the months we'd been apart had been easy. That our love had grown and deepened. That I understood him. That he truly understood me. That absence hadn't just made the heart fonder, but made our connection deeper and more resolute.

But I never liked lying. The distance was killing us slowly and we were fighting tooth and nail to hang on.

It was just after eight o'clock when the car pulled up in front of Scott's place. He was at the curb, waiting for me. A hug and a quick kiss hello, then with one hand he grabbed my bag and with the other he held mine, leading me through the complex to his apartment.

He slung my weekend bag over his shoulder and opened his front door. The wall of windows that dominated the exterior wall was black. I'd missed sunset while I was stuck in traffic. I knew that, but that hadn't been my plan. Sunset over the Pacific, even if only a small line of the ocean was visible from Scott's apartment—that was the stuff of my dreams. I walked to the windows and looked out, the full moon high in the sky and casting white light on the water.

"Pick your poison," he said from the open kitchen.

"Gin," I answered. I wasn't a gin drinker, but Scott liked making cocktails and I liked drinking them and making him happy.

"Cucumber gimlet?"

"Sounds good. Gotta get my veggies in somehow," I called to him over my shoulder. I left the window and joined him in the tiny kitchen, which was, for all intents and purposes, a glorified wet bar. He also survived on cafeteria food and carry-out, so I knew the food offerings were much like the ones at my place: booze and protein bars, but instead of my comfort ice cream and chocolate bars, he'd have his favorite peanut butter cookies and a random assortment of questionable fresh produce that was strictly for cocktail garnishes.

"I'm hungry. Let's order in."

"Called in an order of sushi. Should be here"—he paused slicing the cucumber and glanced down at his watch—"in about fifteen minutes."

I placed my hand over his, stopping his work on the cocktail. "We can work with that," I said, my mind flooding with memories of hurried encounters shoved into our busy schedules when we were back in Boston.

"Yes, we can." His hands came to my cheeks, turning my face up to meet his. "I missed you, Ali," he whispered. His lips dropped to mine and I tried to get lost in his affection, lost in his touch, but he felt far away even though he was right here. *We* felt far away and I hated it.

"I miss you," I said, breaking away a beat before renewing the kiss, trying to find him, trying to find us.

His hands fell to my shoulders to pull me close and my arms wrapped around his waist.

A series of beeps punctuated the moment and we broke apart.

"That's my pager," he explained, snagging it off the top of a pile of mail. He glanced at the screen and looked back at me, raising his eyebrows, neither one of us wanting to jinx the situation by speculating why he was being paged, but his mood had turned.

"I thought you weren't on call this weekend."

"I'm not." Our eyes met. Phone in hand, he walked out of the kitchen.

Well, there goes our fifteen minutes before sushi, I thought. I poured some gin in the bottom of a glass, dropped in a cucumber slice and splashed some soda on top, not even bothering with any ice. I knew it wasn't even close to whatever creation Scott had in mind, but it would do the trick. I sipped my drink and tried to listen in on his conversation in the living room, to catch if he'd been paged by mistake or if a case was cratering, but I couldn't hear.

"Massive pileup on the 405," he called to me across the room, the smile that had been on his face long gone. "Probably explains why it took you a year to get here. They need me. And, since I was waiting for you to have a cocktail, I'm good to go in."

"Go," I said, waving at him. "I'll be here when you get back."

A quick kiss and he was out the door.

~

BETWEEN THE TWO-HOUR time difference and my early bird surgery hours, California sunrises and I weren't exactly strangers. I was fixing my second cup of sugary coffee when the front door opened and Scott walked in. Or some approximation of Scott.

Surgeons on TV never looked like this. They always

looked competent and strong and determined, even at the end of marathon surgeries.

Scott looked rough. Tired eyes, hair standing up in a million directions, and a slump to his shoulders that ran the length of his body.

"Hey," he said.

"It was bad," I said, giving him words so he wouldn't have to dredge them up.

"Yeah," he said with a nod, biting his bottom lip. "It was."

"Go shower, crash out."

"I didn't—"

"I know you didn't plan this, but it comes with the territory. Shower. Sleep. We'll brunch or lunch or whatever later."

"You're the best," he exhaled, dropping his keys on the glass dining table and nearly stumbling down the hall with exhaustion.

I filled the morning with a long walk, checking out house prices on my phone. Kansas City was looking better with every million-dollar, two-bedroom fixer-upper I saw. I wasn't going to take the job in Bakersfield. No matter how sweet the offer, that wasn't our plan. It was a half measure, a stopgap, and I was ready to jump in with both feet. Our plan was an ocean view.

I was enjoying the sunshine and watching surfers from a beachside coffee shop when Caroline texted.

Tot story time is now. Librarian wants update. Hear back?

Haven't messaged the potential granddaughter, I texted back. Though I wanted to know what happened to Elliott, the thought of him and his family suffering in POW camps turned my stomach.

I adored the Elliott I knew from his letters. He was a dreamer and a worker and I couldn't help but to feel some kinship with him. And I wasn't sure if I wanted the real world to intrude on that man and turn him into a real person, a person with some unavoidable rough edges and likely even more sadness. I liked him as this quasi-fictional character. And I liked keeping him to myself. Well, sharing with Caroline didn't quite count, but I wasn't sure I was ready to share him with the world.

I also didn't know how Elliott's family would react. Would this be welcome? Would it upset anyone? Bring up heartache or hard feelings? Would they even care? Because if they didn't care, that would break my heart a little. And if they cared and they asked for the letters back? No. I didn't want to return them. They weren't really his anymore. They were letters to Alice. They were *my* letters.

"Oh, why not," I said to my chocolate chip muffin. I opened Facebook on my phone and messaged the woman Caroline had found.

Hi, I'm looking for the descendants of Elliott G. Keller, originally of Burr Oak, Michigan. He and my great-grandmother exchanged letters when he lived in the Philippines in the 1910s. If you're his descendant, please let me know. I'd like to send you copies of the letters and find out what happened to him.

I read it through a dozen times, fixing words and changing phrases, and trying my best not to sound creepy. Finally, I hit send on the message, and texted Caroline that the deed was done, that I'd tried to contact someone who might be Elliott's granddaughter.

Cool. I hope you hear back! Got bit by the genealogy bug.

Think Stuart and I may be related, but not sure. Either way, pity Bess. She's got us for parents.

Doomed to a lifetime of counting by fives, I texted back.

Caroline met her husband in pharmacy school, which she joked had involved more forgetting than actual learning. "The first thing you do is learn to count by fives. We spend a whole semester on it," she'd told me in her most serious voice. The only giveaway of her joke was the glint in her eye. Every time I wrote a script that was not divisible by five, I imagined a poor confused pharmacist somewhere, having a nervous breakdown by having to count out twenty-one pills.

I flipped over to my email and saw a message from a physician recruiter who I'd been working with to help me make the jump to California. She was the one who'd mentioned the small practice in Bakersfield. It was California, yes. But Orange County it wasn't, and I was ready to let her down easy in hopes she'd find me something closer to Scott and the ocean. I opened the email and tried my best not to cry. The position was filled. I hadn't even gotten a phone interview. Not that I wanted that position anyway, but now that it was off the table I felt like a failure yet again. It was the third practice in California that had passed on me.

Mr. Elliott Keller and Miss Alice Hirshhorn. Dr. Scott Sayer and Dr. Ali Waller. A war wasn't standing in my way. Time and patience and I'd find my place, I told myself. Time and patience.

I returned to my house hunting, checking out sleek condos with ocean views and cozy duplexes with beach access. A home where we'd eat breakfasts, hang Christmas stockings, and one day bring a tiny person home to join us.

What did Elliott's house by the sea look like? I wondered. He mentioned a seawall. Soon I had a map of Iloilo up on my phone and then I was down a rabbit hole of pictures from the nineteen tens. I found what had to have been his club, which had been named Santa Barbara and now was the Iloilo Golf Club. The oldest golf club in the Philippines. American and English membership only at first.

An old photograph showed a two-story wooden building with big verandas and wide shutters propped open to let in the breeze but keep out the sun. I could see Elliott playing bridge there with his friends. I could see him in a linen suit, a flat-brimmed straw hat, and laughing over drinks. I could see him in knee-length breeches playing golf with his European friends, and drunk in a dark suit, mourning the Irish woman who passed from cholera. He was more real to me now than before.

If Caroline could find Elliott online and I could find what I was pretty sure was his club, could I find Alice?

Finding her obituary was easy. *The Seattle Times*. The details were slim. She was born in Indiana. She taught school. She married Frederick in 1918. She'd been a member of the Seattle Tennis Club, the Seattle Garden Club, and a past president of the local chapter of the League of Women Voters. And she was dearly loved.

But other than those simple words, she was a dead end on the internet.

I turned back to my Elliott search and had more luck. I found the obituary Caroline had told me about, but it didn't seem quite right. Too simple for the Elliott I knew.

His name. That he was preceded in death by his parents and a son, and was survived by his wife, one son, and a granddaughter. Four years in captivity and the death of a child? Alice's hurt was just a taste of the harshness life would bring him.

I poked around more, and using his wife's name from the obit, located a photograph of women sitting on the steps of a wooden cottage around nineteen thirty, surrounded by pine trees. Either they'd come home for a visit or this wasn't my Elliott. *My Elliott.* I smiled at the silliness, that I'd think of him with some sort of claim to him, but I downloaded the picture anyway.

TWELVE

ALI

S*eptember*

I ARRIVED BACK at Scott's place around noon to find him stretched out on the sofa, clean and damp from a shower. Some college football game was blaring from the giant TV.

"Hey," he croaked out, his heavy-lidded eyes on me. He was a bit groggy and I didn't make much out of the second it took for his brain to process why I was in his living room. "You are really here."

My gaze swiveled to the bright blue sky beyond the wall of windows. I didn't come to California to watch football. That I could do with my brother any weekend. "Yeah, I am. Want to go out?"

"Sure. This game is terrible," he said, switching off the TV.

We headed out and wandered around Huntington Beach hand in hand in search of lunch.

"What have you been up to all day?" he asked me over salads, after he'd spent our walk debriefing me on the emergency spinal case he'd worked on all night. It wasn't a happy story.

"Took a walk. Looked at some houses. Surfed the web. Did you know that the Philippines still has cholera outbreaks from time to time?"

"Wouldn't surprise me," he said.

"Also, did you know that Japan invaded the Philippines within hours of the attack on Pearl Harbor?"

"Studying up in hopes of a Filipino category on *Jeopardy!*?"

"No, but I realized how little I know about it. I mean, there was the president's wife with all of the shoes back in the eighties, and I vaguely recalled that it was an American colony or territory or whatever its official status was, but that's it."

"Yeah, I'd forgotten about the crazy shoe lady."

"Who is Imelda Marcos, Alex?" I teased him.

"Indonesia next on your list?" he teased me back.

"Nah, sticking with the Philippines. I got more things from Grammie—she keeps unloading stuff on me—and in with some table linens were some love letters to the original Alice."

"The original Alice had an affair?" he asked, his eyebrows arching in surprise.

"No. This was before she got married. Some guy she met on a train. He lived in the Philippines and for years was trying to get her to move there, but he had to save up money and then the First World War started, and it wasn't meant to be, I guess. She married my great-grandpa and here I am."

"Years?" he said, his interest piqued.

"Yeah, three years."

"Sure he wasn't already married or something? Because that's a long time."

My jaw set and my breath stopped for a beat. I tried not to read anything about our situation into his comment about Elliott and Alice's situation. "I'm sure. I've read his letters. He loved her."

"Really? If he loved her so much, he wouldn't have been in the middle of the Pacific Ocean. He would have been with her in Kansas City."

"Seattle," I said, focusing on correcting his facts rather than addressing the meat of his statement that if you loved someone you made things happen. "The original Alice lived in Seattle. That's where my grandmother grew up and my mom was born there too. The family moved to KC when my mom was in high school."

"Wherever. I just don't get it. If you want to be with someone, you be with them."

His offhand comment hung in the air for a minute before taking root in my soul. It stung. I knew this was hard, and that we were both working to make us work, so I brushed it off as best I could to not ruin our time together. "Anyway, I've been trying to run down Elliott-the-letter-writer and try to find his family."

"Hence the research."

"Yeah, but I think Caroline tracked down his grand-daughter."

"Really? That's cool. You should call the lady."

"Yeah. She's on Facebook, so I messaged her."

"I never check my Facebook," he said. "And messages from strangers probably go to some spam filter anyway. Get your sleuth Caroline to run down the woman's contact info. Mail. Email. Phone. Worst thing she can do is tell you to go away, so I don't see a downside here."

"Worse things have happened," I said, remembering the horror he'd witnessed last night and knowing that right now a family wasn't having a happy, lazy lunch like we were.

"Worse things have definitely happened," he agreed with a nod, finishing his second Bloody Mary. "And let's not talk about them again. Want to walk on the beach?"

"You know it," I said.

And all through our walk, I batted away the doubt, batted away the hurt that he didn't want me. I wrestled with the knowledge that if he wanted me, we would be together. And I fought off the realization that if I really wanted him, I would have made the choice to be with him too. I could have made that choice but I didn't. Instead of taking the offer with the small practice in Orange that I wasn't in love with in order to be with Scott, I'd put all my eggs in the UC Irvine basket, only to have that basket break. That bit was the hardest to accept. At the end of the day, my head and heart both knew the fault lay with me.

~

WHEN I LEFT his place for the airport the next morning, I got a hug and peck on the cheek from my boyfriend of three years. It didn't feel like a goodbye, but it didn't feel like love.

The hour drive to LAX sucked. I sat in the back of the

car, ignored the driver, popped in my earbuds, and found some music to fit my mood. Aching and bitter. Things with Scott were as good as they were going to get. And as good as it was going to get wasn't good enough for me. Maybe Elliott's letters had screwed with my head. Maybe I was pining for a guy who lived a hundred years ago. But there was no doubt in my mind that if Scott were Elliott, I wasn't his Alice. He didn't want me in that way that said need and longing. And what was he to me? My once upon a time easy answer to having a boyfriend?

By the time I was back in my own apartment, I had the afternoon to burn and I didn't want to show my sad face to my mom or grandmother or Caroline. They liked Scott. They liked me with Scott. But did Scott like *me*? And did I like *him*? After the weekend, I wasn't sure.

I dumped my carry-on in front of the laundry closet and threw dirty clothes in the washing machine. Laundry started, I called Scott to let him know I was safe and sound. I was half convinced that he wasn't going to answer, that he was going to screen my call.

"Hey," he said, his voice more distant than it had been a short six hours ago. "You got a minute?"

"Always," I said.

"I should have said something to you while you were here, but, Ali, this—"

"Isn't working," I said, accepting the truth even though my mind raced to find a solution to make it work, to make us work, to keep us together.

"Yeah."

"I'll call the recruiter I've been working with and get in touch with a few more. Maybe there's someone better to use. I'll run down folks from Georgetown and Boston and work my network to really focus on getting in with a practice in Orange County."

"Ali—"

I wasn't stupid. I didn't need any more words from him to figure it out. And I could tell by the way my name hissed out of his mouth on a sigh that his mind was made up. He was done. We were done. And the root of it was my fault. My inability to choose being near him and choose a perfectly good small practice over the prestige of a position at a research hospital.

"Got it," I snapped, going into doctor mode. The land where my needs were second and the task ahead of me was paramount. And right now the task was getting off the phone with Scott with some of my dignity intact.

"Ali, don't be like that. Listen—"

"No, really. I get it. You don't have to say more, okay? Let's just say goodbye."

"Christ, Ali. I mean, I know you can be a hard-ass at times. I like that about you, but I thought we'd at least talk about it."

"A postmortem?" I chuckled, fighting back tears. "You don't change your mind, Scott, and I don't want the play-by-play on why six months of being apart somehow changed everything."

"Okay, then. I won't give it to you. It's not you—"

"Just don't," I warned, fighting back equal parts tears from sadness, and laughter from the ridiculousness of our self-imposed distance. The distance that was our downfall. "Don't finish that sentence, okay? Because it *is* me. It's us. And whatever worked in Boston isn't working now and I'm doing my best to fix it, to hold it together."

"Ali—"

And this time, I let him continue. I let him say all the things he wanted to say, but they were only sounds to me. I blocked it out. The apologies, the justifications, the rationalizations, but when he lied, I wasn't having anymore.

"Scott," I snapped. "You loved me. Don't say you didn't."

"Ali, I'm not saying that I didn't—"

"But you don't anymore."

"Ali—"

"I can't do this right now."

"That's fine," he said, trying to soothe me. "I don't want to be strangers. I really don't want that."

That line did it. Because it *was* a line, a platitude, and I was done. "You don't get to choose," I snapped. "And I can't talk about this anymore." I ended the call before I let him have another word.

Anger coursed through my body. Why did he wait until I was home? Why did *I* wait? Because it was over. We were over long before this weekend. But if I'd gotten that position at UC Irvine, would we be engaged? If I'd taken that job that I didn't love, would we be married? Would I be married to him and then only years later find out that he really didn't love me? That I really didn't love him? That we were convenient, but weren't worth any sacrifice? Not even worth the minimal hit to my own pride by taking a good position with a nice private practice rather than the job of my dreams?

I didn't even pretend to salvage the rest of the day. I crawled into my bed and stayed there, alternating worrying over what I had done and fretting over what I was going to do.

THIRTEEN

ALICE

September 1915

Her roommate answers the knock at the door. "Alice," Francine calls down the short hall of their shared apartment. "A delivery for you."

Alice sets her teacup down in its saucer, the fog of sleep lingering at the edges of her thoughts. She stands, unties her apron, and smooths her hands down the skirt of her simple dress. At the open door to the apartment, a delivery boy stands, a bouquet of pink roses, tied with a blue ribbon, in his arms.

"Miss Alice Hirshhorn?" he asks, extending the flowers to her. She nods and gives the boy a dime and her thanks in exchange for the bouquet.

"Your new beau?" asks Francine.

A small envelope is tucked in the green waxed paper, held in place by a slender straight pin.

He was leaving. Or he had left. She wasn't quite sure of the time, but he had to be gone. Ignoring Francine's excitement, she unpins the envelope with care and then tucks her bouquet under her arm so that she can open the note.

A simple, rich, cream-colored calling card, his name embossed in black. Elliott Gustav Keller. And above, written in what she assumed was his hand, a simple *Good-bye, E.*

Seeing the ink, his familiar initial—in that moment, she knows. Her face crumples as her heart does. She has made a mistake. A horrible mistake. Why were they saying good-bye? They had just said hello.

"Take this," Alice says, thrusting the bouquet at her roommate. "I hope my hair is fine." Alice bends to shove her foot into her boot. "Where is my other boot?" she shouts at the world in a panic. The sleepiness from a few moments ago is erased by the need to get to him, the need to fix this, to right their wrong.

"Behind you," says Francine, who grabs Alice's pocketbook and places it in her hands as soon as her boots are laced.

Alice shoots out the door and down the stairwell.

"Good luck! And if you go to the Orient, at least send a message so I know you're alive!" Francine calls after Alice's departing figure.

At the waterfront, Alice isn't sure what to look for or where to go. She isn't sure who to ask. Men hustle and shout amid the gull cries. It's midmorning and that's when his steamer departs. She doesn't have time to lose. It's a

Japanese boat he's booked on. That she is certain. Vancouver then Japan. *Maru. Something Maru.*

She runs to a longshoreman. The man is wrapped in a waxed canvas coat with a cigarette caught between his teeth.

"Pier three, I think," he answers out of the corner of his mouth with a shrug. Throwing the spent cigarette on the gravel and crushing it with his heavy boot, he continues. "Almost all of the Japanese ships have *Maru* in their name. And half of everything out of here is headed to Vancouver."

"A Japanese steamer named *Maru* headed to Vancouver *this* morning?" she demands, staring him down.

The burly man whistles at a group of men loading crates onto a dolly. "Japanese steamer headed to Vancouver? *Maru* something. You know it?"

"There she is." Another man points to a boat in the bay, slowly cruising north.

"You missed your boat, ma'am," the longshoreman states before lighting another smoke and turning his back to her.

"No," she says, stopping herself before she can say more because if words tumble out, then her tears will follow.

On leaden legs she trudges the mile uphill to her boarding house. She'd flown down these streets as if on fire not half an hour ago, the minutes and seconds far too critical to spend waiting for a trolley. Her mind set to jump on a ship, to ask him to stay, to say yes to his unasked question.

Utter insanity, she chastises herself on the brutal walk. Eloping with a man she barely knows, who she met less

119

than a week ago. She'd noticed him watching her while she sketched on the train. His gaze across the observation car warmed her skin. She'd snuck a shy smile in his direction, but his head was turned away, allowing her a lingering look at his profile.

She turned a page in her sketch book, the still life she'd been sketching out of boredom no longer of any interest.

His face would be too obvious, so she drew his legs and shoes in their various positions as he shifted about in his reading chair, never quite settling down or relaxing. And when he would look at her, she felt it and she would pause her pencil, her breath catching and her cheeks warming.

After what felt like hours, he folded the newspaper he was reading and placed it on the side table. Out of the corner of her eye, she watched his feet shuffle to a stand, and watched his feet walk toward her. Her pulse raced. Was he going to introduce himself?

The train lurched around a corner and the accompanying jerk of the carriage sent her charcoal pencil rolling toward the edge of the table. She'd shot out a hand to grab it, clasping it against the tabletop, her hand landing an inch away from the man's hand, his palm flattened against the table for balance. Alice lifted her head to his face and found kind, delighted eyes land on hers.

"Pardon me, miss," he'd said, straightening. He turned from her and with a few quick strides was through the door to the small viewing platform at the end of the train.

His nearness, for however brief a time, flustered her. She wanted to flee, she wanted to stay in place and await his return, she wanted to join him on the platform. Indecision was a stranger and she didn't know how to respond to him.

She watched the door intently, her drawing forgotten. "Alice," Francine had said from her nearby club chair. "Shall we freshen up before dinner? Our seating is in twenty minutes."

Alice had turned to her friend, her roommate since their first year at normal school. "Yes."

Throughout dinner, she'd wanted to tell Frankie about the man she'd crossed paths with. But what could Alice say without sounding foolish? *There is a man on the train. He is so handsome and he was looking at me. I was looking at him. Our hands almost touched. He said "Pardon me, miss" and I thought my heart was going to beat out of my chest.*

No, none of it sounded right. It was far too fanciful. At twenty-eight, Alice and Frankie are not schoolgirls. They are independent women who had jumped at the chance to teach and live thousands of miles away from their Midwestern homes.

And now, taking one step at a time, up the stairs to their third floor apartment, Alice doesn't know what to say to Frankie yet again.

"I'm back," she calls as she enters the apartment.

Frankie spins around, a pen dangling between her fingers, her face surprise then sadness.

"Well, I'll have to start over." She picks up the stationery in front of her and crumples it into a ball. "I was writing Josie and telling her about your whirlwind romance with Mr. Keller and how you were on a boat to the Philippine Islands as I wrote."

"The boat left before I could get there," says Alice, falling into a chair, untying the laces of her boots, and kicking them into a corner in frustration. Sulking, pouting, and utterly exhausted, Alice is thankful that Frankie lets her brood, and doesn't intrude on her scattered thoughts and aching heart.

"Can I ask if you were truly going?" Frankie says after long minutes of quiet.

"I don't know. I don't," answers Alice, standing to gaze out a window, toward the direction of the sea, before turning toward her bedroom. "I'm going to lie down for a bit."

"You look exhausted. And I won't tell anyone about last night."

Alice turns on her heel. "Or any of it," she says, her voice wobbling.

"Or any of it," pledges Frankie.

Alice closes herself in her bedroom, her trunk propped open against the wall. How easy it would have been to have thrown in the quilt she'd pulled from it last night and have boarded the ship with him. Passports and plans be damned.

She unhooks her dress and slips into her nightgown. It's barely lunchtime, but a day in bed, pulling herself together, is what she needs. Before the meetings and preparations for the school year begin. She takes out her sketch book and flips through the pages, staring at the imaginary vase of dahlias she'd been drawing on the train. Before the world was different.

Her fingers drift along the lines and shadings, smudging and working the charcoal. She finds her pencil and begins to work again, losing herself in the task.

She tears the page from the book and writes on the back of the sketch:

Dear Elliott,

You said to write. That there couldn't possibly be too many letters from me. I'm not sure how to start, so I will simply begin.

There is something that you should know, but I'm not sure if I'll ever tell you—at least not until you come back to me. I would have said yes. I would have said yes to going to the moon with you. The Philippine Islands are at least here on Earth.

I'm saying it now, here, on this paper, that I am certain that I will never send you. Because while I would have said yes, you may not know the question. (I'm not talking about whether I like ice cream. I do, by the way.) And if I was wrong, if that question was not on your lips as you bid me good-bye at my doorstep at two o'clock this morning, then I don't want you to pity me.

But I think it was on your lips, lingering there but never pushed out into the world, bitten back by some reason. Maybe this is why I'm certain that you'll be back as soon as you can. Regardless, I am confident in your return.

Is next summer too much to dream of? A year will be easy. I'll gird myself and be strong and noble and proud and confident and think of how a year apart isn't such a big thing. It will be terribly romantic. You on a tropical island in the middle of the Pacific, setting the stage for a life for us. Me, teaching this year's class and filling my trunk with a trousseau and a pink dress.

A pink dress for the roses you sent me. I cannot thank you enough for them. And perhaps that is why I know you'll be back for me. You must have had a thousand things to attend to this morning, and to send me flowers... Well, to be frank, I've never been sent flowers before.

But also thank you for leaving a thing with me. That's what I was mulling over this morning before the flowers arrived—I realized that I had no physical remembrance of you. At least for now. I hope that some of the photographs we took with Frankie's camera will turn out. I will send some your way, if they do. Until those photographs are developed, I don't have a thing to prove your existence.

When I woke this morning (it was very late and I was very groggy, by the way), I fixed a cup of tea and a slice of bread, and sat in my tiny kitchen and wondered if you really did exist. If this past week hadn't been some sort of fantastic dream.

The flowers are in a vase next to my bed. Frankie put them there while I shot down to the waterfront to see if I could catch you (yet again another thing I won't share until I see your face again). When I returned, she asked me if I would have gone. I would have. Ask me next time, Elliott. Ask me to go with you. Ask me to adventure with you. Ask me to marry you. I will say yes.

You never asked (among many things you didn't ask), but I was sketching a still life when I first noticed you on the train. Flowers in a vase. Nothing imaginative or grand. I started this letter with the idea that I would send you the completed drawing as a keepsake. But this letter has taken a rather unforeseen turn and I can't send it to you. I will now write one that I can.

Until we meet again,
Yours for always and forever,
With great affection, and
Love,
Alice

SHE DOESN'T EVEN READ through the letter before she balls

it up and throws it into her wastebasket where it disappears from sight. Regret sweeps over her again. A second
time this day she has thrown something precious away.
Up from bed, she collects the paper from the wastebasket
and smooths the creases with her palms, the words
smudged but legible.

FOURTEEN

ALICE

S *eptember 1915*

DEAR ELLIOTT,

The new school year begins tomorrow and I have been busy preparing in the week since you left. This year I've been assigned a fourth grade classroom of girls and boys. Long division looms. My third year of fourth grade and I hope this is the year that I finally feel that my feet are under me.

With the start of the school year, the splendor of the Seattle summer comes to a close and then gray days and long dark nights will settle in around me, but in a way, they are already here. You left a week ago. I'm eating, I'm sleeping, but I feel drab. Like the colors of the world have been muted.

My thoughts are often with you, somewhere in the middle of the Pacific. Far from my little apartment and classroom.

I haven't had the heart to send you letters yet, even though I *gave you my word I would. I worry that I won't be charming enough or witty enough and, being honest with you, I don't want my letters to tarnish your thoughts of me.*

Today after finishing the first month of lesson plans and straightening my classroom, on my way home I noticed a postal box I hadn't noticed before. It is a few steps away from the trolley stop near my apartment, and I have vowed that I will keep my word and send you words. And here they are—words, from me to you.

Thank you for the roses. They are hung upside down in my bedroom, tied together with a blue ribbon that they arrived with. The blue of the ribbon reminds me of your eyes. Your card sits on my vanity, where I look at it every morning and every night while I brush my hair. Thank you for remembering me before you boarded your ship that morning. Thank you for the kindness. I'm sure that you were quite in a state that morning, as I was. I know I've never been out so late before. Or was it early? Either way, I was an absolute slug the next day.

I know I promised you words, and I don't yet have words for our days. Perhaps one day I will. And perhaps you will have words for me then, too. A question, even. And I will have an answer.

How soon can you return? I will be here, waiting for you, sending you words, and waiting for yours.

Though I am not a true artist, I've enclosed a little sketch. I went up to Queen Anne Hill and brought along my sketch book and pencils. Perhaps I should borrow Frankie's camera sometime. But until I have a photograph, this view of the bay that carries your name, and the city with Mount Rainier in the distance—this is my gift to you.

Write back with plans for when I can expect you to be here with me. And I do expect you.

Truly,
Alice

THE DAY after his boat sailed she spent in bed, as well as the next. She'd ached all over. Only up for the necessities and beyond grateful for Frankie for giving her cover and excuses to the other teachers. Traveling was difficult, and Frankie swore that no one even noticed Alice's absence. The next day she'd had no choice but to plaster on a smile and attend to her life.

She met the new principal and the other teachers. Many of whom were returning, but some were new, replacing women who had left due to homesickness or husbands. Next year she'd be one of the missing. "Oh, did you know Alice?" someone would surely ask as she chatted with friends and exchanged stories of summers spent at home with family. Most of the women were also from the Midwest. Farm girls like her, who for one reason or another weren't suited for farm life. These were her kinfolk. Women who lived in books and art and music and for the children in their classrooms, reminding them of the ones they might never have.

On the morning of the first day of school, she and Francine have toast and eggs and coffee in their tiny apartment, packing simple lunches in a sack.

"And for a box of caramels, how many angels and how many devils?" Frankie asks.

"Don't be silly," says Alice, shooting Frankie a cool look as she hands her a breakfast plate to dry. "They are all angels." The two women dissolve in gales of laughter. "Four angels for every devil is my wager," Alice replies, wiping her eyes. "I can't handle any more. I have twenty-three students this year. Twenty-three! That's six devils in a classroom and God knows that I can't handle any more."

"Amen. Did you know that I still have a small mark on the back of my leg where that little Petersen boy placed that tack on my chair?"

"Really?" says Alice.

Frankie shrugs in response. "It's a tiny little mark. A battle scar."

"He *was* a devil," Alice confirms. "I will be honest, I was so happy that no Petersen child was on my roster, but I'm worried about the new girl who has the sixth grade. Lottie from Wisconsin, I think? I saw Olaf Petersen assigned to her classroom."

"Should we warn her?" asks Frankie, her voice flat and impassive.

"Well, certainly anyone who graduated from a *university* instead of a *normal school* doesn't need our assistance in running a classroom," says Alice dryly.

"Excellent. Now, I have a treat." Frankie disappears into her bedroom and emerges with two candies wrapped in waxed paper. "A caramel for each of us, out of the box. A little sweetness to place in your pocket if the day starts to sour."

In the lobby Alice and Francine meet with the other women and walk to the trolley stop, all chattering excitedly in the crisp morning air. Alice slips a letter into the postal box before alighting.

"Letter home?" asks Ruth, another new teacher who Alice met two days ago, but liked immediately. Alice doesn't want to lie, but she also doesn't want to tell the truth about the letter that is most certainly not going home.

"Alice is a prodigious letter writer," answers Frankie with a wink at Alice. "In fact, it wouldn't surprise me a bit if she posted a letter each morning."

"I'm a terrible letter writer," says Ruth, kicking the long skirts around her ankles. "I never know what to say and my letters sound like a news report."

"Any suggestions, Alice?" teases Frankie. "What was in this letter, for example?"

"Oh," says Alice, shooting her dearest friend a look that says *hush*. "Only my hopes, my dreams and my dearest wishes for the future. Same as always."

FIFTEEN

ALICE

F *ebruary 1916*

DEAR ELLIOTT,

This is the third day that snow has fallen. And my second letter to you in that time. If I wasn't from Indiana and didn't know about snow, I'd probably think that this is how the world ends. Well over a foot is on the ground and it just keeps fluttering down from the sky. It's really quite beautiful, but also a little terrifying. It shouldn't be this cold here. It seeps in through the windows and the wind off the water cuts straight through you. Schools have been closed. Everything is closed and we are stuck indoors.

It's best not to think about it at all. I can't imagine what your January is like, but is it fair to say it's above freezing in the tropics? Some of the girls are staging a variety show to keep busy. I don't have a talent for the stage, so I've been keeping myself occupied by painting and reading. But, oh!—the talent some of the girls have!

I know you like theater, and when you return, you are absolutely taking me to the new Coliseum Theater. It opened a few weeks ago and is spectacular from the outside. I haven't been inside yet, but one of the girls had a beau take her to the opening night and she says that it is opulent like Louis XVI. One day we'll see the palaces of Europe, but I am happy to start with this photoplay palace right here in Seattle. I'm looking forward to watching Mary Pickford (she's my favorite) and then imagining you watching the same movie later in that funny little bamboo hut of a theater you described to me. Or, even better, imagining you watching from the seat next to me. Maybe I won't go at all until you return. Make it something special for us to do together for the first time?

Which brings me to my point, as always. How much longer? Can you and your uncle simply open a bank in Seattle? The city is boundless with opportunity but a touch closer to home. Even better, it's a touch closer to me.

Yours,

Alice

THE SNOW and slush and streams of nearly frozen water destroy her boots. The salt and grit placed on the sidewalk eat through the soles.

"You need to buy new boots," Frankie had scolded her, but Alice had protested. New boots were expensive. She could find a cobbler and get hers repaired. Surely they'd hold together long enough for her to get home and make a purchase at the store that knew what she needed.

But when the freezing water seeps through the leather

and soaks her thick stockings, she concedes. Frankie is right. Penny wise and pound foolish, and certain to catch a cold. It isn't much. It won't ever be much, but Alice has been frugal. But now instead of putting away a few dollars each month so that she won't be entirely dependent upon her family, she's saving so that she can have new dresses made before she leaves for the Philippine Islands, dresses that she can wear as she begins her new life as Mrs. Elliott Keller.

On Saturday morning after the blizzard, the women venture down to the Arcade. Piles of snow as tall as Alice tower along sidewalks. The newspaper claimed it was only two feet, but it has devastated the city. The dome of the cathedral has collapsed and people swap harrowing, secondhand stories of being stuck in offices and shops without sufficient food and fuel for heat. The assistant principal resorted to breaking up furniture to feed a fire to keep the small band of people trapped in the school warm. Buying a new pair of boots isn't such a great hardship in light of what others have endured.

The women meander through a department store, admiring the offered dresses, and hats, and kitchenware, and stationery, but not making a purchase. Alice lets her eyes linger on the elaborate valentine cards on display. Some of the cards are imported from France and trimmed with lace. Others have embossing or moveable parts or picture windows. A few even pop up to little standing displays. How she'd love to find something like this in the mail. Perhaps she could send one. But none are right for him. Or, more properly stated, none are right to send to him. So, she moves on, wishing that they were more fixed, that she could send him some token of affection that was more than ink scrawled on paper.

Back on the sidewalk, they reach their destination. A large blue and white sign extends over the sidewalk. *Wertheimer Shoe Company* it proclaims in a bold script. A pair of glamorous embroidered satin pumps are on display in the window. The women pause to admire them before pressing through the door of the shop

"Good morning. How may we help you?" asks a shopman, a neat white apron tied around his waist.

"I need new boots," answers Alice, forcing herself to look away from the fashionable displays and toward the utilitarian black boots that she needs.

"Anders, can you assist the gentleman while I work with the ladies?" booms a deep and cheerful male voice. Alice looks at the handsome man as he approaches. Dark hair with silver at the temples and a smile that reaches to his eyes, making his whole appearance radiate joy.

"Of course," says Anders as he slides away.

"Now, Miss..." continues the new shopman.

"Geiger," offers Frankie, a mirroring smile on her face at the handsome man.

"Miss Geiger," he says with a nod, "and Miss..."

"Hirshhorn," Frankie says with a smile.

"Well, Miss Geiger and Miss Hirshhorn, we have some lovely new boots and we will get to them, but perhaps you'll be willing to demonstrate those pumps you were admiring?"

Frankie nods at him eagerly.

"We're only here for the boots, I'm afraid," says Alice.

"Won't hurt a thing to try on the shoes," says the man. "Tell me your size and I'll fetch them from the backroom."

"Really—" says Alice, shaking her head to refuse.

"We'll try them," says Frankie, nodding with glee.

"Excellent," the man replies and takes the information offered by Frankie.

"Frankie," Alice hisses as soon as the man steps away. "They are gorgeous, but I'm sure those cost a fortune! And where would you wear them?"

"Like he said, it won't hurt to try them."

"Don't seek out temptation," Alice counsels.

"Hello, pot. I'm kettle," she says, extending her hand. "And since we're on the topic of temptation, what's the latest from the sunny tropics?"

"He's asked me to meet him in Japan this summer," Alice confesses as she looks more carefully at the display of women's boots, entirely avoiding eye contact with her friend.

Now it's Frankie's turn to look scandalized. "Japan? By yourself?"

"He can't return to the States until next April at the earliest because of his business, but he can meet me in Japan."

"And then whisk you away to the Philippine Islands?"

"We shall see," Alice answers, running her finger over a row of neat buttons on a delightful pair of black and white boots that would be entirely suitable.

"Really, Alice!" Frankie scolds in a whisper. "Japan! And you're getting onto me over a pair of shoes."

The handsome shopman returns and the women settle on a bench to try on the delicate shoes meant for the theater or parties, and definitely not designed for teaching school children. Frankie preens in the shoes, swanning about the store, gazing in mirrors angled along the bottom of a wall. She holds her skirt indecently high, her calf on display. Alice expects the shopman's attention to be on her spirited friend and is surprised to find him looking at her.

"And you, Miss Hirshhorn?"

Alice goes to refuse again, but the shopman insists and kneels in front of her.

He holds the shoe out for her to admire. The decorative stitching gleams in the light. Bold red and orange flowers amid a riot of green leaves. They are a painting in thread and she adores them and the skill of the woman who no doubt did the stitching.

"Chrysanthemums," he explains, turning them so that Alice can more carefully admire the workmanship. "They are well made, too." He extends a hand, palm up, requesting to aid her in trying on the shoe.

Still, Alice doesn't extend her foot. She blushes and looks at her hands in her lap, where she's twisted her fingers together in her discomfort.

"May I?" he says, giving voice to his request.

"No." She shakes her head, wishing that she could sashay around the shop. "I'd like to try boots. Also, I'm not sure you can do it in-house or if I'll need to find a cobbler—"

"We have a cobbler on staff," he answers brusquely.

Alice nods in relief, her shoulders loosening and chest deflating at learning she'll only have to explain herself once. "I'll need the sole built up on the left. An inch makes the world of difference to me."

Understanding dawns in the man's brown eyes, but there isn't pity. There isn't sadness that she's somehow broken, that she's somehow unfit. "That's an easy enough fix," he assures her. "I'll speak with the cobbler about which pairs we have that would be suitable to the adjustment and bring them around."

He places the floral shoes in the box, nestling them in the delicate tissue paper before closing the lid. Alice bids a silent good-bye to the beauties. Gorgeous, expensive, and entirely impractical for her in so many different ways. She watches with envy as Frankie waltzes around the shop.

The handsome man soon returns with another man in tow. "Mr. Grumman is our cobbler," says the shopman, and Alice realizes she doesn't know the shopman's name.

It feels too late to ask, and before she can gather her courage to ask, he steps away to greet another customer, leaving Alice with the cobbler for a few minutes to work through the details of her needs.

"All good, Grumman?" the shopman asks upon his return.

"Yes, sir," the cobbler answers. "It isn't a complicated fix, but she says she spends all day on her feet so I want to get it right."

"All day on your feet, Miss Hirshhorn?" asks the shopman with concern.

"I teach school. Fourth graders. They keep me on my feet and on my toes," she jokes.

And he laughs. "I'd wager they say the same about you," he says with a smile.

"I do my best. Long division is a tricky beast. And yes, I'll take the black and white button-ons."

"Excellent," he agrees with a nod, extracting a pad from his apron pocket to take down her details. "The quality on these is good. They should last a good long while."

"I hope so," she says, her smile fading a bit as she grows serious. "Frankie," she calls out to her friend. "I'm almost ready to go."

On the walk home, Frankie raves about the embroidered satin shoes, pining for them. "But they were six dollars! Six whole dollars!" she says, trying to talk herself out of the shoes.

"Perhaps you can create a pool of sorts," teases Alice, knowing that her specially tailored boots cost more than five dollars, which explains why she owns exactly two pairs of shoes. "You can find out which other girls wear a size near enough to you and you can take turns wearing them out."

"To the Coliseum! I could borrow that outrageous stole that Marcie has. Now to find a man to take me. Perhaps the man from the shop. He was quite dashing."

Alice agrees. He had looked confident and unflappable. His dark hair was slicked back neatly from his face, letting the whole world easily take in his brown eyes. "He is very handsome."

"When will your boots be ready? Perhaps we can visit together to pick them up."

"By next Saturday. I'm frankly impressed by how quickly they'll be able to make the adjustment."

"Excellent. We'll go back next Saturday, visit our new friend, and retrieve your boots. This week can't pass by quickly enough."

SIXTEEN

F*ebruary 1916*

ON THURSDAY AFTERNOON, Alice and Frankie relax after the children have extracted every bit of patience and energy from them. Alice works at the small table on an intricate card to send Elliott. He'll get it late, no doubt. She should have worked on it months ago, so that it was already across the Pacific at this point. But it's her first time having someone to send a valentine to, and the idea that she might send one to him only crossed her mind as they had milled about the department store over the past weekend.

On Tuesday she'd painted a small watercolor image of blue forget-me-nots, and now she finishes the card. She carefully glues a piece of blue and gold ribbon to encircle the flowers. She signs her initials to the painting in a soft pencil, so that he'll know it was not only from her, but by her. Maybe he won't know the name of the flowers. Maybe he'll think she'd sent him some blue flowers, but she's confident he will know. He will recognize the flower and notice her initials. He will see the care she has placed into this gift for him. She places it in an envelope addressed to the post office box in Iloilo whose number she knows by heart. On the way to the shoe shop tomorrow, she and Frankie will stop by the post office to ensure she's paid proper postage for this bit of affection to travel halfway around the world.

There's a knock on their door and Alice opens it.

"Hello, Lottie," says Alice, in the friendliest, breeziest tone she can muster. Lottie is far from being on a list of Alice's favorite people. She's five years younger than Alice, a complete snob about how her university training makes her classroom far superior to everyone else's, and unabashedly husband hunting. If she lasts another year teaching, Alice will be surprised. She'll either be married or will have moved on to bigger things than their frontier grammar school.

"There's a man with a delivery downstairs for you in the sitting room. I told him it was allowable for delivery boys to carry things to boarders' rooms, but he said he would appreciate it if I asked you to come down to him, rather than him coming up to you."

"I'm not expecting a delivery," says Alice, confused by the statement, but her heart leaps at the idea of another bouquet from Elliott.

"Well, he has a delivery, whether you were expecting one or not. Several boxes."

"I'll be right down," says Alice, wondering what boxes Elliott could have sent.

"You tell him yourself," says Lottie, turning on her heel.

"Want me to come with you?" halfheartedly offers Frankie from the settee where she's curled up in a ball.

"No. I'll be back in a jiffy," says Alice, slipping into her worn boots. She unties the apron she is wearing and pats at her chignon to check that it is in place. It will be nice to have new boots, even if the leather might be stiff for a few days. She hopes the cobbler made the adjustment appropriately, so that she doesn't limp.

Downstairs in the sitting room, the handsome shopman stands by the fireplace, a few boxes tied together with string at his feet. The electric lamplight is golden and it dances in his eyes.

"Miss Hirshhorn." He straightens and greets her.

"Mr.—I'm sorry, but I didn't get your name."

"Wertheimer. Frederick Wertheimer."

"Mr. Wertheimer, nice to see you again," she greets him, entirely confused by his presence in the sitting room.

"You as well, Miss Hirshhorn. Your shoes were ready, so I thought I'd bring them to you."

"Thank you," she says, truly appreciative.

"Care to see if we made them correctly?"

Alice looks around the room. They are alone, but the double doors are open. She should get Frankie.

"You're safe, I assure you," he says, anticipating her worry and assuaging it. He extends a hand and gestures for her to take a seat in a nearby chair.

"I haven't paid for them yet," she reminds him. "I owe the store five dollars for the shoes and cobbler's work."

"We'll deal with that later," he says, kneeling in front of her as he'd done a few days before. He unties the boxes.

"Do you have other deliveries to make? It's getting late and I don't want to keep you. I can bring the boots back to the store if they need adjustment," she says. The words rush out in a wild stream from her nerves at his nearness in this quiet room.

"No other deliveries," he says calmly, opening the first box, and she watches carefully as his fingers push through the delicate tissue paper. The black boots with the tall white uppers she selected appear. She smiles, happy with her decision. They are the first boots she has ever owned that aren't entirely black, but with her long skirts, while she's at school only the black will be visible and therefore entirely acceptable. And in the spring and summer, with the shiny buttons contrasting against the white, she'll feel more fashionable. She congratulates herself on the smart compromise.

She unties her boots and slips her stocking feet into the new ones. The leather is sturdy and stiff. Yes, these will do fine, she thinks with a smile. They will hold up. They will last. She looks up and finds him ready with a buttonhook. She extends a foot and in a flash, he's twisting the buttons into place.

"Quite the service," she says, smiling at him, thankful that he didn't make a production out of her need to have the shoes altered specifically for her. She hadn't been looking forward to trying the shoes in the store in front of strangers who might pity her. She didn't want anyone's pity.

"We do our best," he says, patting her ankles and indicating that she should stand.

"Proof is in the pudding," she says, rising to her feet as he rises to his. She slowly circles the room, trying to determine if her gait is steady. If her slight discomfort is from the newness of the boots or something more critical. The doctors had cautioned her to take care with her shoes unless she wanted to end up with an even more pronounced limp, or be confined to a chair.

"Looks good," he says, breaking the quiet.

"Yes," she says, her smile pulling from ear to ear as her steps become more assured.

"If they need adjustment, stop by the store and we'll fix you right up."

"Thank you, Mr. Wertheimer."

"You're very welcome, Miss Hirshhorn. Now, on to the next?"

Alice's eyes shift from side to side in confusion. "I only bought one pair."

"No woman has ever complained about having too many shoes," he says, motioning for her to sit in the chair again.

"Mr. Wertheimer." Alice exhales in frustration. "I thank you for your thoughtfulness, but I'm a school teacher. I can only really afford one new pair of shoes."

"That kind of thinking will put me out of business." He clasps his hands behind his back and nods at the chair.

Alice tilts her head, trying to figure out how to get away from the aggressive salesman who doesn't seem to know how to listen. "And the kind of thinking that involves you giving away shoes won't put you out of business more quickly?"

"Miss Hirshhorn, you misunderstand. This is *my* shoe company, The *Wertheimer* Shoe Company. And these," he says, gesturing to the two closed boxes on the floor, "are a present for *you*."

"But why?" she asks, not giving an inch, and being careful not to telegraph her surprise at mistaking the shop owner for a clerk.

"Because women like shoes," he says in explanation, his hands held out, palms up, as if an explanation is entirely unwarranted. "Really, I've never had to work so hard to *give* a woman a pair of shoes before," he says under his breath.

"You regularly *give* women shoes?" Alice asks in puzzlement, now questioning his sanity.

"No, of course not," he says, a hand raking through his hair, the strands of silver at his temples shining in the warm electric lights. "What kind of businessman would I be?"

"I'm not sure you want me to answer that," says Alice, folding her arms across her chest, "seeing as how I ordered one pair of shoes and you've appeared with three."

"Miss Hirshhorn," he says, hands coming to rest on his hips. "Are you always this difficult?"

"This isn't me being difficult, I assure you. This is me being rational. Really. Three shoes for the price of one? What sort of sales tactic is this?"

"It seemed like a good idea at the time," he says, his hands flying out from his sides. "*Oh, Mr. Wertheimer*," he says in a falsetto, "*The shoes are lovely. Yes, you may take me to the theater.*"

"Why would you take me to the theater?" asks Alice, confused by the entire situation.

"Because I'd like to take you to the theater. If you like the theater, that is."

"I do."

"Good," he says, his open hands resting on his hips as he rocks back on his heels. "Saturday, then?"

Alice's brain suddenly organizes the conversation in a way that it makes sense. "You *want* to take me to the theater?"

"And to dinner, if you also eat," he answers with a nod.

"Yes."

"Yes, you eat or yes you'll go to dinner and the theater with me?"

"Yes, to both, I suppose." The words slip from her lips before she can think them through, before she can recall the handmade card sitting on her desk, waiting to be posted.

"I suppose I should stop while I'm ahead," he says with a smile.

"Does this mean that there really are other shoes for me in the boxes?"

"Ah, so you are in fact a woman. Yes. Sit. Let's see what we find."

She sits and he quickly dispatches the new button-on boots from her feet. The second box reveals a pair of short, cream leather pumps with a set of thin straps across the open top.

"These were some of our top sellers last summer. And I've reordered them for this spring, as well, but this time with the two straps across, rather than a single strap." His eyes move from where she's slid her feet into the pumps to her face. "These aren't leftovers that I'm trying to get rid of, Miss Hirshhorn. And the cobbler made your adjustments, so you can't send them back even if you tried."

She covers her face with embarrassment.

"I'm sorry," she apologizes through her fingers. "I've never had a man give me shoes before and I wasn't sure what to make of it. What to make of you. I thought you were a clerk. I didn't know you were the owner."

"On to the next?" he asks, ignoring her apologies. She slips out of the pumps with a nod.

"Thank you," she answers. "Forgive me."

"Nothing to forgive, Miss Hirshhorn."

"Alice," she corrects him, once again scanning the room to ensure they are alone.

"Alice," he says when her gaze returns to meet his. "Call me Fred."

He settles the pumps back in their box and cuts the string off the third box.

"This feels like Christmas," she says, embracing the joy.

"In so many ways, it does. Merry Christmas in February, Alice." He hands her the box and she places it in her lap. She opens the lid and pulls back the tissue.

"Oh my!"

"Are they good enough?"

"I don't know what to say."

"You don't have to say anything. I can see your delight."

A giggle rises from her. "It's too much. Really too much," she politely protests.

"It's a done deal, Alice. They are yours."

Overwhelmed by him, but not a bit cowed, she pulls the shoes from the box and admires how the red and orange satin stitching glows in the warm light.

SEVENTEEN

ALI

S*eptember*

"SWEETHEART, HOW WAS CALIFORNIA?" Mom asked over the phone around lunchtime. I heard the worry-tinged hope in her voice and I was certain my sister Jess had told her that Scott and I were over.

I'd been home a few days and had been sending my mom's calls to voicemail. Our texts were short and informative. Mainly about what I wanted to do for my birthday next week. I hadn't breathed a word to her or anyone else other than Jess about my breakup with Scott. Jess had put me on speaker in the car while she sat in line for after-school pickup and listened patiently while I huffed and sniffled. I hadn't even told Caroline. Talking to Jess was easier because I couldn't see the sorrow and concern etched on her face. If I told Caroline, she'd want to talk about it and I didn't have words. It was too fresh. The wound had stopped bleeding but the scab was only beginning to form.

"Fine," I said, again punting on having this conversation, but it was far from fine. It wasn't fine and it wasn't good and it wasn't bad. It wasn't anything anymore, other than over.

"Can you go over to Grammie's? The move is coming up and she's a little low. Patrick's going to visit tomorrow and Jess spoke with her this morning. Having you kids around her really keeps her mood up, but she's just very sad right now."

"Understandable." Our moods would match in that respect. And while we were both setting aside parts of our lives to be in the past, her move was the scary one. We all knew where it led, even if we didn't say the words.

At dinnertime I arrived at Grammie's house empty-handed. I'd meant to pick up dinner for us, but the steam I'd been running on for the last few days had given out. I had nothing left. She greeted me at the door with a glass of wine in hand. One glass of red wine a day. She'd negotiated a hard bargain with her doctors—those who treated her and those who loved her.

"Ali," she said with a smile.

"Good to see you moving pretty well."

"I'm not dead yet," she said with a rueful smile as she passed me the glass of wine. "Looks like you could use this more than I could."

I shook my head no. "Keep your wine. Bar cart still stocked?"

"Whose house do you think you're in, sweet pea?"

I followed her to the formal living room. The big space

looked even bigger with only two wingback chairs, a coffee table, and the brass and glass bar cart that I'd known all of my life. She prided herself on her hostessing skills. Taught me how to make a Scotch and soda for my grandpa when I was about eight. *Just a splash to open it up. You don't want to drown it, sweetie.* The small dish that always held a fresh lime and lemon was empty, but the ice bucket was stocked. I reached for the decanted Scotch and fixed my grandfather's signature drink for myself.

"You should take the bar cart," she said, making herself comfortable in a chair.

"Grammie," I exhaled. "I mean, I love it, but I don't have room."

"And it's probably not your California style."

I swirled the amber drink in my glass, the two ice cubes clinking, and sat in the other chair, the exhaustion I'd been keeping at bay overtaking me.

"Oh, sweetie." She sighed.

"Yeah," I said, taking a sip of the fiery drink and hoping the burn would help tamp down the tears. I blinked against them. "Yeah," I repeated, pursing my lips together and nodding my head. "Yeah."

"He'll come around," she said, reaching over to pat my knee.

"That's the thing," I said, scrubbing my face with my free hand and deciding to come clean. "I don't think he'll come around. And I won't come around and it's just—" I waved my hand in the air, letting the motion supply the words I couldn't say.

"You're young, Ali. I'm sure it doesn't feel like it, but this isn't the end of the world."

"I know. It's not. But—"

149

"But nothing. Life is too short to be married to someone who you don't want to be married to. Or, even worse, being married to someone who doesn't want to be married to you."

"Yeah, but it still sucks."

"Language," she corrected me.

"Sorry," my ten-year-old self squeaked.

She accepted my apology with a nod. "Even if you don't take that bar cart, the decanter would look lovely on the top of the buffet."

"It would," I said, eager to agree to take more of her things if it only meant that we could stop talking about Scott. "You ready for the move?"

"I won't ask about Scott, and you won't talk about my move, deal? Honestly, anything else is fine—your birthday. How anxious your mom gets about Thanksgiving dinner. Strange patients. Something awful that Patrick or Jessica did to you when you were children. The weather."

"Definitely not my birthday. How about Alice?" Before she could answer, I continued because Grammie wasn't just having a good day. She was having a great day. If only I knew how to bottle the magic of a great day, I'd never be sad again. "I read those letters."

Her head tilted slightly to the left. *I was wrong about her having a good day. She doesn't remember.*

"In the buffet you gave me. In the bottom drawer. There were a bunch of love letters to Alice from the guy in the Philippines," I explained, hoping to trigger her memory.

"Sweetie, I have bad days, but not that bad. I remember. And I'm not sure I want to know about the letters.

They must have meant a lot to my mother to keep them all those years."

"They are so romantic. And it's heartbreaking because they were going to get married, but the First World War ruined things."

"That is sad," she agreed, taking a drink from her glass. "I knew there was someone else. When she was happy with my father, he'd gloat about how right she was that she'd 'picked this fella.' In all honesty, I thought there was a chance she'd been married before, and I thought there was more than a chance it was this man with the letters from the Philippines."

"No. No secret marriage," I assured her. "He constantly wrote her about them getting married one day. The letters are all about his plans for their life together and he even talks about them taking a honeymoon trip to Japan. I hope you don't mind that I read them."

"I don't, and I don't think she'd mind that a bit, Ali. I didn't read them because everyone is entitled to their secrets, but I couldn't throw them away either."

"Was she happy?"

"I suppose I should say that I don't really know, that no one can really know how someone else feels. But I can tell you what I think, and I think she was happy. When I think of my mother, I see her smiling and laughing. And, as long as I'm being honest, I remember some screaming matches between my parents—they were both very hardheaded— but I never remember her saying that she wished she'd chosen that other fella or that she regretted marrying my father. She might have felt that, but I don't remember her saying it and I don't remember her acting like my father was anything but her love."

"So she loved Fred?"

"I'd say very much. When he died, she was heartbroken. This was well before you came along. They lived in the house I grew up in on Volunteer Park until my father couldn't handle the stairs, and then they moved to a high-rise condo near the floating bridge. They had the most terrific view across the lake to Mount Rainer."

"Heartbroken but with a terrific view of the mountain? Doesn't sound so bad," I quipped, the liquor warming me from inside out. "Beats my view of the hospital."

"You'll be fine. I promise. My mother became less than herself after my father died. I can't explain it well. But that's how I know you'll be fine. You look tired, but you don't seem distraught."

"So, back to Alice," I said, again steering the subject away from Scott or how tired I looked on the cusp of my thirty-fourth birthday. "The man who wrote the letters was Elliott Keller. And I think I've found his descendants. My friend Caroline did some online genealogy research and found a woman named Gail Keller Copley who lived in New Mexico and I'm trying to contact her. I sent her a message on the computer and I haven't heard back, so I'm going to send her a letter in the mail, if that's okay with you."

"You should. They're your letters, Ali. They aren't mine. And if you want to give them back to his family, you don't need my blessing."

WHEN THE RECRUITER called a few days later, asking me if I'd be interested in joining a group that was forming in

Orange County, I hung up on her. I didn't have the bandwidth to have a normal conversation because that conversation was months late. Seven months ago, right after UCI told me they were passing, it would have been different. I would have been over the moon at the opportunity to be in California with Scott regardless of what job it was. I scolded myself for being childish.

"Okay," the recruiter said, a little too patiently, when I called back and apologized. She was sweet to me, and let us pretend that her call had just dropped, but I knew she was reminding herself that she got a paycheck from placing jackass doctors in their dream jobs. "So any Orange County is out unless it's got a strong research component?"

"Yeah. I'm sorry. That's really non-negotiable. No Southern California."

"That's a one-eighty from the direction we've been moving."

I could tell she was frustrated and fishing for an explanation, but I wasn't going to give her one. "I know. Let's see what else is out there."

"What's your top want in your next position?" she asked. "Other than a permanent position. I know you want that, but if you've changed your mind and want another locum tenens contract, that's easy to do."

"No. I still want something permanent." That much I knew. Another year of the in-between wasn't what I wanted.

"Okay, so tell me what your top wants are. Maybe that will help me get you some good options."

It was a fair question and one that I hadn't thought about since I was seventeen, applying for colleges, and dying to get away from home. *What I want... What I want... Not what I have to do, not what needs to be done, but what I want.*

"Ummm..." I didn't have a good answer because there wasn't a good answer. Caroline. My parents. Grammie. Even my siblings and their families. I liked the hospital, the staff, my patients. Did I want to stay here? Did I want to leave? "I'm not sure," I finally answered truthfully.

"That's fine. A change of pace is a good thing. You'd prefer the West Coast still? If no California, what about Seattle? The children's hospital system there is massive and needs folks all the time. I can put feelers out there. Or Portland. Everyone's dying to move to Portland these days. Or maybe you go back east? Have you thought about North Carolina? Charlotte is hopping and—" She tried her best to sell me, but it was if I was getting over a stomach virus. Nothing sounded appetizing.

EIGHTEEN

ALI

ctober

<<From: Ben Copley
    To: Ali Waller>>
    Dear Ms. Waller,
    I don't know who you are, but I ask that you leave my mother Gail alone.
    Sincerely,
    Ben Copley

That was not the email I was expecting. Out of surgery and on my way to clinic, I pulled up my personal email to check in with the world. This was the third day since Grammie's move and she'd been short of breath and had some swelling in her ankles. We knew the care was better at the assisted-living facility, but the stress of the change was the unknown in the equation. And with her retaining fluid, we all were sweating whether we'd made the right call to move her or whether we should have kept her at home. I didn't have time to deal with Ben Copley or the mystery of Elliott, and so I moved on to the morning message from Grammie's nurse. Grammie had lost almost two pounds in twenty-four hours, which was an excellent development. She was breathing easier too.

Relieved, I shoved my phone back into the deep pocket of my white lab coat and walked through the clinic. A quick knock on the exam room door to announce myself, and I stepped through. "Mr. and Mrs. Ursini," I said. Jackson was in his dad's arms and swiveled his head to look at me. "And hello, Jackson!"

"He knows his name now!" his mother told me as she planted a kiss on her toddler's round head.

"That's so great. I'm so glad that he's responding well."

I pulled up Jackson's file on my computer and flipped through the reports. Everything looked promising. Good, even. I asked about concerns while I examined the surgical site. Three months post-op, and I was a little surprised to see them on my schedule.

"No concerns. Not at all," Mrs. Ursini said.

"Yeah. Couldn't be better. But," Mr. Ursini said, jostling Jackson on his knee, "let's talk about going bilateral." His eyes were bright with expectation and hope.

I nodded and launched into my spiel. "Having two ears helps normal-hearing listeners distinguish speech from noise in two ways—spacial separation, and redundancy where the auditory system gets two 'looks' at the sound," I said. "And, like we talked about before, doing the procedures closely together will hopefully allow his brain to better develop pathways to both systems rather than become more focused on the first installed system."

"Sign us up," said Mr. Ursini, raising Jackson's arms in triumph.

I looked over at his wife, who was staring at her son. "I guess the risks are the same," she said after a beat.

"Yes. No procedure is without risks. The good news is that Jackson managed the first procedure well. I have no reason to believe the outcome will be different, but you never can be certain." The couple looked back and forth at each other and at Jackson. "How about you guys call my office and we'll set up another visit in a week or so? Give you time to discuss it."

"We're ready now," Mr. Ursini said, pressing on, over-riding his wife's concern.

I looked at her. Every so often, I'd see this. One parent being too bullish on the future and the other, often the mom, wanting to be conservative, not wanting to press their luck.

"Really, honey, let's get us on the books," he urged her.

She nodded and I typed notes in my chart to schedule them for an office visit without Jackson. A nod from her wasn't enough. This was elective surgery and Jackson would live a rich life without it. I needed buy-in from them both before we booked an OR.

～

THAT NIGHT AT HOME, I was curled up with a glass of wine on my sofa, some mindless home renovation show on, when I remembered the email from the Ben guy.

I grabbed my computer out of my bag and read his message again. Sure enough, the dude was telling me to stay away. Had I been pushy or rude? No, I assured myself. I'd sent the Facebook message into the great void of the internet only to have no response. Scott was probably right that it'd gotten caught in a filter. I'd sent letters to several Gail Copleys because Caroline and I couldn't find addresses for any Gail Keller Copley. So I sent letters to all the Gail Copleys we could find who we thought were in the right age range to be Elliott's granddaughter— New Hampshire, Atlanta, San Diego, San Jose, Santa Fe, Mesa, and one to a suburb south of Seattle.

And even though Santa Fe was most likely where she lived, I liked the idea of Gail somehow living in Seattle, of her walking the same streets that her grandfather did. Maybe Seattle would be a good option for me. Grammie would definitely approve of me going back to a "home" that had never truly been my home, and there was no denying that it was a gorgeous place to live.

Dear Ms. Copley, I'd written each time by hand, using my best, most legible, non-doctor handwriting on the monogrammed stationery that Grammie had given me for a birthday present years ago.

My name is Ali Waller. I believe that your grandfather Elliott Keller wrote love letters to my great-grandmother Alice Hirshhorn when Elliott was living in the Philippines in the 1910s. I have these letters, and if you are interested, I would be happy to share a copy with you. I look forward to hearing from you. My contact information follows.

Sincerely,
Ali Waller

I READ through Ben's snippy email again and wrote back, channeling my best bedside manner and angling for polite and professional.

<<FROM: Ali Waller
    To: Ben Copley>>
    Mr. Copley,
    Thank you for writing me. I really would like to share these letters with you or your family, if you are interested. Please let me know.
    Sincerely,
    Ali

I HIT SEND, and found a happy email from the recruiter letting me know that Children's in Seattle might have needs. I was excited, but tamped it down. No way that's happening, I told myself. I mean, I had the credentials, but that system was world-class and if I couldn't land any position in California, why would they even want to talk to me?

What you can *do is often simply a matter of what you* will *do.* I heard it in my head, said to me a million times by Grammie, and I knew it came from some children's book—and one that I'd likely read at some point—but I couldn't remember which one. Nothing ventured, nothing gained, I said to myself before I typed back. *Sure, Seattle would be awesome. Let's make it happen.*

When I woke up in the morning, I had a message from the recruiter saying she was going to do her best to get me an interview if they did have an opening. *Do your best, fairy godmother.* Also in my email was a bit of bile.

<<BEN COPLEY to Ali Waller>>
I don't know what kind of scam this is, but stay away.

SCAM? My hackles shot up. I set my laptop down and snagged my phone. Stomping over to the sideboard, I pulled out the letters and snapped some pictures, taking care to capture Elliott's signature and return address, complete with his Philippines post office box number. I immediately tapped out a reply on my phone. This time I couldn't muster polite.

<<ALI WALLER to Ben Copley>>
Mr. Copley,

This is not a scam. Here are some pictures of the letters. If I've reached the wrong family, I apologize and will leave you alone. But I assure you this isn't a scam. Your mother is perfectly safe. I'm not some Nigerian prince. I'm a physician in Kansas City. Google me. My grandmother gave me the letters and I'd like to find Elliott's family.

Sincerely,

Ali Waller, Real Person

A FEW MINUTES PASSED, and I thought that if I'd scared him away, that was entirely fine. If it wasn't meant to be, it wasn't meant to be. But at least I tried and I could run down the other Gail Copleys, if I could figure out which of the Gail Copleys had a son named Ben. Another sleuthy request for Caroline's tot time library adventures. I fixed another cup of coffee and had begun scrolling through the morning news when my computer dinged.

<<BEN COPLEY to Ali Waller>>

Dr. Waller,

Very nice résumé. Consider improving it by adding another title. If not Nigerian royalty, Duchess of Kansas City?

To be honest, when two letters arrived for my mom within a few weeks of each other, it was very odd. Who sends handwritten letters anymore? It seemed off. And one was forwarded from an old address. Then she mentioned how she'd been on Facebook and someone had tried to contact her there about some old letters as well, but she'd ignored the message.

I'll talk with my mom about your Elliott Keller. Yes, that's the name of my great-grandfather. But before I share anything about us, do you have any more details about your Elliott that I can use to crosscheck against my Elliott?

Sincerely,

Baron Ben von Copley

P.S. Ten thousand gold doubloons can be yours, if only you advance my loyal footman ten silver drachmas.

<<ALI to Ben>>

Baron Ben,

Or should I open with Your Grace or My Lord or something? Not sure of the etiquette.

Based upon the letters, "my" Elliott is from Burr Oak,

Michigan, but I believe he spent most of his childhood in Indiana. He graduated from the University of Michigan and taught school in the Philippines during the American occupation (or whatever the appropriate word is for that. Colonization? I don't know.) He left teaching and worked with his uncle in a pharmacy. They were based in Iloilo. "My" Elliott eventually took a job with what I think was a division of Standard Oil in the Pacific. He met my great-grandmother Alice on a train to Seattle, where she taught school.

In addition to the letters, I have a few photographs I'd be happy to share with your family as well.

Sincerely,

Countess of Kansas, M.D.

P.S. Drachmas set to arrive by passenger pigeon on the 30th of February.

SATISFIED with myself and the potential progress on finding Elliott's family, I stared at my screen a bit before hitting send, then turned to scroll through social media updates. A minute later, my laptop dinged again.

<<BEN to Ali>>

Dr. Waller,

Yeah. I'm not sure about the Philippines thing, but he worked for an oil company. Pretty sure that's us.

Let me talk with my mom.

Ben

NINETEEN

ALI

O*ctober*

"OH, A REAL PHONE CALL!" Caroline teased for a second before her voice dropped to a serious tone. "Are you breaking up with me? Over the phone? Not a text message?"

"Of course," I deadpanned, though the slight sting from the way Scott and I actually ended it lingered. Only Jess knew the hows and the whys. "Only jerks break up with their best friends by text, but I don't like you enough to want to see your face, so phone it is."

"Excellent. What are you doing?"

"Not much. Laundry, errands. Going to check in on my grandma. Might go to the gym. Might go read in a coffee shop. I've got the day off."

"Oh good! If you see your grandma, you'll be out our way, then. Come have lunch with me and Bess."

"You don't have to bribe me with Bess, you know. Lunch with just you is fine."

"Trust me. I love her, but I'd really love for her to have someone else to climb all over while I eat."

"So, I should wear my finest silk blouse and other dry-clean-only clothes?"

"Absolutely. And I'm demanding that we do KC right. Barbecue ribs."

"I'll wear my finest yoga pants and rattiest sweatshirt, then. It's not Bess I'm worried about. You always make such a mess."

At noon, I was back in the suburb where Caroline and I had grown up, sitting at a table that I'd undoubtedly sat at during some point in my more than thirty years on this planet, but this time, I had a squirmy seven-month-old in my arms.

Caroline tucked into a slab of ribs and a giant side of mac and cheese, justifying the plate to herself by muttering something about nursing and her extra calorie allotment. I didn't care what she ate or if my sandwich and fries went cold because I was happy to feed Bess some Cheerios while I updated Caroline on my job search and how Providence was now on my radar thanks to a med school classmate.

"Can't you just stay here?"

I made a comically large frowny face.

"Really." She laughed. "It's not bad. I didn't think I'd come back after college, but I did. KC's not glamorous, but it's a good place to raise a family."

"Because, oh, look!" I exclaimed in mock surprise. "I've

got one of those family things in my back pocket! Huh, wonder how it got in there?"

Caroline stuck her tongue out at me. "You know what I mean."

"I do," I said, taking a break from my silliness. "And KC will always be home, but it's not what I want."

"What do you want?"

"That conversation is way too deep for barbecue," I said. "That chat requires drinks. I've got an interview in Seattle next month. I don't want to say more because I don't want to jinx it."

"Understood. How's your grandma?" Caroline asked.

"Good, I think. Her vitals are trending better and she's settling in well. It's a nice place. It doesn't feel like assisted living," I said, bouncing Bess's diapered bottom on my knee. "It's more like a swanky hotel. They have a concierge and two different dining rooms. Laundry service. Room service, if you like."

"How do I sign up?"

"Yeah, I thought the same thing."

"Say hi to her for me," she said, returning her focus to her meal.

"Will do," I said, taking my opening for the big news I'd been wanting to share with her in person. "I'll also say hi to Ben Copley, son of the mythical Gail Keller Copley."

"You found the family?" she said around a mouthful of mac and cheese. "Shut up!"

"I know! The internet and your librarian are magic. I sent out handwritten letters and then this guy emailed me. Thought I was running some sort of scam on his mom," I said with a laugh.

"Yeah, you're like the least scammy person ever. Hey,

remember the saga of you trying to return the lipstick when Sephora sent you an extra tube?"

"Let's just forget that," I said, blushing at the memory.

"No, really. Let's not. It was hysterical. The saleswoman thought you were insane and you were being all earnest about it, how you hadn't paid for it and you needed to return it. 'It was the company's mistake,' she kept saying. 'I wouldn't worry about it, if I were you.' And you kept saying no and she kept saying that she couldn't take it back without giving you a refund and you kept refusing. I was cleaning out a closet during Bess's nap the other day and found that lipstick at the bottom of an old purse. Looks good on me, doesn't it?"

She smiled and I noticed the bright plum lips.

"Pretty," I agreed. "It's probably what, five years old?"

"Closer to ten, I'd say. But hey, free lipstick! Now tell me about the scam you're running."

"Yeah, so he thought I was trying to con his mom or something." I quickly caught her up on my emails with Ben.

"When was this?"

"Middle of the week."

"Heard back?"

"Not yet."

She wiped her hands again on her napkin and pulled out her phone. "Ben Copley, let's find you."

"No," I said.

"Why not?" she asked, not pausing to look up from her screen. "You told him to google you and clearly he did. Fair game to google him back."

"I feel a little creepy about it. I mean, if you're just going to look at his—"

"LinkedIn profile. I'm pulling up Ben Copleys now."

"Caroline," I exhaled.

"Don't even pretend. You want to know."

"I'm not denying that I want to know, but I don't want to be the googler."

"Plausible deniability works for me. I'll do the dirty work."

I waved my hand in front of me, encouraging her to keep on Caroline-ing while I enjoyed some baby snuggles and french fries.

"Ben Copley. Several of them. Any clues?" she asked.

I thought for a minute and realized that he hadn't shared anything about himself with me. "No idea," I said.

"Most of the Ben Copleys that I'm finding are British, or at least live in the UK."

"Anything is possible."

"Hey, Benjamin Copley. Tech guy."

"Tech guy?" I asked as Bess began to nuzzle her tiny face into my chest.

"I fill prescriptions and change diapers. I don't computer. You computer."

"Computer is not a verb," I said, drolly responding to our long-running joke.

"See, I don't even know that much. But really, here's a LinkedIn bio of a guy in Seattle who works for—"

"Microsoft."

"Nope. Google."

"Huh."

"Yeah, it's nice when you're wrong for a change." She smirked.

"I wonder if that's him. What else?" I urged her on.

"He's a hottie."

"Really?" I wasn't going to lie. I was interested in seeing if Baron Ben was as cute as he was funny.

"Oh, yeah. Wanna see?"

"Of course," I said, shooting my hand across the table to snatch the phone but before I could get it, Caroline pressed it to her chest.

Her eyes got big. "You have a crush on him."

"Are you crazy?" I asked, feigning insult.

"Ben. Copley. Come on. Spill. We've got like three minutes until she's going to demand to nurse," she said, nodding at Bess before shoveling another forkful of mac and cheese into her mouth.

"Fine, but I don't have a crush on him." I caught her up on a bit of the email I'd held back while she finished her meal—the nicknames.

"Countess of Kansas and Baron Ben?" she said, taking Bess from me. "That's adorable."

I shrugged, playing it off. "I think it was his way of apologizing when he realized I was a real person and wasn't trying to scam anyone. Anyway, phone, picture, now."

I reached across the table to try to snag the phone again and she whipped it out of my reach. "Promise me you'll tell me when he emails you back?"

"Yeah."

"Cool," she said, passing me her phone. "No picture. Sorry for teasing you like that. It's just a bio."

My heart sank a little. Ridiculous, I scolded myself. *So ridiculous to let a friendly bit of banter with a stranger make me feel so good.*

TWENTY

ALI

N *ovember*

MY INTERVIEW with Seattle Children's went well, but I knew when I left the hospital in the afternoon that I was far from a shoe-in. I was having dinner with some of the doctors in the group, so they could make sure I was easy enough to get along with, but I had a few hours to kill. I looked up the Astoria on my phone, wondering if the hotel-slash-boarding house where Alice lived was still there. And it was. It was now condos, and I wondered how much of the interior was the same, and if I moved there, whether I could rent in the building.

I ordered a car. "Minor and Pike," I told the driver, checking the time to make sure I could make a quick run downtown, get cleaned up at the hotel, and make the dinner reservation, considering the clogged Seattle traffic.

During the drive, I googled a bit more and turned up some historic pictures of the building that was built in 1909. It would have been pretty new when Alice lived there.

I got out at the corner and stared up at the building, counting the six stories. It was taller than I'd imagined, but being completely honest, I hadn't imagined it being an actual place. I shook my head and looked down the street. Alice walked here, on this very sidewalk. She lived here with her friends. She went to work. She probably wrote letters to Elliott while sitting by one of the windows that I looked up at, and then dropped them in a postal box on this street.

And at that moment, Alice became real to me. I could be her. I could be the woman writing letters. And a hundred years later, she could be me.

The wind began to pick up and I walked across the street to a brewpub, where I made myself at home at a table by the window with a hoppy northwest IPA in hand and wondered more about her and her life when she lived at the Astoria. What was in this building when Alice lived here? Clearly not a trendy pub filled with an eclectic assortment of chandeliers, guarded over from above by a statute of some six-armed dancing goddess. A bakery? A restaurant? A grocery store? Some sort of clothing shop? Or maybe a fabric store? Or a printing press?

I flicked my phone back on to do a little more internet sleuthing about Alice's Seattle and scrolled through my emails, stopping when I found one from Ben.

<<BEN to Ali>>

Hi, Dr. Waller,

I spoke with my mother and then did a little legwork of my own.

Looks like we do share the same Elliott Keller.

My mom says that I met my great-grandpa Elliott a few times when I was very small. She says I didn't go to his funeral because she thought I was too young, but that she did take me to the hospital to see him before he died. I have this vague memory of going to a really big hospital when I was little. I always thought it might have been a dream, but now I'm thinking it actually happened and I was visiting my great-grandpa.

Anyway, here's what you probably want to know—

My mom doesn't know much about Elliott's childhood. She thought the family was from Indiana. She does know that he was a school teacher by training and that's how he ended up in the Philippines. My mom says she thinks that several of our relatives moved to the Philippines in the early 1900s, but she doesn't know what they were doing there or how any of them made a living, and everyone moved back to the States later. Elliott worked for an oil company, running their Asia division for a while, but she says it was Mobil Oil and not Standard Oil. And, thanks to Google, I've learned that Mobil Oil and Standard Oil are connected.

Elliott married Pearl. They had my grandpa Ted (aka Theodore) and his brother Eugene. Eugene died young.

Elliott and Pearl and Ted moved to San Francisco when WWII ended. That's where Grandpa Ted met Grandma Louise. They had my mom, Gail Keller Copley. She's an only child. Then, my sister and I came along.

My mom would like a copy of the letters and anything else you have. She has pictures of Elliott, Pearl, and Grandpa Ted, but nothing before the end of WWII.

My mom also wants to know about your great-grandmother.

Thanks,

Ben Copley

I WAS ABSOLUTELY FLOORED. I read the email at least a half dozen times, wishing it had more. More information. More of anything that would answer my question about whether Elliott was happy. But mainly I was amazed that the Elliott I knew was a real person. Who lived, and loved, and had children, and now I was emailing with his great-grandson. Would Elliott's romance with Alice have been different now with emails and Skype and airlines? Of course. But would it have ended differently?

TWENTY-ONE

ALI

November

I TEXTED Caroline to see if she was around to talk. She said she'd call once she got Bess down for the night. I needed to talk now, about how I'd found Elliott's family, so instead of heading home, I headed to see Grammie. But first I swung by the local grocery for fresh berries. Even if she couldn't have a glass of wine, we could enjoy a little treat.

"I don't see your deal with the doorman," I said after kisses and hugs, with a few fresh blackberries in a bowl for us and a glass of wine in my hand. My mother had laid down the law and Grammie's hard-bargained-for glass of wine was no more, but Grammie insisted that her visitors be welcomed to her apartment with a stocked bar cart.

"He's Eddie Haskell from *Leave It To Beaver*."

"I don't see it. He always seems perfectly nice to me."

"That's it. 'Good morning, Mrs. Markham.' 'Good evening, Mrs. Markham.' 'Off to the chair exercise class, Mrs. Markham?'"

"Yeah, that's called being friendly."

"It's called him not minding his own business. Is he trying to get into my will? Does he gather information for some sort of report on us?"

Yes, all of the staff do, in fact, I wanted to tell her. From the nursing staff to the activities director, we got regular email updates on Grammie, but I didn't want to creep her out. She was here because she needed care. She needed eyes on her around the clock and a crack medical team a moment away.

"Friendly," I asserted, ending that conversation and knowing exactly how I was going to distract her. "I've tracked down the family of the letter writer."

"The Filipino man?"

"American man," I corrected her. "Elliott Keller."

"He was American?"

"Yes," I said and I gave her a rundown of what I'd learned about the man and how he'd met Alice. "And through some internet sleuthing and the help from a librarian, Caroline and I found his descendants, including Elliott's granddaughter. I've been emailing with the great-grandson."

"That's amazing," Grammie replied. "That you were able to find him at all is absolutely amazing."

"It really is. The world is so small in so many ways now. Elliott's family wants to see the letters."

"They don't belong to them." Grammie bristled.

"Don't worry. I haven't offered the letters. I'm going to send them copies. Do you want a set?"

She folded her hands and unfolded them, watching her fingers work. "Yes and no, I suppose. I never read them before, but maybe I should. No reason not to."

"You really should. It's fun to think about Alice on this big adventure, but I found some stuff about Elliott that is sad and I'm not sure if his family knows."

Grammie leaned toward me and patted my knee. "We all have sadness, sweet pea."

"Yeah." I exhaled. "I mean, it's not like he killed anyone, or anything, but he—and his family—were POWs during World War II. It looks like he was held by the Japanese in China for over four years while his wife and children were held in the Philippines during the war. And one of his children didn't survive."

"That's awful," she said after a minute. "The war was awful. But why don't you think they know?"

"Ben, Elliott's great-grandson, told me a little bit about the family. He said Elliott and his wife had two sons and one of the sons died young, like he didn't know the circumstances. Do I tell him?"

"Has he asked?"

"No." I sighed. "But I feel like he should know. Like they should know."

"Well, at least it's not one of those stories you hear about babies swapped at the hospital and raised by the wrong family, or parents who turn out really to be the grandparents. It's awful and sad, but it's not the same as a lie."

"That's true. I'll let him find out himself. Now tell me about Alice. Do you know how she met Great-Grandpa?"

"I'm not sure how much is exactly true, but she was teaching in Seattle, needed new boots, and bought them from his family's shoe store. They dated or were engaged for a long time. Over two years before they married. That seemed ridiculously long to me. Especially when your grandfather and I were engaged within two months of meeting. And my mother and I fought about that. Which way was the 'right' way. She thought you should wait and really know the person. I thought your grandfather hung the moon. And he did. At least for me. 'Marry in haste, repent at leisure,' she would tell me. And, let me tell you, I didn't regret it. Not a moment of it. But you didn't ask about me. My mother was warm and funny and got around just fine."

"'Got around just fine'?" I asked, baffled by the comment.

"She had a limp."

"A limp? No one told me this before."

"It wasn't debilitating. She didn't need a cane until she was older, but she'd contracted polio as a child and it caused her left leg to be weaker and a bit shorter than the other. Looking back, I think that's why her parents let her become a teacher and then move to Seattle. Farm life was going to be too hard on her."

"And that may explain why she didn't get married until later in life. She was, what? Thirty-five?"

"Thirty-one, and I think so." Grammie nodded sadly. "I hate to think that men would have passed her by because of her limp, but it's probably true. Such a good thing that she married someone in the shoe business. One sole had to be specially built up so that she could walk more evenly. She still had a little limp at times from the muscle weakness. But she went to college and taught school and then jumped on a train to Seattle and here we are."

"I can't believe no one ever told me this about Alice."

"Well, I didn't know you didn't know, and it wasn't that big of a deal."

"What else don't I know?"

Grammie laughed. "What *do* you know, sweet pea?"

And I told her what I'd learned. Facts and dates and glimpses of her through Elliott's eyes in his letters.

"She did love art. She was a talented painter. I'm glad to know that Elliott appreciated that about her. Again, something that was probably better suited for life in a city than on a farm."

"I can't believe how brave she was. To get on a train alone in the early nineteen hundreds and head for a city she'd never been to before and look for a job—"

"No, that isn't how that happened."

"How did that happen, then?"

"There was a group of her friends from normal school. The city of Seattle was in desperate need of teachers because its population was exploding and, so, as part of a teacher drive, she and some of her school friends were recruited. They went together. I don't remember how many of them. Maybe six? It was a sizeable group. They had contracts with the city to teach on a yearly basis and they lived in a boarding house, which is sort of like a hotel, but it wasn't a hotel like you and I think of a hotel now."

"I walked by the building when I was out there for my interview. It's condos now."

"The building is still there? That's wonderful that the city's history is being preserved. I worry about it changing too much. Anyway, the girls shared tiny little apartments, that didn't have proper kitchens. A cook prepared their meals and they ate in a dining room. She'd tell me stories about how much fun they'd had. About how they'd sewn white dresses and marched in a suffragette parade, and how they'd done work in support of the war effort. She always made it sound like they had a good time together."

"She was a suffragette?" My voice filled with pride.

"I suppose, but it wasn't all that radical in Washington. Women had the vote in state elections by the time she moved there, but they still weren't able to vote in presidential elections."

"I saw the League of Women Voters mentioned in her obituary."

"Yes, that was her passion. On Tuesdays we always ate oatmeal for dinner because she had her meetings during the day and was too busy to cook and that was the only thing my father knew how to make."

"And Great-Grandpa was cool with that? That's a lot for a husband back then to be okay with."

"Oh, Fred loved her very much. She wasn't a servant to him. Or to us. Sometimes I think TV shows have gotten in your head that everyone's life was like *The Donna Reed Show* or that TV show with the ad executives—"

"*Mad Men*," I supplied.

"Yes, that one. And yes, there were awful things about then. Like how the bank didn't let me have an account without your grandfather's name on it even though it was *my* money. But whatever the world thought of women, my father adored my mother. I remember when she was elected chapter president of the League of Women Voters. My father bent her back in a big kiss right there in the kitchen and then opened a bottle of champagne. I was seven and they let me have a small glass to celebrate with them."

"So that's why you remember that."

"I thought she'd been elected president of the United States," Grammie said with a laugh, patting her chest solidly as a cough followed.

"Did Alice stay politically active?"

"Oh, no. It wasn't that at all. I don't think it was politics that drove her. Not in the sense of what party you belonged to or what issues you supported. She was focused on participation. That women should participate."

"That's fascinating," I said.

"She was a wonderful woman."

"I'm sad I didn't get to know her."

"I am too. But Ali, she'd be so proud of you. You and your sister and your mom."

TWENTY-TWO

ALI

N*ovember*

AFTER MY GIRLS' night in with Grammie, I paid for access to a few genealogy databases and research tools. I was searching for Alice. And sure enough, I found her. Pictures in the social sections of the Seattle *Post Intelligencer* and *Times*. Mentions of dinner parties that Alice and Fred had attended. Even a little article about their vacation to Hawaii in 1934, and a few years later, their trip to New York via a ship through the Panama Canal.

And something I'd known all of my life struck me for the first time. I called my mom.

"If Great-Grandpa Fred owned a shoe store, how come he and Alice were able to travel to New York and Hawaii during the Great Depression? Wouldn't he have been wiped out?"

"He sold the store well before then," said my mom. "He made a lot of money during the First World War by selling shoes to the government. Both US and Canadian troops. There was some sort of scandal about the quality of the shoes, but by then he'd sold out and I don't know the details. He went into investments and managed the money."

"What happened to the shoe store?"

"He sold it to some folks who sold it to some other folks who sold it to Nordstrom."

"*Nordstrom* Nordstrom?"

"That's the family lore, at least. Do you feel better about shopping there now?" she teased, a smile in her voice.

"Weirdly, yes. So they just got lucky in the Great Depression?"

"I know he had losses and had to sell some land, but they weren't starving."

"No." I laughed. "Going to Hawaii for a month isn't starving."

Late that night, I wrote Ben.

<<ALI to Ben>>

Ben,

Please, call me Ali.

I cannot believe that I've found Elliott's family. Well, I didn't find you. My friend Caroline found you with the help of a librarian.

I'll get copies of the letters and scan or mail them to you. Whichever you like, let me know.

As far as my great-grandmother, I didn't know much about

her. Until your email, asking about her, I knew she was my great-grandmother and I was her namesake, but that was it.

I relayed what I'd learned about Alice, and by the time I was done, several screens were filled with words.

This is possibly the longest email I've written in years. I didn't mean to dump all of this on you, but it's not like there's any secret I've revealed. And it's too late and I'm too tired to read through it all again. So, it's yours to read or not read or share with your mom or just delete. Whatever you like.

Is it weird to also think that I wouldn't be here and you wouldn't be wherever you are if Alice and Elliott hadn't been kept apart? If they'd gotten married and had children and sailed off into the sunset? They both really wanted to visit Europe, by the way. I hope Elliott got to go because I don't think Alice ever did.

Let me know about how you want copies of the letters. Look forward to hearing back.

Ali

THE EMAIL SENT, I flipped over to my social media accounts. I wanted to see if I could find Ben. Scrolling through the stream of memes and baby pictures and political posts that greeted me, a selfie of Scott popped up. Him next to his surfboard, the end dug into the sand. He was backlit by the setting sun, the edges of his hair a golden halo, and tucked under his arm, a woman. I ached at the image, at the thought of him being with someone else. I clicked and the picture filled my screen. At least I didn't know her. Sure, it had been two months. Two months. And he was a catch, as my mom would say, and as she *had* said. Many times.

But I hadn't thought of him being with anyone else. More than anything, I hated that distance from him. That we hadn't spoken. That the man in the picture wasn't someone I knew anymore. That I didn't know that there was a woman in his life. That I learned there was a new woman in his life in this way—through a photo on Facebook. Three years together and, suddenly, we would forever be strangers. Seeing a picture of him happy stung too. Because I wasn't happy. I wanted to be happy for him, but I couldn't find a way to be a grown-up about the situation. I closed the lid on my laptop, no longer caring about tracking down Ben, and I crawled into bed with dreams of Elliott in my head.

A few days later, I heard from Ben.

<<BEN to Ali>>

Ali,

I liked comics a lot when I was growing up. So much that my childhood dream was to be a comic book artist. As you may have guessed, middle school was less than fun for me. Anyway, in some of the old Superman comics, there's this alternate reality. It's a planet called htraE, aka Earth spelled backward. It's like Earth, but everything is opposite. Add in the slew of Sci-Fi I read during those awful middle school years, and I'm convinced that there is an alternate universe or dimension where we don't exist. Okay, that seemed really weird once I wrote it out. I hope you get what I'm trying to say.

Anyway, scanned or photocopies work. Whatever is easiest for you.

Ben

I PULLED out the box of letters, and with my trusty phone, tried to take a few pictures. But the dark ink had soaked through the thin paper, making each letter written visible on the reverse. Add in the fact that Elliott's long, fluid hand was on both sides of the stationery, and the pictures were barely legible. I fiddled with the lighting. I tried putting the pages against light surfaces, against dark surfaces, but I couldn't get images easy to read. I'd need a professional.

<<ALI to Ben>>

Ben,

I know exactly what you're talking about. You don't make it through medical school without having known more than a few comic book geeks. Also, I have a big brother who was most definitely one of those med school comic book geeks. My thoughts were more along the lines of A Wrinkle in Time, *if you ever read that book. It's the first book I read with alternate universes. Confession—I haven't stopped. Alternative histories or parallel universes are my favorite things to read. So, yes, I understand exactly what you mean. World War I never happened and Bizarro Alice and Bizarro Elliott lived happily ever after and we don't exist.*

I've attached some photos of the letters, and I know they are terrible and hard to read. I'll chat with someone and figure out logistics of getting good images made. I want to get a nice set of copies for my mom as part of her Christmas present. I'll see about getting you a set or at least some cleaned-up images.

Ali

<<BEN to Ali>>

Ali,

I'm in tech. I can't go a week without hearing a comic book reference in a meeting. And that sounds awesome.

Ben

<<ALI to Ben>>

Ben,

I've found a vendor that can make scans and bind a physical set. I'm going to order a set for my mom, one for me, and a set for your family. Should be ready in a few weeks.

Ali

<<BEN to Ali>>

Ali,

That's cool. Thanks.

Ben

TWENTY-THREE

ALI

D*ecember*

<<BEN to Ali>>

Hey, Ali. I know you said Christmas and life gets busy, but could you get me an ETA on the letters? My mom is asking about them. And if something's come up, that's cool. Let me know. I hope you're okay.

Happy New Year.

Ben

TWENTY-FOUR

ALI

J*anuary*

<<Aʟɪ to Ben>>

Ben,

I'm so sorry. Happy New Year!

I've been super busy. I've been interviewing for a new job and that's been eating up my life right now. And my grand-mother—Alice's daughter—isn't doing so well. I know I'm lucky that I'm thirty-four and still have my grandmother, so I'm not complaining. She has congestive heart failure, which is miser-able. She moved into assisted living a few months ago, so we've been cleaning out her house, putting it on the market, and otherwise pretty much getting things in order for when she's no longer with us. My parents are both in Kansas City, as is my brother and his wife, so the load isn't all on my shoulders.

But between her situation and my job hunt, I've been juggling a lot of balls and, to be honest, I'm dropping some. Amazon to the rescue for all of my Christmas shopping this year.

I haven't gotten the nice photocopies made yet. I've got the company's contact info, but I haven't gone out there yet. It's in the burbs and they are open normal people hours, which don't match up to my weird hours, so I just need to block out the time on a weekday and do it. I'll get it done. I promise.

Ali

<<*Ben to Ali*>>

Ali,

I'm sorry about your grandmother. That's rough. To tell you the truth, my mom's health has been up and down. That's part of the reason that I made a big life change a few years ago. Switched jobs, moved up to Seattle. She had a cancer scare and it was easier to be closer to her than down in Phoenix.

Ben

<<Ali to Ben>>

I thought you were in Seattle, but I wasn't one hundred percent sure and I didn't want to be the creepy person from the internet who asks you to meet up. I was just there before the holidays, interviewing with Children's. I'll get my act together on the copies.

<<Ben to Ali>>

Yeah, I'm back home. Grew up in a suburb, but I live in the city now. Upside, my commute is a fifteen-minute walk. Down-side, I live in a tiny place with my big dog. But we make it work. You thinking of moving up here? That's a great hospital.

<<ALI to Ben>>

It's an amazing hospital. The interview went really well. I had dinner with some of the other docs and the team seemed nice. I'm on a year-long contract here in Kansas City. It's up in May. I've been filling in while one of their doctors does a stint in South America with Doctors Without Borders, and while it's been great to be home in order to help out with my grandma, the hospital doesn't have room for another permanent ENT. One of the Seattle surgeons is coming down to KC to observe me in a surgical case soon, so...fingers crossed.

<<BEN to Ali>>

Sounds like it's almost a done deal. Welcome to Seattle! When I moved back, it was a bit of a shock. I was in an actual house in Phoenix, and Thompson, that's my lab, had a pool and space to run around. Now he's got a thousand square feet and goes to work with me. Yes, I bring my dog to work with me. Let the mocking commence.

<<ALI to Ben>>

No mocking of the dog going to work. I'm kinda jealous on that front. Maybe I shouldn't have gone to medical school, so I could have a cool job where I could bring my dog along. I don't have time to keep a goldfish alive, but one day I'd like a dog. I had a golden retriever when I was growing up. No offense to this Thompson character, but Charlie Bucket was the best dog ever. And as soon as I'm settled somewhere I want to get a dog.

<<BEN to Ali>>

As much fun as I'm having emailing with you, this is an important question. Charlie and the Chocolate Factory *from the 70s or the one with Johnny Depp? Answer carefully.*

<<ALI to Ben>>

Is this a trick question? Because I don't even recognize the Johnny Depp version as being Charlie and the Chocolate Factory.

<<BEN to Ali>>

Excellent.
Marvel or DC?

<<ALI to Ben>>

The comic books? Whichever one has Wonder Woman.
Pancakes or waffles?

<<BEN to Ali>>

Close enough. And she's DC.
Waffles. Belgian style. Real maple syrup.

<<ALI to Ben>>

I'm nodding with approval. The hospital where I did my fellowship had a cafeteria with waffles so good I didn't care that the syrup wasn't the good stuff. If you're ever at Mass Eye and Ear, go to the main cafeteria and get the waffles. You will write me a thank you note.

Football or baseball?

<<BEN to Ali>>

If I'm honest and say something along the lines of real football—aka soccer—are we done here?

~

<<BEN to Ali>>

What's the verdict? A week of silence and you're still considering, or are we really done here? If so, I change my answer to football and let you suffer the consequences of my intentional ambiguity.

<<ALI to Ben>>

Oh, sorry. I haven't forgotten you. I've been busy with my family and work. Soccer is fine. Observation surgery went well. Also I had a phone interview with a hospital in Orlando.

I took the letters out to the place to get scanned and bound. Should be ready in a few weeks. The woman didn't quite know how long it would take because it depends on how much computer magic she has to do to the images to get them cleaned up where the ink that's bled through isn't so visible. What's new with you?

<<*BEN to Ali*>>

Not much. Work's good. Looking for a new place. Thompson's got a girlfriend. Or a boyfriend. I'm not sure what Bailey is, so I probably just should say he has a friend. He keeps playing with Bailey who is a gray standard poodle. Yes, he probably has more friends at my office than I do. Orlando would be...awful in August. And that comes from someone who spent a decade in Arizona. When will you hear about Seattle?

<<*ALI to Ben*>>

If things go through with Seattle, a few weeks for contract negotiation. Orlando? Who knows, but I thought the phone interview went well. And then the recruiter I'm working with has a phone interview set up with a hospital in El Paso. It's almost February, and my gig here is up in May, so I've still got some time to get a plan together. Physician placement either moves at warp speed or is painfully slow, and with me being under contract through May, no one's been in a hurry on getting me an offer.

What's new in Thompson's life? I've been cruising shelter websites for a puppy and every time I see a lab mix, which is every time I look at puppies, I think about him. What color lab is he, anyway?

~

"WHAT'S THE PLAN, ALI?" Caroline asked.

"Margaritas and queso and chips. Here's to finally getting a day off tomorrow." I took a salty-fruity sip of my electric green drink.

"Well, since that's what we ordered, duh," she said,

gesturing to the table. Bess was at home with Caroline's husband and we were having a post-holiday girls' night at a Mexican place that didn't skimp on the tequila or the food coloring in its artificially flavored mix. "But you know what I'm asking. How'd it go with the guy from Seattle?"

"Ben?"

"Sure. The surgeon who was coming to observe. I don't know his name."

"Oh," I said, the heat of a blush creeping up my cheeks. "Wrong guy. Will Lannings was the guy who came down to observe. It went well. It wasn't a particularly tricky procedure. We had dinner afterward and he gave me some more insight into the group."

"That sounds promising."

"Yeah," I agreed with a nod. "It did. I also had a call with a hospital in Orlando this week and the recruiter is setting up something with a hospital in El Paso."

"Okay, so I'm going to put a pin," she said, holding up one hand flat like a piece of paper and using pinched fingers to show how she was placing a pin in it, "in the Ben thing. But El Paso? Orlando? Can you get any farther away from Seattle than Orlando?"

"There's Miami."

"I'm being serious and you're being technical. Are you going to let your job decide the rest of your life?"

When I didn't answer, she continued, talking to me in a way that only someone who had known me for decades could without making me mad.

"You get to pick. You jumped through all of the hoops. Dotted every *i* and crossed every *t*. You get to pick now. Pick. And if you pick wrong, pick again. But you have to pick. You don't need to let someone else make this decision for you. Don't let Will Whatever from Wherever make this decision for you. Don't let some hospital administrator or some recruiter make this decision for you. Pick. Commit."

I took another drink of my margarita, pursed my lips and nodded. She was right. I needed to make a decision about what I wanted my life to look like, but I didn't know how to do that. "So like, how?"

"Where do you want to be? Seattle makes sense to me for you. It's a city. But Orlando and El Paso are just sprawling hot messes. Personally, I vote for Orlando, so we can see you and do Disney World trips when Bess is bigger. But don't let Scott scare you off from California. You want to be in Orange County? Then be in Orange County. It's big enough for both of you. And we can visit you and see Disneyland."

I snagged a clean napkin out of the pop-up dispenser and a pen from my purse and began drawing out a game we'd played so many times.

M-A-S-H I wrote at the top, and underneath I drew an empty box. As I began to draw sets of empty lines around the box, Caroline pulled the pen from my hand.

"Hey!" I protested.

"That's not picking. That's letting randomness pick. That's no different than letting someone else pick. You. Have. To. Pick," she said clapping her hands on the beat of each word for emphasis.

"Seattle," I said. "It's a city. It's near the ocean. It's a great hospital system. I'd get to do the work I want."

"Your life isn't your work. So let's try this again without mentioning work."

"It's a real city. It's near the ocean and the mountains. It doesn't get really cold or really hot. The food scene is great. There are lots of people from all over the world."

"And…"

"You got something else to add to my list?"

"Yeah, Ben Copley."

"We've been emailing," I said with a sheepish smile on my lips.

"Like about your ancestors?"

"And about his dog and my job hunt and—"

"You have a crush on him. For real you do. I was teasing you before, but you really do have a crush on him."

I wasn't ready to admit my crush to anyone, but I couldn't keep the smile off my face at the thought of Ben. "I'm not talking to the Seattle hospital because of him. I was talking to Seattle before I knew he was there."

Caroline balled up a napkin and tossed it at my face. "You silly goose. You've been emailing with him all this time?"

"Yeah," I said, my smile now proud. "I have."

TWENTY-FIVE

ALI

J*anuary*

I USUALLY SAT on the sofa while she dozed in her recliner. She didn't sleep in a bed anymore. She hardly moved. But the cough. The achingly persistent cough that left her wheezing for air, the cough that sounded painful because her whole body was sore and tired and filling with fluid. And I knew it would be soon. We all did. My sister Jess flew in for a long weekend and sat with her. My mother was at the assisted-living place all the time. My father and brother and sister-in-law too. We all were there, taking shifts. To be with her. To monitor the nurses that we'd hired to care for her. The room service that I'd mocked, it became our lifeline.

We were in the waiting game. She could linger like this

or her heart could tumble into a-fib, but the when was much more important than the how. Too many doctors in the family for us not to all know the progression. But none of us talked about it. So we talked in circles or we didn't talk at all.

Patrick and I had a hushed conversation in the hallway when I came to relieve him this evening. He'd joined Grammie for dinner and told me that she'd enjoyed the strawberry yogurt.

"You want to have dinner with me and the kids on Saturday?" he asked.

"Sure," I said with a shrug. I didn't have much else to do, and I liked my family, but it wasn't exactly a hot date.

"Grace will be in Chicago on a girls' trip..."

"And you need help with Becca and Charlie?"

"Would be nice, but if you've got plans, it's no big deal. We'll watch *Scooby Doo* and eat pizza in the den and play preschooler *Lord of the Flies*."

"I'll pass on the *Lord of the Flies*, but the rest sounds great."

"You good, Ali?"

"Yeah," I said, not wanting to be babied by the forty-year-old man in front of me. He'd always been my protector, always been Jess's protector. And while I'd leaned on him plenty—teaching me how to climb down a tree as well as up one, picking me up from a high school Christmas party and not telling our parents when I'd puked cheap vodka on the floorboard of his car, and helping me move out of the apartment after my college boyfriend and I broke up—I was determined that I didn't need him in that way anymore. That I wasn't his baby

197

sister anymore. That I was a grown-up. "I'm good. See you Saturday."

I slipped into Grammie's apartment, fixed a Scotch and soda from the bar cart, and tiptoed to the sofa where I'd hang out until I was tired and then drive home to crash out in my own bed. This was Patrick's and my new Tuesday and Thursday night routine, tagging off in a relay race that was going to end sooner than anyone would like.

While Grammie slept in her recliner, I tried to read, but I was antsy. I couldn't settle down from my long day at work and the decisions that lie ahead. I took out my laptop and checked the news, watched a replay of a late night comedy show from the day before, and cruised websites about Seattle neighborhoods and things to do. I wanted Seattle to make me an offer. I could see myself there, both at the hospital and in an actual life outside it. I checked my email again, but there wasn't any news from the recruiter, so I decided to write Ben.

<<ALI to Ben>>

Hey. I know I just wrote you yesterday. And I know we usually do this ping-pong thing where we volley emails back and forth. But I'm sitting with my grandma and she's asleep, and well, I'd rather not talk about that.

Let's talk about anything else.

I'm still waiting to hear about Thompson's special friend the poodle. If all goes well, I'll need a rec for a doggy daycare in Seattle soon. And as much as I'd like a big dog, like a golden or a lab, I'm not sure how that works in a city.

I've been to Seattle off and on, growing up. And a few times as an adult for conferences and things. But I don't know the city, so it seems a little scary. I remind myself that I've moved before, that I've made life-shaping decisions before. That I can do this. But I think I've kinda forgotten because it's unlike before, when the path was clear—the best college I could get into, the best medical school that would take me, and the absolutely best fellowship program. Where are the U.S. News & World Report's *rankings for how to make grown-up decisions?*

I kid, but in truth, I'm gun-shy. That's the bottom line. I was up for this dream job last year. And I don't know exactly what happened, but I didn't get the offer. They went with another candidate and I spent the next few months being angry and feeling sorry for myself, but I needed a job and got the temporary position that I have now. I'm a grown-up and a surgeon and on paper I have this great life yet I feel like I'm at loose ends. And I know that I have to create this life for myself that's in reality only slightly different than the one I thought I'd have, and some days I don't know how I'll do that. Or if I can do it.

And I think that's what I've really loved most about finding Elliott's letters. He and Alice both went on big adventures. He went to the other side of the world and she went across the country. And it wasn't like their futures were guaranteed. The world was at war. Ships sank and trains derailed and bad stuff happened.

And bad stuff still happens.

And I guess I don't need to be so scared of bad stuff happening or the stuff that I want not happening that I don't enjoy the good stuff that will happen, that can happen even if bad stuff happens.

But I guess it'll be a leap of faith, right? Like when you made your move from Arizona? You just have to jump and see if it works. And if it doesn't work, then you jump again.

I mean, Alice is the perfect example. She fell in love with a stranger on a train and spent the next three years swapping letters with him, hoping he'd come home. But she didn't shut herself up in a cave. She didn't hide. She ended up meeting and marrying my great-grandfather and having a very happy life, from what I can tell. But she kept those letters. She didn't forget Elliott. She didn't throw out his letters or her memories of him. I don't think she ever dreamed that she'd fall madly in love with a stranger on a train. Or, after she met Elliott, that she dreamed she'd end up with someone else.

You'll figure out from this nonsensical ramble, the reason that I was a computer science major and not an English major. Feel free to laugh with me. I trust you well enough to think that you're not going to laugh at me. But you laughing with me? I'd like that.

And now that I'm at the end of this email, which took a weird turn and became my diary. I have to keep reminding myself that I don't really know you, because I feel like I do. I hope we get to meet in person sometime. I hope you have a life-time of happiness. And, I hope—

"WHAT ARE YOU DOING, SWEET PEA?"

"Hey, you're awake," I said, my attention fully on my grandmother as I put my computer down on the coffee table and closed the lid.

"Still exhausted," she said shifting in her chair.

I walked over to her and dropped a kiss on her forehead. "Love you."

"Love you too."

"Can I get you anything?"

"Some lip balm."

I gently dabbed some balm on her lips. "Anything else?"

"I love you and you're going to do amazing things."

I laughed and sat on the small wooden chair next to her recliner. "I love you too."

"Talk to me. About anything," she said, her eyes closing.

"I've been emailing with Ben," I confessed in a whoosh, not sure what she'd think about it or if she'd even realize the implications of what I was saying. "He's the great-grandson of the man who wrote Alice all of those love letters. We've been emailing for months now."

"Is he nice?"

"I think so. And he's funny. He makes me laugh."

"Is he coming to visit?"

"No," I said, giving her hand a squeeze. "I don't really know him. If I get the job in Seattle or if I go back for another interview, I think we're going to try to meet up for coffee."

"Always pick the man who can make you laugh. That's what my mother told me. And I told your mom and I'm telling you. Money, a handsome face—those things can be lost. It sounds silly only because you hear it so much, but it's what's on the inside that counts." A deep cough racked her frail body.

"I'll keep that in mind," I said with another squeeze on her hand, the skin paper-thin and cool. "But I'm hoping to have coffee with him before we plan a wedding," I teased, wanting to lighten the mood, wanting to fight back against the deep sadness that was creeping up on me.

"Tell me a story."

I smiled. The woman who had told me stories was asking me for one.

"Okay, let's see what I've got." I pulled up the book app on my phone and read out the options. *"The Lion, The Witch and The Wardrobe. The Story of Ferdinand."*

"What are you doing with children's books on your phone?" she said in surprise and I didn't answer because I knew I'd shatter into a million tiny pieces if I told her why.

I cleared my throat and continued. *"Rudyard Kipling's Just So Stories. The Velveteen Rabbit."*

"That one," she said. "It was one of my favorites as a little girl. Both my parents read it to me often."

And so I sat, on a small wooden chair, holding my grandmother's hand and reading her a story about a rabbit that was loved so much that it became real.

TWENTY-SIX

M *arch 1916*

"I DON'T UNDERSTAND," she tells Frankie as she buttons the new boots. She's always had laces before, so she struggles a bit to fasten her boots with the hook. Fred and the cobbler had made it look so easy with doing up the buttons. She looks at the buttonhook in frustration, wondering if it somehow works differently than other buttonhooks because she simply cannot fasten the buttons, regardless of how soft the white kidskin is. The slim metal hook is embossed with *Wertheimer Shoe Company, Seattle, Wash.*, and she already knows she'll keep it no matter how this evening with Fred turns out. "I don't understand why he gave me those shoes," Alice says, gesturing toward Frankie with the hook.

"Well, I wouldn't complain ever," says Frankie, walking

around their small apartment in the adored satin pumps that haven't yet met a sidewalk.

"You realize you'll give yourself a permanent limp if you don't stop."

"They're beautiful and they are worth it," says Frankie, stumbling a bit.

"Trust me. They are not worth it."

"I think they are, and anyway, he gave you shoes because he owns a shoe company."

Alice looks to the ceiling in exasperation before resuming her fight with her new boots. "That bit I understand. I don't understand why me."

"Why not you?"

Alice pauses her work and ticks off the reasons on her fingers. "One," she says, holding up her index finger, "I'm twenty-eight. Two"—middle finger—"I'm bland."

"Who says you're bland?" Frankie interrupts her. "No one who knows you."

Alice shakes her head in disagreement. "To other girls maybe I'm not, but men have never found me interesting. And now I'm to believe that at my age, I've caught the eye of not one, but two men?"

"You are certifiable sometimes. You know that, right?" says Frankie, gently taking off the satin pumps and nestling them among the tissue in their box. "What about that medical student who we met on the lake two summers ago?"

"The Canadian man?"

"Yes, the Canadian man. P-something."

"Peirce."

"You honestly don't think that if he hadn't been about to be sent off to war, he wasn't going to pursue you?"

"You think he was? Truly?"

"He asked about visiting your family, Alice. He asked about train tables," Frankie all but screams. "And then last year, there was the fellow with the logging company who took you to dinner. Several times, if I recall correctly, and sat next to you at Easter service."

"Stephen Farber?"

"That's the one."

"He married Meredith," Alice objects.

"After you introduced him to Meredith based upon their mutual love of baseball. Truly, they should name their first daughter Alice."

Finished with her boots, Alice stands and checks her gait. She's had the new boots for a few days, but they are still not entirely familiar.

"It's not you," Frankie softly continues. "I know you think it's you or your leg, but it's not you. It's them. It's men from home. They worry too much. City men, businessmen, don't care about your limp."

Alice lets the words roll around in her brain. *Is that true? Is that the difference?* All of her life she's known that she'll always be a burden to another and that she'll have to fend for herself, create a life for herself because she's never had faith that she'll be able to build a life with anyone. Men have options and likely won't take her on, no matter how charming or pretty she can be. And as much as the idea of building a life with Elliott seems like something she could do, something she could make real, it is still a fantasy. She is in Seattle, what feels like the edge of the world already, and isn't sure she'll ever be brave enough to press farther across the horizon.

"Truly, truly. Fred has asked you to dinner for only one reason. He wants to spend time with you."

"But Elliott—" Alice protests again, something vicious beginning to eat away at her stomach as she realizes her betrayal of Elliott.

"It's dinner, Alice," Frankie answers. "He's invited you to dinner. And I hate to think it and I won't say it, but you never know. You simply never know. What if we enter the war, what if there's an accident, what if a million things happen? A bird in hand, and all. Go."

∿

ALICE WAITS in the sitting room, too nervous to sit, so she paces.

"Alice." Fred greets her with a smile.

"Hello," she says with a shy wave.

"Ready for dinner?"

"Absolutely." She takes her coat from a nearby chair and as she begins to slip into it, she finds Fred's hands helping. "Thank you."

"You look lovely, Alice."

"Thank you."

"Up for a bit of an adventure?"

"What do you have in mind?"

"Have you been over to Chinatown?"

"I went last year with some of the girls. We walked around a bit during the day."

"Well then, let's go exploring."

Outside the building, Fred opens the passenger door to his car and Alice settles into the tufted leather seat. She isn't sure what to do. She's only been in a car a handful of times and never one built for two people.

"It's not raining, so do you mind keeping the top off?"

"It's nice," she agrees and he passes her a lap blanket before cranking the engine.

"Electric starter," he says with pride. "No hand crank."

"It's beautiful," she says, admiring the shiny green paint and rich leather.

"It's a Chevrolet roadster. I bought it in Chicago and had it shipped here. First one in the city. And probably the fastest car in the state, too."

Alice's frame stiffens. Who is she out with? A man with a fast and fancy car? A man who owns a store?

"Ah, but don't worry, sweet Alice, you're safe with me."

They wind through the city streets and reach Chinatown, passing under tall, glass-globed street lights and into a new world. Birds are on display in windows. Some alive in cages, others smoked and hanging by twine wrapped around their legs. Busy stands fill the sidewalk, overflowing with produce. In the daytime, when she'd visited last year, there were some other women like her, but now she stands out.

Fred slows the car to a crawl and looks at her, assessing her mettle. "A night market. Are you up for it?"

"Without a doubt," Alice answers, eager to explore with him.

Fred finds a nearby garage for the car and they wander through the bustling streets.

"This way," he says, taking her hand in his, and, as he pulls them toward an alley, she worries for a second, her stride faltering a half step. Fred stops and turns toward her. "It's a noodle restaurant," he explains. "A very good one, just there," he points to a door. "Have you had Italian pasta?"

She nods in response. "I know what noodles are," she says. "I know how to make spätzle."

"Yes, it's like that, but entirely different. And if you don't like it, I promise you a big steak and potatoes and a slice of chocolate cake."

She follows him again, more confident, and when they emerge from the restaurant, she is bubbling, eager to learn more about this corner of the city. "What else can we try? What's that?" She points to a street vendor who pulls a cage of fried golden balls from a large vat.

"Rice balls, I think," he says. "Would you like to try one?"

"You speak Chinese?"

"A very little. Enough to order food, but I'm working on it. And Japanese."

"That's impressive. I only speak a little German. Do you?"

"No," he says. "My parents were born here, so I don't know any."

"Mine immigrated shortly before I was born," she says, "but we weren't encouraged to speak it outside of church. Prayers are the only things I really know. Well, prayers and a few curses."

He laughs and orders a waxed bag of fried rice balls for them to enjoy.

~

"ALICE," he says in the car in front of her building, not yet cutting the engine. "I'd like to take you out again, but I need to be very clear about something."

The warmth that has built within her immediately fades and she steels herself for whatever hard fact she is about to face.

"I'm leaving in a few months for a trip. I'm going with my father to Japan. We're part of a mission to do some business on behalf of the city and to bring back some specimens for the zoo."

"What kind of animals?" Does she even know what kinds of animals live in Japan? She'll have to look it up in case a student ever asks.

"Probably some birds, but mainly plants. I think the plan is for a Japanese garden."

"I'd love to see it."

"And I'll be happy to show it to you when it is finished and you're back in Seattle. I assume you go home for the summers?"

"Yes, I do. I'll be back in September." She thinks about leaving it there, and not telling him the rest, but he's been open and kind with her. Harboring a secret isn't something she wants to do, and if he wants to see her again, and if he knows about Elliott, then it's fine. She isn't being a liar toward Fred or betraying Elliott. "Fred?" she asks in a quiet voice, after he cuts the engine and begins to open his door. He turns his face toward hers, expectant and patiently waiting for her to continue. "I appreciate you being forthright with me about your trip, so that I don't get my hopes up. And I'll repay the favor—"

"And tell me that I'm presumptuous and you don't want to see me again? I knew that I shouldn't have bought you the rice balls. I should have made you wait for the rice balls so that I could take you out again."

"No, that's not it at all, you silly," she says with a laugh. "I'd be happy to go out with you again, but there is someone else."

"Who?"

"You don't know him."

"Seattle isn't a big city, Alice."

"You don't know him," she says again.

"Doesn't matter really," he says with a shrug. "As long as he's not here and there isn't a ring on your finger, that's all I need to know about this other fella."

TWENTY-SEVEN

ALICE

M*ay 1916*

UP THE STAIRS and in her apartment, Alice takes off her coat and boots while Frankie quizzes her about her afternoon picnic on the slopes of Mount Rainer with Fred, and Alice provides all of the details.

"You have to find out if he has a friend. Or even better, a brother. Oh, Alice, wouldn't that be lovely? If we found brothers? Then we could be sisters."

"I have two of my own already. Plus, if we were sisters, I think we might get in spats and I really don't like quarreling with you."

"But I only have the one sister and she's so much older and so serious."

"Evelyn is lovely, and hush."

"Ah ha, you can be the bossy older sister. You're doing

your level best already. See, we can make this work. Just find out if Fred has a brother."

"I'll ask," Alice says, "but we don't have any plans set, so he may change his mind about taking me out again."

"Bah," she says. "You always say that, and then a couple of days later you're dancing or at the theater or out for dinner and now a picnic. He won't change his mind. And neither will someone else, apparently. You got a telegram this evening!"

"A telegram!" *Elliott.* She knows it's from him. Elation and guilt rip through her in equal measures. A telegram is extravagant, expensive, and it was here, waiting for her, while she was out with another man.

Frankie hands her the envelope with *Alice Hirshhorn* visible through a cutout window. "Open it," Frankie encourages.

Caught up in the excitement of the telegram, Alice turns the envelope over and tucks a finger under the loose seam before she realizes she wants this to be private. That whatever Elliott has sent her must be exceedingly important to be rushed around the globe via wires and Morse code. Maybe he's on his way to her already. Maybe he's enlisting in the war. Maybe he's saying good-bye. No, she thinks. It's good news, and good news that she doesn't want to share immediately. "I'm going to read it in my room."

"Spoilsport," teases Frankie. "If I ever got a telegram from a beau, I'd read it from the rooftop."

Alone in her room, Alice sits on her quilt-covered bed and extracts the canary yellow pages.

Her heart stops for a full minute and her world tilts.

Father died. Please come home. Suzanna.

∼

DEAR ELLIOTT,

I'm home (well, if you can count Lake Michigan as home). I met my family here at a little camp on the lake shore that I mentioned. We spend August here each summer. It's a simple cluster of cabins. But it's good to be back home with my mother and sisters and nieces and nephews. As for the menfolk, we all try not to think about them being bachelor farmers for the time. Heavens knows what they do or how they survive, but they seem to manage fine. Perhaps next summer you can join us here. When I mentioned it to you, I meant it. Both of my brothers-in-law are here for a few days off and on, so you wouldn't be the sole man about the place.

The return train was filled with happy memories of you. It was long and slow, though, and I spent most of the journey daydreaming. No strange man on the train to chat with this time (or to enter my sleeping compartment in the middle of the night). Oddly enough, though I was moving farther from you, I felt closer to you as the carriages rocked their way east.

I hope you enjoy the little painting I've done here on this letter for you. Another Aesop's fable for you—the tortoise and the hare. (I counsel myself to be patient, but it's so difficult. I wish you were here. You'll simply have to come to fetch me as soon as humanly possible.) I hope my last letter with the photograph arrived. I sent it two months ago, and I don't expect that your letters will find me back home, much less on the lake shore, and I know things can take an age to reach you, but when you get it, please let me know.

Have no worries that you will find me in Seattle when you return. April cannot come soon enough.

Love,

Alice

"ARE YOU DONE WITH YOUR LETTERS?" says her sister Suzanna.

"Yes," says Alice, tucking the letter to Elliott in an envelope addressed with his name. She stacks the two letters on the corner of the desk in their bedroom. She and Suzanna share a bedroom that has the only bit of quiet in the small cabin. The space is loud with four children, but none are Suzanna's. Yet. Next year that will have changed. Suzanna married in the spring and Alice has no doubt that this time next year, Suzanna will have a child or one on the way. But she might not be a spinster aunt after all, Alice thinks wryly.

Suzanna picks up the letters and shuffles them in her hands. "Two men!"

"Suzanna!" Alice hisses, stomping her foot. "Those are my letters."

"I'm not reading the contents. I'm reading the addressees, which are entirely public. Frederick Wertheimer and Elliott Keller? Two men?"

"It's not as scandalous as you'd think." Alice lunges toward the letters, but Suzanna whips around and holds them high in the air.

"I hope it's scandalous!" says Suzanna, her eyes bright. "You have to tell me!"

"Fine. You can't tell Mama," says Alice, using her stern teacher voice.

Suzanna sits on the edge of the bed and signs a cross over her heart. "I promise."

"Or Judith," cautions Alice, knowing their eldest sister wants Alice to be married as much as their mother does.

"Or Judith," Suzanna agrees with a nod.

Alice crawls onto the bed next to Suzanna and confesses to her younger sister. "I don't want them to pin their hopes on anything. I'm twenty-nine next month."

"But two men! Two! That's double the odds! Who are they?"

"I met Elliott on the train to Seattle last summer. He's a businessman—from Ft. Wayne, strangely enough—who is in the Philippine Islands now. Fred owns a shoe store in Seattle."

"And…" prompts Suzanna.

"And—" Alice exhales, deciding to spill all of her secrets to her sister. "I'm older than Elliott by two years. He doesn't know that yet. And he lives across the Pacific Ocean. Fred is older than I am. He's funny and charming and he's here. I mean, he's not *here*. He's *there*, in Seattle."

"Do you think either will propose? Or both?" Suzanna clasps her hands together in excitement.

"I don't know," says Alice, falling back on the bed to stare at the ceiling.

"But you want to be married, yes?" asks her sister.

"Yes. I never thought it was for me, but I think I'd like it. That I could belong to someone. And now with Father gone, I hate to say this, but I really think hard about getting married. I do, Suzie, I do."

"So which one?"

"Would I pick or do I think might pick me?"

"Will you tell me who you'd pick?"

"No." Alice isn't even sure herself. She and Elliott seem

like plunging headlong into a swirling destiny, while she and Fred feel easy and light. And she's entirely grateful that her younger sister doesn't push her to give an answer.

"Then who do you think will ask?"

"Elliott. He will when he returns. I'm confident of it."

"And if Fred asks first?"

"I'm not expecting that. If he'd wanted to be married, he could have done that a long time ago. He knows everyone in the entire city. We can't go anywhere without seeing people he knows. I thought he might ask, though. Shortly before I left, he took me out for an entire day. He has a car and we drove to the mountains and picnicked and played in patches of snow and I laughed so much. And occasionally, he'd become a little quiet, and I thought —" Alice purses her lips and shakes her head before taking a big breath and letting it escape in one giant whoosh. "But he didn't. So, here I am."

Suzanna pats Alice's knee. "I won't tell Mama or Judith. I promise. But you have to promise to tell me more. I want to hear all of it."

And out of Alice's trunk come the embroidered shoes and the pink rose petals, now dried and pressed between the pages of her bible.

TWENTY-EIGHT

ALICE

S*eptember 1916*

A YEAR, she thinks. A year and nothing has changed, except the students in her classroom. The week has been filled with confusion and wariness and the expectation of great things to come. A fresh slate. She laughs to herself, looking at the blackboard at the front of the room, quiet now that the students have gone. The board is neat and clean except her name and a simple list of rules for the children, expressed as virtues: honesty, courage, loyalty, fairness. Adding one more to the list for herself: patience. She will need that for navigating the children and these next few months as she awaits Elliott's return.

That night, she begins another letter to Elliott, her pencil hovering over the margins of the paper, planning out the pumpkins and gourds that will be seasonal when this letter reaches him in late October. Her mind fills with the daydreams that she has of their future when she paints for him. Frankie interrupts her watercolor dreams of the tropics, asking if she'd like a cup of tea.

"No," she says, setting her pencil down and opening her pan of paints. "And before you ask, no, I haven't heard from Fred."

"It's only been a week since we returned. He still has time. My wager was that he'd call within the first two weeks. I've got three days left."

"I think he's entirely forgotten me. I didn't have a letter from him all summer."

"And it could be that the moon is truly made from cheese."

"Really, Frankie," sighs Alice. "Do I never get to be the optimist here or are you claiming the title of Miss Sunny Sunshine?"

"I can't help it." Frankie laughs. "Who knew it would take boys turning thirty before they wised up?" She looks down at the ring on her finger, placed there by one of Fred's friends just yesterday.

"You should resign now, you know? Before the children settle in with you. You can marry next week. I'll find a new roommate."

"I spoke with the new principal this morning. He's contacting the superintendent, but he says that until I'm married, I can hold my position. I don't want to leave the school short a teacher, but as soon as they do find a replacement—Oh! Alice! I still can't quite believe it," she says, admiring her ring again. "And my serious wager is that they'll have to find replacements for both of us."

Alice shrugs, dipping her paintbrush in the glass of water before gently dabbing the oranges and ochres.

"Have some faith, Alice."

"I left a card at his shop the other day," Alice says, focusing on the paper.

"You did? When? Without me?"

"Yes, yesterday after school let out, I took the new girl to show her the shops in the Arcade."

"Sneaky sneak."

Alice doesn't answer, keeping focused on painting the perfect little pumpkin vine to dance along the edge of the page.

"I know we've talked about it until we're both blue in the face, and I wish so hard that Elliott would come back for you, but—"

"I know, okay? And, Frankie, you don't know if Fred's even the least bit interested in marriage. He could have gotten married years ago."

"Maybe it's catching." Frankie laughs, looking again at the ring on her finger. "His friend Charles certainly got bit by the marriage bug and I couldn't be happier."

Alice places her paintbrush in a glass of water and picks up her pen to write Elliott. "And I couldn't be happier for you, either."

Dear Elliott,

I'm marking the months and weeks and days until I can see you again. I didn't say this to you earlier because I didn't want to share my sadness with you, but my father passed away this spring. Time has passed, and my mother has settled in with my elder sister and her family. The grief isn't quite as sharp, so I feel strong enough to tell you now, but I don't wish to write about it at length. I mainly share to tell you that there isn't a need for us to travel to Indiana before we set out on our adventure, provided that you're still interested in an adventure with me.

Perhaps knowing that it would be a shorter journey here would make it easier for you to get away. I've done my research with the timetables, watching shipping bulletins in the papers, and if all goes right, travel will only take a month. And I don't come with much more than I can fit into a trunk.

And I don't need much. I'm not accustomed to fancy things and I don't wish for them. A modest house with sea breezes and you at my breakfast table.

I know you want more, want to give me more, but I'm letting you know right now that you don't need it. You don't need anything other than yourself.

Love,

Alice

∽

"CLASS DISMISSED," Alice tells the students two weeks later, and the room breaks out into a din of happy chatter as the children gather their things from the cloak room and strap their books together.

"Am I dismissed, Miss Hirshhorn?"

Alice whirls to face the doorway and takes in the tall man standing there in a blue suit, hat in hand, arms open to greet her.

"Fred!" Her heart leaps at the sight of him.

He smiles, the edges of his eyes crinkling with happiness as she weaves through the children to reach him, catching herself before she entirely forgets her place and falls into his embrace. She takes a step back from him, to give him suitable space.

"Oh," she says, remembering that her classroom isn't the place for the affectionate hello he offers. "I mean, Mr. Wertheimer. Welcome to my class. What are you doing here?"

"You're here." And Alice's own smile grows at his simple statement. "Do I need a better explanation?"

Bubbles of joy rise up within her, making her light-headed with happiness. She had won her bet with Frankie and enjoyed an entire box of caramels as her reward for being right that Fred hadn't found her within the first two weeks of their return, but she will gladly eat crow.

"That answer works for me," she says, patting her hair to make sure that the chignon hasn't fallen into too much disarray after the long day. "But truly," she continues. "How did you find me? I'm assigned to a new school this year."

"I need to get back to the shop, but to answer your question, I wasn't sure where you were living this year so I tracked you down through the school's central office."

"Resourceful. And I'm living in the same place as I have for the past few years."

"Then I'll pick you up at six for dinner?"

"I'd like that."

"Excellent."

And with a quarter bow, his eyes giving her the caresses that he cannot, that he should not, he turns and leaves.

Following dinner, Fred takes her on a long drive

around the city. The top is down and the cool evening nips at her nose.

As they crawl along the waterfront, he speaks to her in a low voice that she can barely make out over the engine and wind.

"Before you think that I forgot, I've been in Vancouver for business and returned yesterday to find your note at the shop. I was half convinced that you would have run off with that other fella while I was gone."

"I didn't."

"Clearly. And I'm glad. But I also notice that you didn't tell me you won't run off with that other fella. The world is wide, Alice, and I am here."

"Why haven't you married?" she asks, the darkness and solitude making it easier to be frank with him.

"Lots of reasons, I suppose. I was having too good a time and I was busy with the business. I don't want to put the cart before the horse, and clearly I'm running second to someone else, but until you tell me to stop, I intend to spend time with you."

TWENTY-NINE

ALICE

N*ovember 1917*

THANKSGIVING DAY HAS ARRIVED. With a warm apple pie balanced on her lap, she sits in Fred's green car. She didn't go home this summer and was free to paint and draw from her small apartment that she now shares with her new roommate, Ethel. Free to spend as much time as was decent with Fred, and she enjoyed his company more with every passing hour.

While the pie baked, she wrote, but not to Elliott this time. It had been a month since she'd written him. She would try to write him later, but the letter writing seemed more like a duty, an obligation, and the words didn't spill from her heart any longer. The words hurt, because with the world at war he wasn't coming home and she wasn't going to him. Over two years had passed since their days together, and while she didn't like to think of the number, she was now thirty.

The sermon at church the previous Sunday had resonated with her. She'd heard the verse read at weddings, including Frankie's, but it wasn't the recitation of the glories of love that struck her. It was the part that she'd never truly listened to before that struck her between the ribs and lodged there.

When I was a child, I spake as a child, I understood as a child, I thought as a child: but when I became a man, I put away childish things.

It is far past time for her to grow up, to stop living a tropical dream in her head and fully live the dream that is within her grasp.

Dear Frankie,

I'm happy to hear that the population of Olympia is rising by one. I know you've been thoroughly enjoying your little love nest, and, to be frank, I've been awaiting this news since your wedding last winter. In fact, I may even have tried my hand at embroidering a bonnet for this occasion. And I may have retrieved it from its tissue paper wrapping and I may be posting it along with this letter.

As for me, no happy news, but no sorrowful news either. Fred turned thirty-seven in October and, I'm (well, let's just say I'm a number that you and I know, but I don't like to dwell on) and I keep thinking of what I might have, if I'd just say yes. He keeps hinting and I keep demurring, and I think I'm done with that now. I think that if he hints again, I may hint back. With the war taking so many men, I know I should latch on to every bit of happiness I can when I can have it.

All continues to rock along otherwise. Ethel is a fine room-mate, but she doesn't care for caramels so I'm left wagering with myself over silly things. Last week I wagered on whether one of my students would earn three demerits. If he didn't, then I'd treat myself to a single caramel on Friday afternoon. He finished the week with two demerits and I enjoyed my caramel. It was sweet even with the knowledge that I had turned a blind eye to several of his sins. See what I have become without you? Not even honest with myself.

And that brings me to the rest of my confession. I love Fred. I haven't told him but I know it to be true. And I'm going to do my best to convince him to give up his bachelor ways and build a life with me. Sometimes love burns slowly like a smoldering coal and sometimes it's a flaming forest fire. Those flames I felt before have waned and Fred is the one who warms my heart and fills my dreams.

I wish you all of the best luck and happiness in the world. Until children are old enough to learn to read, I haven't a clue what to do with them! Write and let me know if I may visit over Christmas, otherwise it will be our first Christmas apart in five years.

All of my love from Seattle,
Alice

FRED'S FAMILY is warm with her as always, but underneath the welcome his mother watches them like a hawk. Alice sees the hope that lives in her eyes, that has lived in her eyes for a year since she was first invited to Sunday dinner with his family. Alice helps clear the table as the men retire to the porch for a smoke.

"Thank you, Alice," Mrs. Wertheimer says.

"Of course. Thank you for inviting me."

"You're always welcome here."

"You truly make me feel welcome. Thank you."

"No need for thanks. And no need for you to help with the dishes today. Why don't you see if Fred will take you on a stroll before the sun goes down?"

"Oh, I'm happy to help," Alice says, collecting the silverware in her hands.

"Put those down, please, sweet Alice." Mrs. Wertheimer brooks no argument and Alice sets the forks and spoons and knives back down on the linen tablecloth. "Now, outside and tell Fred that you want to stretch your legs."

"Yes, ma'am," Alice says, not sure why she's being shooed away, but she does as she's been asked.

On the house's front porch, Fred leans against the railing and his eyes light up when Alice steps out of the front door. "Nice afternoon for a walk," he remarks to his father. "I'm going to take Alice around the block." Fred stubs out his cigar on a large glass ashtray that the two men have balanced on the rail between them. "Alice," he says, offering his arm to her. "Shall we go on a walk?"

Alice nods, takes his arm, and they set off down the porch steps.

The first pass around the block is silence. On the second, her tension grows. Is something terribly wrong? Fred has never been this quiet.

"Fred?" she whispers as they begin their third turn around the block, looking up at his strong profile and noticing his eyes are fixed on their path. "Is everything all right?"

"It will be, I hope," he says, gazing down at her, and the teasing smile she adores returns to his face.

"Can I help?"

"Yes, very much so." He stops their walk and turns to face her in the middle of the sidewalk, taking both her hands in his. "Alice, it's time. It's well past time and we're not waiting any longer. I love you. I've been waiting to hear from you about this other fella—"

"Ask me," she says, squeezing his hands to give him encouragement, strength, and love.

"Will you marry me?"

THIRTY

ALI

February

<<Ben to Ali>>

Ali,

I'm very sorry to hear about your grandma. I'll talk about that or not talk about that as much or as little as you want. I want so badly to be able to make this better for you, but I know I can't. I know that you can't make it better either, and that's the worst part.

I'm also very sorry that it took me a few days to write back.

Your email was cut off in mid-sentence, so I wasn't sure if part of it got deleted by accident or whether you didn't mean to send it in the first place.

Anyway, I went back and forth on whether to even acknowledge that I got it, then I remembered that you're a friend. You're my friend, so email whenever you want. I'm here.

I wish I could tell you that you'll get through this chaos and that you're stronger than you think and this is a beautiful part of life and you need to embrace it, but I can't. I've worked in corporate America long enough to know that the poster of the cat with its claws dug into a tree branch with "Hang In There" under it only makes people—well, it makes this person, at least —feel worse about the situation.

And I wish I could tell you that bad stuff doesn't happen. But it does. I know it and you know it. And you're completely right. We can't let the bad stuff rob us of the good stuff.

When I moved up to Seattle, my mom was going through a medical thing. Ovarian cancer. (I'll tell you that even though thinking about it now still makes me want to throw up.) She's good now, and we all hold our breaths at her checkups, but it was bad for a bit.

Bad is underselling it. It was awful and my dad was a wreck and my sister was with her kids up north and I had to be the strong one. Or at least I thought I did. I pushed forward so hard to do what needed to be done and hold everything together that I didn't realize I was being held together too. By my job who didn't fire me when I worked remotely more than I should have. By my family. By my friends. Even by my dog. It may feel like you're in pieces and alone, but you're not. And even if I'm a stranger on the internet, I'm here.

If you're in Seattle for an interview or a visit or I find myself in Kansas City or wherever you land, let's meet up. There's no good way to mention meeting up that doesn't sound like I'm trying to pick you up, so I'm glad you brought it up first. I've written a sentence about meeting up with you about a dozen times in our emails and deleted it every time, but there you go—coffee or a beer or an entire cocktail menu, on me if our paths ever cross in real life.

In the meantime, what I can tell you is that yeah, it does get better. That when I made the move home to help with my mom, my life was a mess and I wasn't sure if the move was going to be a good thing or just another snowball in an avalanche of disasters. But it was good. It was the best thing. I'm in a good place now and that's not about where I physically am. And it's not even been about being near my parents. They're in the suburbs and I'm in the city, so it's not like I see them every day or even every week.

Sometimes stuff just works out in ways you couldn't ever expect. So whatever it is you were hoping for yourself or hoping for me or hoping for whoever in that email, keep hoping it.

I wasn't an English major either, so don't sweat anything. Keep in touch. Check in with me when you're ready. You've got a lot on your plate right now and I'll be right here if you ever want to talk or not talk or whatever you need.

As for Thompson, he's a yellow lab.

Gummy bears or jelly beans?

Your friend,

Ben

THIRTY-ONE

ALI

F*ebruary*

SEVEN IN THE morning and my phone rang. A Sunday. A day off. I was in PJs and curled up on the sofa with coffee and a magazine. I knew it wasn't good news. But when the display showed it was my mother, I steeled myself for whatever horror would greet me. And I was pretty sure I knew what I was about to face.

"Hello? Mom?"

"Grammie died last night," my mom said, the words rushing out of her. There was no warm-up, no preamble. Just the unvarnished truth.

I knew this was coming. We all did. And we'd known it for a long time. Christmas Day made that painfully clear. Her heart wasn't going to pump forever. It wasn't going to get stronger. The medicines wouldn't be able to keep up.

We'd watched her weight rise and her blood pressure fall for a few weeks, leaving the consequences unspoken. She hadn't even been able to get up from her favorite chair when my parents and I had joined her for dinner in the dining room at assisted living on New Year's Eve before heading to a party at Caroline's house. Her legs had been wrapped tight in compression hose and she didn't try to hide her discomfort from me. And after my last visit to see her just two days ago, I knew she could leave us anytime.

But knowing and experiencing were two wildly different things. Hearing the words, the sobs leapt from me and I didn't even try to hold them back.

"She died in her sleep," my mom reported, her tight professionalism teetering on the edge of collapse.

"It's for the best," I said, using my own doctor voice. I tucked my phone under my chin and wiped my tears with the palms of my hand, pressing my cheeks hard just to feel something other than sadness for a moment.

"I know," my mom said, her brittle voice breaking into heaving grief.

I blinked back the endless tears from my eyes and took a deep breath. "I'll be right over."

In doctor mode, I forced it all down and focused on the tasks before me. I showered and dressed and threw some spare clothes into an overnight bag. I drove to my parents' house and was greeted by my brother at the front door.

"Mom's napping."

"She's actually asleep?" I asked, amazed that she'd spiraled into the exhaustion of grief so quickly.

"I doubt that, but that's what Dad says, so I'm going with it."

"Where is he?"

"Running an errand."

I rolled my eyes because of course he was running an errand. My father, the doer, the fixer. He couldn't fix this, but he could rewire a lamp that worked fine or hire a landscaping crew to resod his already neat lawn. "When is Jess getting in?"

"Tomorrow morning," said Patrick. "I thought we could run shifts."

I didn't roll my eyes at my big brother's plans and I was relieved he was there to take charge, to take care of us. I followed his lead for the next few days as tears were shed and my grandmother was laid to rest next to my grandfather. Well, most of her anyway.

"She wanted what?" my mother had nearly shouted, her eyes big.

"I'm not telling you that you have to do that at all," said our family lawyer in a measured voice. "I'm telling you that her stated preference was for no lilies at her funeral, that passages from *The Velveteen Rabbit* be read, and that half of her ashes be interred in the family plot in Seattle. No one is going to make you do any of this."

"But it's what she wanted?" my brother asked.

"It's what she requested," said the lawyer. "My advice is that you do what's right for your family."

And that was how, a week later, with the funeral behind us, my family ended up on a plane to Seattle.

My brother brought Grammie in an urn in his carry-on. He assured us it was okay and while I thought for sure there was some sort of procedure, some sort of paperwork that we had to obtain, he barreled on. I stared at that blue rucksack tucked under the seat in front of him. My mom was two rows ahead of us and I was glad she couldn't see the bag.

I slept in a hotel room with my sister, and in the darkness, we talked in low voices as the sounds of the city crept past the double-glazed window. About her life in Texas. About her struggle to juggle her work with her kids and a house and their new puppy. And how she'd gained twenty pounds and how it made her sad, but she didn't see how she'd ever be able to fix it. We talked about my time at home and how I thought Kansas City had changed, or I'd changed, or everything had changed and it wasn't chafing against me. About how much she liked Austin and how I should look there. We talked about anything other than the reason for our ersatz family vacation.

"We should go somewhere with Mom," she said. I heard her toss in the bed. "A girls' trip. And if Dad wants to come, that's cool."

"Spring, maybe?"

"I'll have to look at the school calendar, but yeah. Let's do something this spring," said Jess. "Anything you want to do this weekend?"

"Weirdly, yeah, I do."

"Besides get day drunk?"

"That can be on the agenda. I say we do family stuff tomorrow and then we sleep in, have a lazy boozy brunch and do some tourist stuff, and I want to go by this place that Great-Grandma Alice lived."

"Isn't her house right by the park?"

"Yeah, it is," I said, nodding against my pillow. The

house Alice and Fred lived in was only a few blocks from the cemetery where they were buried. "But I want to stop by where she lived before then. When she taught school. She lived in a hotel that was like a boarding house. The Astoria."

"Where is it?"

"Minor and Pike. I went by when I was up for my interview. It's condos now, but I want to swing by."

Jess was quiet for a few minutes as I stared into the darkness of the room. I thought she'd finally fallen asleep, and I was halfway asleep myself when she spoke.

"How do you know where Alice lived?"

"I have her letters," I began. Sleepily and slowly, I told her the story of Alice and Elliott.

~

THE TALL EVERGREENS rose along the edges of the hilltop cemetery and the lake spread out at our feet. *Alice Lenore Wertheimer* was carved into a flat headstone, partially obscured by the green rug of fake grass that was hiding the pile of dirt to cover Grammie's urn after we left. The internment was simple. No priest. No pastor. Just our family and a few staff members there to assist. With my dad's help, my mom kneeled down and gently lowered the white urn into the ground. They rose and we all stood and stared at the ground.

"I know I'm the baby, but I'd like to say something." My voice broke the heavy mantle of silence that had settled over us. I rocked back and the heels of my pumps dug into the soft earth. "I know Wallers are doers, not talkers, and we did all of that talking a few days ago at the funeral." My voice cracked over that word that meant the end. "She requested a reading from *The Velveteen Rabbit*, and Jess and I spent time trying to find the right passage to read at her funeral, but starting around Christmas I've been thinking about all of the books she gave us. All of the books she read to us. And I started thinking about which ones I remembered most, and I've been reading them again. I guess it's my way to say goodbye and thank you and I love you. Anyway, I've read *Charlotte's Web* and *Where the Red Fern Grows* and I cried over the books like I did when I was little, and I'm crying over her now because she's gone, but it's not sadness."

I looked at my mom, whose face was burrowed in my dad's chest as he embraced her, her sad eyes peeking at me above his arms. At that moment I knew that one day, I'd be her. I'd be the one aching so deeply, and I hoped that I'd have someone to wrap his arms around me. But if that wasn't the case, I'd still be fine. I took Jess's hand in my own and squeezed it.

"It's this amazing love. It's this amazing feeling of fullness. And it's bittersweet. That she lived a good life. That she did amazing things and that we got to be a part of that. That we had her love and her time and that we're richer for it. And I didn't understand why she wanted part of her to be in Seattle forever. But I think I'm beginning to understand. Because her parents are here. And the house where she grew up is here. And she met Grandpa here. And Mom was born here. And while she hasn't been a part of Seattle for fifty years, Seattle is a part of her. I wanted to find a quote from one of those books about death and grief and love and home and family, I couldn't find one. I found hundreds. So thank you, Grammie. I love you and I miss you."

The silence filled the spaces between us again. My brother took my free hand in his, the three of us siblings holding hands together like we hadn't in decades. "I love you, Grammie," he said, and his words were echoed by Jess. My mother's face turned back into my father's chest and her shoulders began to shake. My father dropped his head next to hers, rocking her back and forth. The wind picked up and her cries quieted. Mom lifted her head and nodded her thanks at the staff. Hand in hand, my parents began to walk away, and we followed.

Back at the cars, my parents said a quick goodbye to us. "I'm taking your mom back to the hotel," my dad told us.

Patrick loaded his kids and wife into their rental car. "I'm taking the kids down to the Seattle Center and Pike Place and maybe the oddities store. They've been troupers. Let's circle up later about dinner."

We waved them off and Jess turned to me. "Lunch? Coffee?"

"Glass of wine?" I laughed, trying to shake off the sadness, but my joke was hollow. We wandered around the neighborhood, looking at the stately homes.

"I think that's where Alice and Fred lived," I said, pointing at a great wooden Victorian that sat on the park.

We stopped on the sidewalk and gazed up at the two-story house. Wooden siding, painted green with crisp white trim. A large bay window looked over a small, neat front garden. The entire neighborhood would have been new when they moved in, I realized. The tall trees in yards would have been saplings. Or not even planted yet.

"I noticed the pink roses that you brought for Great-Grandma's grave," my sister said, not looking at me.

"Yeah," I said, keeping my eyes on the house as well, my mind turning over daydreams of newlywed Fred and Alice moving in, of him picking up the morning paper from the front path, of her tending to dahlias and roses and the other flowers that grew so well here, drawing upon the stories that Grammie told me in my childhood to give names and colors and texture to their life in my imagination.

"That's what Elliott left her, right?"

"Right," I said. A gust of wind bit at us and I wrapped my arms around my coat. It wasn't cold. Not like the cold I was used to, but the gray of the sky tricked my body into a shiver. "Now I know why they drink so much coffee here," I joked. "Let's go find a cup."

A few blocks away, we settled into a small coffee shop.

"So tell me more about Elliott. Do you think they—you know..." she said with a smirk.

"I don't know. I don't think so. It's all the restrained passion. There's a reference to a kiss, but nothing more. I'll send you copies of the letters. I had them scanned and then all of"—I waved my hand over my shoulder in the direction we'd walked—"that happened and I meant to send it to Elliott's family, but things just got..."

"Busy."

"Yeah. It took me a bit to find a company to make digital images of the letters, that promised that they would be careful, and then I got busy and I kinda forgot to pay the people for the longest time so it was almost embarrassing. Like, worse than showing up at the dry cleaners because you've found a claim ticket in your car, and not having any idea what you dropped off, or when you dropped it off, and wondering if the dry cleaners had sold your clothes yet. Anyway, I got around to getting the scans and I did manage to load them onto my cloud, but then I wanted to write a nice email to send along and I kept putting it off and then last month—"

"Oh, you don't have to tell me about life. I don't remember the last time I had a weekend without the kids around. I felt crappy about not bringing them, but they were at the funeral and then Patrick's kids weren't exactly charming on the plane, from what Mom told me, so it's for the best. But Elliott's family? You found them?"

"Yeah. It's amazing what you can find online these days. Grammie knew. It was kinda our project." I cupped my hands around the coffee cup, trying to let it warm my bones, but I knew that it was sadness and not the weather that had me chilled.

"So, tell me."

"Well, I learned a lot about Elliott. Thank goodness he basically wrote his biography in a letter to her because it would have been a lot harder to track him down if we hadn't known where he was born and where he went to college. By the way, those class notes that are in the alum magazines? Where people brag and update the world about their lives? Those live forever. Forever. We found some from the nineteen thirties. Class of 1911. Elliott Keller reporting that he'd been promoted by an oil company and could be reached through the Army and Navy Club in Manila. But Caroline gets the credit. She really got the ball rolling. I was able to find out about Elliott, but she found his descendants."

"Are you going to give his family the letters?"

"No," I said, shaking my head. "I mean, they haven't asked and I haven't offered anything more than the electronic copies. The letters were Alice's and she kept them, so I feel like I should keep them."

"You should send them the electronic copies."

"I will. Remind me when we get back to the hotel. And Elliott's great-grandson—he's the one I've been emailing with—his name is Ben and he lives here."

"You should meet up with him."

"Maybe I'll ask if he's free," I said, drawing out my response as I drank more of my vanilla latte and gave myself time to think about Ben Copley and his funny emails, but I wasn't sure if I'd be brave enough to ask him to hang out, especially last minute.

THIRTY-TWO

ALI

F*ebruary*

<<ALI to Ben>>

Ben,

I'm sorry that it's taken me forever to get back to you. My grandmother died.

I'm in Seattle for the internment of her ashes, so Alice and Elliott have been in my mind all day. My sister and I walked by the house that Alice lived in with her husband Fred. Tomorrow, I'm going to the hotel-apartment building-boarding house where Alice lived. You'll read it in the letters, but Elliott sent her flowers the morning that his boat left for the Philippines. I've got his calling card where he wrote "Good-bye, E." You can see the holes where it was pinned to a ribbon or some tissue paper. It makes them so real when I hold that little card. And I like to think that some of the flower petals that are stuck in the family bible are from that bouquet your Elliott gave her—but that's probably silly.

I left some flowers at Alice's gravesite today. Pink roses, like what Elliott sent. It seemed like a good idea at the time and I hope my great-grandfather Fred, who is buried next to Alice, forgives me.

Anyway, I didn't know much about my great-grandmother, and while I can't say that I know her, she's now real to me. A woman who went on a big adventure, fell in love with a stranger on a train, and made a life for herself. I'm proud to have her old-fashioned name.

The link to the cloud storage with the scans of the letters is below. Password is Seattle.

And jelly beans, definitely. I like the black ones that taste like licorice.

Ali

<<BEN to Ali>>

Ali,

I'm very sorry to hear about your grandmother.

Alice is a good name. And isn't any more of an old-fashioned name than Ben is.

I'm Benjamin Wilbert Copley. Everyone thinks the initial W is for William and I just let them go with it. The Benjamin is because my parents liked it, but the Wilbert is after a great uncle on my dad's side.

So your Alice could be worse. Much worse.

Do you remember that TV show Mister Ed *with the talking horse from the 60s? It was in reruns when we were little and my sister thought it was hysterical to say "Hello, Wilbur" like the horse did. So in the family names lottery, you're the big winner. Alice is a pretty name.*

You're probably not up for it, considering the circumstances, but I'll ask anyway. Let's grab a coffee tomorrow. I've got a beer-coffee-entire cocktail menu offer to make good on. Take your pick. I can be free whenever you have time. I'm just north of Lake Union, not far from the zoo.

Ben

<<ALI to Ben>>

Ben,

Sounds like a plan. I thought about asking if you were free, but it was last minute and I didn't know what you had going on or if you were serious about the coffee-beer-cocktail offer. I don't fly out until Sunday morning. I don't have any plans for tomorrow other than walking by the place where Alice lived— the Hotel Astoria—and then heading down to Pike Place Market. That's probably too touristy for you though. What about coffee? Let me know when and where.

And your sister missed a golden opportunity. I would have gone with Wilbur from Charlotte's Web and called you "Some Pig."

Ali

<<BEN to Ali>>

Ali,

Let's do it. Google tells me there's a branch of this coffee shop that I like right near there. They roast their own beans. How about Victrola at 2? Okay if I bring Thompson?

I can't believe you remembered that kids' book. And yes, a

couple of years ago she sent me a T-shirt that says "Some Pig"
on it. No clue where she found it.
 Ben

<<ALI to Ben>>
 Victrola at 2. See you and Thompson then.

∾

"IT'S A DATE," my sister announced that night when I
asked her about her thoughts about me meeting up with
Ben for coffee and leaving her high and dry for an hour or
so the next day. "I mean, I haven't been on a first date in,
what? Ten years? But it's a date."

"It's *not* a date. We've emailed some and I'm in town.
It's a 'let's meet up.' It's not a date." I said the words, but I
wanted it to be a date. I wanted Ben to be as funny and
kind as he was in our emails. I wanted him to be cute. But
most of all, I wanted him to like me in person. I felt like I
knew him and I felt like he'd be the same in person, but I
also knew that I really didn't know him.

"Well, hello, Miss Defensive. I was teasing you. *Teasing*
you, but now I'm thinking that it is a date."

"It's not. Trust me," I told her, reminding myself that it
wasn't a date. That as charming as our brief emails had
been, I didn't know anything about him. But as I put on
my makeup the next morning, I took my time to get my
eyeliner just right. I wished it was a date.

I pushed through the glass door of the coffee shop at
two o'clock on the nose, and I was more nervous than I'd
been at any of the job interviews I'd had over the past few

months. I knew what to expect with those. But this? I didn't have a clue.

The coffee shop was nestled in a cozy block of brightly painted single-story buildings and was next door to the bar where I'd had a beer when I was up for my interview. Light spilled in through the large plate-glass windows onto the exposed brick. I looked around, but then remembered that I didn't know what I was looking for. I didn't know *who* I was looking for. There were four guys entranced by their various electronic gadgets and Ben could have been any of them. I scanned their faces, trying to match one to Ben. Was he handsome? What color were his eyes? Did he have a beard? Was he short? Please don't let him be shorter than me, I thought. And I knew it was stupid of me. I knew it was shallow, but I was taller than average and liked dating men taller than me. *It's not a date, it's not a date, it's not a date.* I kicked myself for getting my hopes up.

At the counter I ordered black coffee and started doctoring it up my favorite way—heavy on the half and half, with more than a touch of sugar. I stirred my brew, dropped my dirty spoon in a crock, and as I turned around with my mug in hand I heard a crash behind me. I'd knocked over the crock of clean spoons with my purse. Every head in the place swiveled to stare at me and I stage-whispered a "sorry" in an apology to the universe.

I set my mug on the counter and bent down to clean up after myself. The ceramic crock had survived but its embossed *clean* label was an utter lie. I began dropping the scattered spoons into the vessel, thankful that I hadn't made more of a mess.

"Let me help," a man said.

"Thanks," I said, grabbing another couple of spoons without looking up. "But it's my mess. I've got it."

His hand shot into view as he grabbed a spoon that I was about to reach. My fingers brushed the back of his hand and I jerked back. I muttered another apology and I looked up to his face. Warm brown eyes framed with thick glasses. A mess of brown hair with threads of silver at his temple and a friendly smile.

"No worries," he said from his crouch next to me. "Happy to help." He dropped the spoon into the crock I was holding before standing up.

I looked around to make sure we'd picked up all of the spoons and then I stood myself, readjusting my purse. "Thanks."

"Ali?" he asked, his smile growing.

"Ben?" He was handsome. I don't know what I'd been expecting, I couldn't have drawn a picture of what I expected, but I hadn't been expecting him. And he was taller than me.

"Yeah. You this graceful with a scalpel?"

I smiled and rolled my eyes at his tease. "I've got a great deal on some oceanfront property in Arizona that you might be interested in," I shot back, feeling my smile grow because with that simple exchange, I knew that the man I only knew through his words, the man who I liked because of his words, was the same man I found in front of me.

"I'm about to come into thirty pieces of eight or some gold doubloons on February thirtieth, so I think we can cut a deal. Nice to meet you, Ali," he said, the smile still on his face as he hoisted a messenger bag up on his shoulder and extended his hand for a shake.

"Nice to meet you," I said, shaking his hand. Warm and soft and enveloping mine—the crush I'd been secretly tending roared to life, making my heart do a little waltz. Maybe I could pretend this was a date in my head, to get ready for dating again. A secret practice date. Yes, that would work. I was on a secret practice date. I reached down to pet the yellow lab sitting neatly at his feet. "And nice to meet you, Thompson."

THIRTY-THREE

ALI

F *ebruary*

"CAN I GET YOU ANYTHING?" he asked.

"I've got coffee," I said, picking up my mug, "so I'm good, but thanks."

"Cool. Let me get something." I watched him walk to the counter and I reminded myself that I didn't know him. That a few friendly emails and a nice smile and a handsome face didn't make him a real friend, and that I didn't need to make my secret pretend practice date into anything more than it was.

While he ordered, I scored us two seats at a big communal table. A mug in hand, he found me and made a slight frown at the table full of people typing away on laptops.

"Mind if we get this to go?"

"Works for me. I'll nab a go-cup," I agreed, happy to explore and breathe fresh air that didn't have a hospital smell. Plus, the day was warm for February and the wind didn't bite through my coat.

"So Alice lived around here?" he asked as we stepped out on the sidewalk.

"That building across the intersection." I pointed. "The Astoria. It's condos now."

"It was really cool that the letters didn't have a street address. Just the hotel name."

"You've read them?" I was surprised because it hadn't even been a day since I sent him the link.

"Last night. I was printing out a set for my mom and I got sucked in."

"It's so easy to get sucked in," I agreed. "At first I felt like some sort of creep, peering into his letters, but—"

"It's not creepy. It's this amazing window into his life a hundred years ago." We crossed the street and stopped in front of the red brick building with its white stone trim. "I wonder when it was built?"

"1910ish," I answered, scanning the windows and wondering which one was Alice's.

"It was new when she lived here."

"What, five years old? And I don't know where she lived before she met Elliott. There are some letters to her at other addresses in the box with Elliott's letters, but those are later."

"Letters from another boyfriend? Did your Alice two-time my Elliott?" Ben teased, bumping his shoulder against mine.

"No, letters from her family and friends from her normal school," I said, bumping his arm back with my shoulder. "I think the only two-timing she did was with my great-grandfather and I'm not sure that counts."

"What's normal school?"

"Teacher's college," I explained. "That's what she was doing here. She was a school teacher."

"She and Elliott had that in common, then."

I nodded in response and sipped my coffee, savoring its warmth.

"Elliott was married before my great-grandmother," Ben said.

I turned toward him, thoughts roiling in my brain. But Elliott wasn't married to Alice. All of the evidence I had said they weren't married.

"To Alice?" I asked because maybe I was wrong.

"I thought so. Well, my mom thought so. She'd heard rumblings that he'd been married before Pearl, but it wasn't something she actually knew anything about. And she'd never looked into it. So, when she learned about the love letters, she was convinced that your great-grandmother was Elliott's first wife."

"She wasn't," I said, certain that they weren't married. "They weren't married."

"I know. We did some research. Turns out he was married to a woman named Penelope."

My breath caught in my chest as I fit the puzzle pieces together. "Penny Powell? But she married his friend—"

"Joseph Carlisle. I know that from the letters now."

"He was sent off to Europe in World War I," I said, straining to remember what Elliott had written about Penny and Joseph.

"I don't have the image of the marriage license, but the

index online shows Elliott marrying a Penelope Carlisle in July 1919. She died less than a year later."

"Wow," I said, blown away by the revelation. "I guess Joseph died in the war and then Elliott married his friend's widow?"

"Yeah. That's my guess too, so it was pretty cool to see Elliott's future wife show up in his letters to Alice. Family secrets come to light through the wonders of the internet. Want to keep walking? Thompson's up for it," he said with a nod down at his dog.

"Sure," I said. "Mind heading down to the waterfront? I know it's touristy, but—"

"Sounds like a plan."

As we walked, I peppered him with questions about his research skills. He brushed it off, claiming that he didn't have any skills. He just had a computer, paid subscriptions to a few services, a message board where he asked serious genealogy buffs for help, and a mother who kept pestering him to find out whether Alice was Elliott's first wife.

"Never underestimate the power of my mother to get me to do stuff. Even at forty," he confessed with a self-deprecating huff of laughter.

"You're forty?" I said before I could shut my mouth.

"Yeah. Something wrong with being forty?" The tease was back in his voice and he sipped his drink.

"No. Absolutely not. I mean, this sounds strange, but I hadn't given you much thought. I've spent all the time thinking about Elliott, but I hadn't thought much about you." It wasn't true, but it wasn't a lie. I'd thought about Ben a lot, in this abstract sort of way. But until he'd mentioned meeting up, I hadn't thought about him in a way that meant wondering what he looked like, what he sounded like, whether I would melt in the soft chocolate that was his eyes. The answer to that question was an unequivocal yes.

"It's not really fair. I don't have much of a web presence."

"Okay, I'll admit I looked you up online, but how do you work in tech and not be all over the internet?"

His smile crinkled the corners of his eyes and he tapped the side of his nose twice. "I work in data and I'm a private person."

Wanting privacy made sense to me. It was amazing what I'd been able to find out about Elliott through genealogical records and that was before everyone started posting pictures of their dinners on social media. "Did you look into Alice?"

"Some. Saw that she married. Found an image of her marriage license to your great-grandfather. Her name wasn't Alice Keller on it, so I thought maybe they'd been married in secret. Alice Hirshhorn to Frederick something."

"Wertheimer," I said. "She was Alice Lenore Hirshhorn Wertheimer and I'm Alice Lenora Waller."

"You're a Lenore?"

"Alice Lenor-a. My parents wanted to make it slightly different from Alice's name."

"Still beats Wilbert."

"I'm not arguing that," I said with a smile, happy to discover that being with Ben in person was as easy as emailing with him.

"But that's about all I learned about Alice. My mom

has had me chasing down rabbit trails on our family tree since then."

"It's kinda fun. It's like your own personal mystery to solve." I looked up and down the street, trying to imagine what it looked like a hundred years ago. "There would have been trolleys all around here," I remarked more to myself than to Ben.

"I still wish. It's all buses now, except these two electric street car lines that don't quite go where you want them to go. Did you know that the transportation is such a nightmare that some of the big employers have their own shuttle systems around the city?"

"You're kidding me."

"Nope. The children's hospital has one, and there goes a Microsoft shuttle right now," he said, pointing to a white van.

We kept walking toward the water and fell into silence. "How long have you lived here?" I asked, knowing the answer, but looking for something to talk about.

"About four years. I've been in Silicon Valley and Phoenix off and on."

"And your parents?"

"Issaquah. It's a suburb where I grew up."

"You're a native Seattleite?"

"Yes and no. Suburbs aren't exactly the city. Seattle is its own thing. You know about the troll? Or the gum wall? Or the mystery soda vending machine?"

"You had me at troll. My sister lives in Austin, which claims to be weird, but I don't think it has a troll."

We walked through Pike Place Market, checking out the crafts vendors, and the fish, and the cheese and veg, and the random specialty foods, but we were mainly weaving through tourists with Thompson right by Ben's side. The dog was aloof and although I'd petted him hello when we'd met, he hadn't paid much attention to anyone or anything other than Ben, even in the crowded market with its fish displays and butcher shops.

"I gotta get out of here," I said after a bit. "Too many people."

"Agreed," said Ben.

On the sidewalk, the daylight was golden. "Do you know how to get down to the waterfront?"

His head tilted a few degrees to the right. "Want to see where his ship would have left from?"

"Yes," I said with a smile, thankful he understood. "I know it's completely different. Just like the Astoria and this market—was Pike Place even around then?"

"Let me check," he said, pulling out his phone and tapping away on the screen. "1907, so yes."

"Is the art museum far?"

"Umm—Is it bad if I say that I know it's downtown, but I'm not quite sure?"

"Nope. My great-grandfather had a shoe store near there and Google told me that the building was torn down, but really—I don't want to drag you and Thompson all over the city as my hijacked personal tour guide. I've got my phone to get me around."

"Not a problem at all. It's a Saturday, and we don't have any plans."

"Well, I don't want to keep you," I said.

"Not keeping me from anything. Really."

"Oh. Okay. I didn't want your wife worrying about you hanging out in the city with some stranger you met online."

"Funny you should say that. Her running around the city with a stranger she met on the internet is why we're divorced."

"Ouch," I said, with a grimace, feeling terrible that I'd stumbled upon this particular topic. "I'm sorry."

"This way," he said, pointing to a set of steps. I followed him down to a park. "It's okay. It's fine. It's been a few years."

"That sucks."

"Yep," he bit out. "At least we didn't have kids. You have kids?"

"No. And I'm not married."

"Married to your job?"

"No. I'm an otolaryngologist. ENT is what we're normally called. The joke is that ENT doesn't mean 'ear, nose and throat' but means 'early nights and tennis.'" I thought about holding back, but I hadn't held things back from him yet and I didn't feel the need to start building a wall now. There was something freeing about being with him. He was warm and open and easy to be with and I felt safe in that. "Broke up with my boyfriend a few months ago. He dumped me."

"I guess now it's my turn to say I'm sorry."

"It's fine," I said, waving my hand in the air, batting away any trace of Scott lingering in my psyche. "He's in California. I'm in Missouri."

"Ah, the long distance thing. I gave that a try after college. Disaster."

"Well, this wasn't his fault at all. He's from Orange County and the plan was that we'd move there after our fellowships ended, but I didn't get the job I wanted and that's how I ended up in KC on this contract."

"Worth it?"

"Yeah," I said, pushing out a breath and realizing it was true. It wasn't a decision that I regretted. "I really wanted to be at a big hospital. I specialize in ear surgeries and cochlear implants, and while I could do tubes and sinu-plasties at any hospital, that's not why I chose the specialty. I was a computer science major in college. I like geeking out on the tech of what I do. Don't let the two x chromosomes fool you. This girl likes math."

"Very cool. I was a humanities major. Anthropology."

"How'd you go from anthropology to doing whatever computer thing it is that you do?"

"I'm really good at math too. I didn't realize it until my junior year of college though. I was doing some summer work for a professor. We were compiling and analyzing data about *quipus*—Inca talking knots—it's rope that looks like a mop when it's not unfolded. All of the strands have different styles of knots at different intervals. It's mainly an accounting system—census, crop yields, and the like, but there's also a color code that's still somewhat of a mystery. I ended up helping a few professors out with some research and I found I really had a knack for the data analysis side of the world."

"That's the most amazing career path ever," I said, truly impressed by how he'd stumbled upon his talent.

"It's pretty random, but what I do is a good fit for me. And it's probably no more random than a school teacher becoming a vice president of an oil company."

The bay at our right, we strolled along the wooden pier toward the towering Ferris wheel, stopping at the very end of the pier and gazing out at the water. I looked up at the Ferris wheel, wondering what the view was like at the top.

"We can ride it, if you want. Really commit to the whole tourist thing."

"Ehhh," I said, refocusing my gaze out across the bay to the islands in the distance, blue and purple in the waning daylight.

"Or we can snag a table and a couple of drinks and watch the sun go down."

"I think you read my mind."

"Follow me."

THIRTY-FOUR

ALI

F*ebruary*

W<small>E REVERSED OUR COURSE</small>, weaving through the thinning crowd of tourists as the sun began to sink lower. "I looked up his ship," Ben said. "Elliott's. The letterhead from the ship he took on his way back to the Philippines—the *Sado Maru*. I found some pictures of it online."

"I hadn't even thought to look up his ship."

"It was used for Japanese troop transport in World War II and was sunk during the war."

"Wow."

"Yeah." We settled in at a small table on a wooden pier, overlooking the water. "Beer or wine?"

"In the land of plenty up here, I'd say wine for right now?"

"No wrong answer. But do you drink beer?"

"Oh, yeah I do. The sun goes down so early," I said, zipping up my down jacket against the chill.

Ben poured water into Thompson's portable bowl. "Do you trust me?" he asked.

"With my life? I mean, maybe?"

A dimple appeared in his left cheek when he smiled at me. "Let's start with beer and see how that goes."

"Deal. Want to split a tasting flight?"

"Sounds great."

He ordered the beer, waters, and a bowl of roasted nuts from the server before turning back to our conversation. "And yeah. The long winter nights take some getting used to, but the long summer days make up for it."

"I'd imagine. Hey," I said more to Thompson than to Ben, after he'd walked me through the four beers, taking a sip from each small glass before passing it to me. "Do you think he'd mind if I pet him again? I miss having a dog."

"Mind?" he scoffed. "Yeah, not at all. He hasn't been able to take his eyes off you since you met."

I rolled my eyes at his playful exaggeration. "That's a lie. He looks at you nonstop, like you've got some bacon in your pocket."

I wished that Thompson had paid more attention to me, but more than Thompson, I really wished that Ben hadn't been able to take his eyes off me because I knew I hadn't been able to keep mine off him.

"Thompson," Ben said, pointing his finger at the ground next to my chair. Thompson got up and sat next to me, and I ran my hand across his fur. "Release," Ben said, and I felt Thompson settle into my pets, leaning into my hand, and coaxing me to rub him behind his ears.

"He's really well-trained. So chill for a lab."

"That he is. So why did you become a doctor?"

"Genetics, I guess. Both my parents are doctors and my brother is. My sister is the smart one and is a physical therapist, but her kids keep her busy so she works part-time right now. What about your sister?"

"She teaches art in a small town up near the Canadian border. She's married and has three kids."

"My brother is in KC, and getting to be the cool aunt to his kids has been a big plus of being home this year."

"Could you stay in Kansas City?"

"If I really wanted to I could, but there isn't an immediate need for my specialty there. And it's a good time in my life to explore."

We watched the sun dip down behind the islands across the bay. The sky was streaked with orange and purples, the water shimmering with silver and gold. And I kept sneaking glances at his profile. Could there be something? If I moved here? Could we be friends? Could we be more? Because I'd like that. I'd like more time with him.

As the deep, inky purples of evening filled the sky, I picked up the tiny glass of golden ale and held it toward him, realizing that he hadn't had much of the beer. "Want it?"

"Nah, that's cool. You enjoy it. Think you'll get an offer?"

"Yeah," I said, finishing the glass. "I'll be honest and not modest about it. I'm kinda expecting one. They were serious enough for someone to observe me in surgery, and with surgical position interviews, that's a big step. But I've got a few more months left on my contract in KC, so no one is in a rush to make me an offer."

"I hope it works out, then."

Me too, I thought with a nod. The gulls cried overhead and boats blew their horns.

"This afternoon has been really nice," I said, realizing that our time together had come to a close and I needed to let him go back to his life. My secret practice date was in the books. Too bad my date didn't know that we'd been on one of the best dates of my life. If this were a real date, I'd be staring at my phone for the next few days, begging for it to light up with his call.

"It has. You need to get back to your family or do you have time to grab dinner? I need to eat."

"I can do dinner," I said, happy that our secret practice date wasn't ending, that we were going to get to hang out more. "Let me text my sister to let her know that I'm alive." I took out my phone and began to text Jess.

"Can I see that?"

"Sure?" I offered him my phone. He held it up and I heard it make the shutter sound.

"Sending her a picture. Proof of life. You look happy." He tapped away at the screen.

"Sunset, beer, ocean, Thompson…this," I said, biting back against my instinct to say *you*. "Life doesn't get much better."

"Sent her my phone number too. Sign of good faith in case this hostage situation gets dicey," he said, handing me back my phone.

A thumbs-up from Jess popped up on the screen and I shoved it back into my jacket pocket. "Worried that she won't want me back, like in *The Ransom of Red Chief*?"

"What's that?"

"It's a story by Mark Twain or someone like that. It's about some bad guys who kidnap a child, but the child is so awful that the parents don't want him back and so the bad guys have to pay the parents to take the kid back."

"Yeah, not that at all. I was hoping that you'd develop Stockholm Syndrome."

I felt heat rise on my cheeks as I let out a short laugh. He was flirting with me and I liked it. Maybe my pretend practice date wasn't all in my head. "There's a good chance it's headed that way. Where to for dinner?"

"There's a place not far from here that serves really good fish."

"They're cool with Thompson?" I knew Seattle was laid back, but I also knew pets weren't universally welcome in restaurants.

"No worries. Everyone's cool with Thompson," he said. "You want to walk him some?" Ben asked after he'd settled up our beer tab.

"Absolutely." I took the lead from him, our fingers brushing against each other and sending sparks down my spine. I wanted to twine our fingers together, but I didn't want to be weird. Even though he felt like someone I'd known for a long time, we'd just met in person and I didn't want to be some desperate, clingy girl who mistook friendship for something more.

Ben didn't have those same worries because as soon as I got Thompson's leash situated in my right hand, he took my left in his, leading us to dinner. And I couldn't have wiped the smile off my face if I tried. We didn't talk much on our way to the restaurant and I didn't care. I was with him and he wanted to be with me. He wanted to hold my hand. And that happiness I'd found with him on the pier while watching the sun set hadn't faded. It grew.

"Ali," he said, slowing down our pace as the restaurant

came into view. "I didn't move home from Arizona because of my mom. I moved home because of my mom and my marriage and because I needed to be in a city with public transportation and where I could walk to everything I needed. Thompson isn't my pet. He's my service dog. My diabetes isn't well controlled sometimes and he alerts me when my blood sugar gets out of whack. He's faster than the technology by about ten minutes. It's pretty amazing."

"Oh," I said, processing what he'd just shared, and realizing that he'd kept it from me because he wasn't sure he wanted me to know. I looked down at Thompson and noticed that Ben had dressed Thompson in a simple leather collar and leash and not with a vest or other markings that would tell the world that Thompson was anything other than a pet.

"Yeah, I don't like to make a big deal out of it, but because he's a service dog, he can go anywhere with me. Restaurants, coffee shops, airplanes. And he's with me all the time, even when I sleep."

I looked down at the yellow lab at the end of the braided leather leash I was holding. Thompson sat patiently, looking up at Ben for direction with his big brown eyes.

Ben reached down and scratched him behind his ears. "Good boy," he said softly.

"That's really cool."

"Yeah?" Ben said, turning his face to me. His eyes were open in surprise and I could tell he was waiting for the judgment.

"Of course."

"And I don't drive, which is—"

"Ben?"

"Yeah?"

"It's getting cold. Think we can keep talking inside?"

"Oh, yeah. Of course."

At the hostess stand, Ben asked for a table for two. The hostess looked at Thompson and paused. "He's a service dog," Ben said. "Diabetic alert."

"Okay," smiled the woman. "Right this way."

"Type I?" I guessed as I studied the menu with Thompson at Ben's feet.

"Yes." He pulled out his phone, studied the screen, and tapped away.

Clearly, I'd overstepped my bounds and he didn't want to talk about it. I should have known better than to ask about someone's medical condition. "Listen, I don't want to pry, so I won't ask more. I'm sorry."

He laid the phone down and held his hands out wide. "Ask away. I was just checking my glucose."

"You have a pump?"

He nodded. "Yeah, and the continuous monitoring is sent to my phone."

"Okay, so you know I do cochlear implants and am a bit of a med device geek, but the tech on those pumps has made major leaps. It's pretty astounding."

"You're telling me. Huge change from when I was jabbing myself in the stomach all the time."

The waitress took our orders and I asked for a glass of wine.

"Water for me," he said and I knew better than to question him about what he wanted and what he needed. "And while we're on the subject of me coming clean, my mom's cancer scare wasn't the only reason we made the move. It was a lot of things. My ex and I are both from around here, so family was nearby. We both missed the green and we thought a big change of scenery would help. It didn't. And, what I was telling you before—I don't like to drive."

"Related to your diabetes?"

"Yeah. I blacked out while I was driving. The one and only blackout in my life. It was bad. My ex was in the car. We were arguing and I hadn't eaten and... She's fine, she's fine." I wasn't sure who he was reassuring, me or himself. "Everyone is fine, but I got Thompson and I don't like to drive unless I have to. So I needed to be somewhere with public transportation and Seattle, as much as the traffic is a nightmare, was the answer."

"Are you glad you came home?"

"Yes," he said. "It was a good move. You ready to leave home?"

"Yes and no," I said before I paused to think about my answer, and gave him the truth. "Well, this sounds silly to say out loud, but I'm ready to find a home."

"Seattle is a good one."

"We'll see."

Back on the sidewalk after dinner, it was my turn to make things awkward. "Well, it's been fun," I said, trying to figure out how to end this date that wasn't a date but was feeling more and more like a date every second.

"You ready to get rid of us again or do you want to hang out some more?"

"I'm not trying to get rid of you. And I'd never try to get rid of Thompson."

"Then don't."

"My flight isn't until midmorning, so I've got, what? About twelve hours to kill?"

"Who needs sleep?"

"Exactly. Who needs sleep when there's a gum wall and a troll and lots to explore?"

"You really want to see chewed up wads of gum stuck to the walls of an alley?"

"Is it far from here?"

"No, but it's gross."

"If this might be my new home, I think I need to see it. Warts and all."

"Your funeral. Oh—" He stumbled over the words, and in the streetlights I could see his face pale from embarrassment, the happy dimple slipping away. "I'm so sorry. I'm so, so sorry."

"It's fine," I said, and this time I reached for his hand. "Really, it's fine. Lead the way."

The gum wall was indeed gross.

"Other cities have love locks on bridges or shoes on trees. Why in the world is this here?" I said as I marveled at the slight sweet stench, even on a cool night.

"Yeah, Austin keeps trying to say it's weird, but Seattle is weird. Ready to go? Hey, I mean, let's keep walking and talking, and I swear that I'm not a germaphobe, but this alleyway is starting to make my skin crawl."

"No worries. Remind me to write you an antibiotic script," I joked, pretending to touch the gum and enjoying the gagging face he made in response. "I'm going to ask Jess if Austin can top this. Hey, can I share something that I didn't before?"

He stopped his playacting and looked at me square in the face.

"It's not about me, and it's not about you." And I saw the breath he was holding escape and his shoulders relax.

"I think Elliott was a POW in the Second World War."

"Really?" He turned to walk out of the alley and I went with him, hand in hand.

"I think he was held by the Japanese for years. One website lists him as the longest-held civilian during the war. And your great-grandmother Pearl is listed on another POW site, along with your grandfather and his brother. Your great uncle Eugene? He didn't survive the camp."

Ben blinked at me a few times, but didn't say anything for a long moment.

"There are Red Cross indexes of POW records online," I said, not sure what else to say other than to give him facts.

"I didn't know that. I don't know if my mom knows that. She never said anything."

"I can send you the link. Where to next?"

"The art museum isn't far."

"Cool."

"I really don't think my mom knows that. But that also explains why she doesn't have any pictures of them from before they moved to California. She said she thought there'd been a house fire at some point and family stuff had been lost."

"More like the entire world was on fire."

"Yeah."

"I'll give you the pictures. She can have them, but the letters—"

"I'm not taking Alice's letters."

"Oh," I huffed out. "Thanks. I know it's weird, but—"

"They aren't mine to take."

"What can you tell me about Elliott?" I asked as we

strolled past the art museum. "Because I've got this whole idea of him in my mind and I'm really curious about how much is completely wrong."

"Not much, to tell you the truth. My mom said that Elliott was serious and quiet and liked classical music and opera. I still can't get over the whole POW story. Years being captive? Not knowing if your family was alive? Not knowing what would happen to you? Man."

"Maybe he didn't want to share? Maybe they didn't want to remember? I read about the place he was kept. The Japanese moved a lot of the important—and valuable, I guess—prisoners to one camp in northern China. The rest of his family was held in Manila. I kept hoping it was another Elliott Keller, but the pieces kept coming together."

We slipped into silence, walking with our fingers still laced together.

"How far away is the troll?" I asked.

"A long way. Not walkable."

"And the mystery soda machine?"

"Also a hike. Back toward where we came from and then farther. If you're going to live here, you're going to have to learn the bus system."

I glanced at my watch and wondered if my sister was going to kill me for leaving her alone all day. I hadn't heard from her since the thumbs-up at sunset. "Troll or soda machine?"

"If I had to pick? Troll. But this is your tour."

"Troll."

THIRTY-FIVE

ALI

F*ebruary*

"Is now when you tell me that you're really a psycho killer, and instead of me luring your mom into some sort of scam, this has been a scheme to lure me into a well in your basement?" I asked when we stepped off the bus in a quiet residential neighborhood.

"Your skin is pretty on you. Let's keep it that way. And I think the serial killer confession is more of a second date topic."

Second date. Somewhere this had turned into a real date, not just the imaginary date I'd wished for, and I couldn't stop the happiness that bubbled up inside me at the idea of going on a second date with Ben.

"You want to hold his leash again?" Ben offered.

"I would, but I don't want to take him from you."

"He's not a guide dog, so you're more than welcome to walk him."

"Yeah, I'd like that," I said, happily taking Thompson's leash and wrapping it around my hand.

"It's this way," he said and we began to walk. "*Star Wars* or *Star Trek?*"

"Eh…" I said, cringing slightly. "Is this over if I say neither?"

"Nope. I kept going when I found out you like licorice," he said, taking my hand in his again, and sending a thrill of happiness directly to my heart.

"Good. Because here's a critical one. Toilet paper over or under?"

He looked at me sideways, the dimple in his left cheek more pronounced in the shadows cast by the streetlights. "You're going to have to explain that one."

I wiggled my hand free from his and with a series of awkward gestures, tried to show him how toilet paper could be installed to hang over the roll or under the roll.

"If I say that I've never thought about it, is this over?"

"No, I think that's fair. I'm an over-the-roll girl, and as long as you're neutral, we won't have a problem."

"I'm Switzerland when it comes to toilet paper."

"Swiss chocolate, yes. Swiss watches, yes. Swiss toilet paper? Probably not so much."

"To be fair, I've never thought about toilet paper as much as I am right now."

"I get it, but we're hitting the high points. You're neutral on toilet paper and I'm indifferent in the Luke Skywalker versus Captain Kirk debate. What else do we need to cover?"

We came to a stop under a street lamp and this time he

took both of my hands in his, pushing my hand through the loop of the leash so that we could weave our fingers together. "I like you, Ali."

Thompson sat on my foot and I giggled and Ben's dimple disappeared as the smile fell from his face.

"Oh, I'm not laughing at you," I said, regretting anything I did that made him feel that I didn't like him. "That was a happy laugh. I'm happy. You make me happy."

"It's Thompson, isn't it? All the ladies love Thompson."

"Now you're fishing for a compliment," I scolded him with a smile on my own face.

"And did I catch one?" His dimple was back.

"How's this?" I said leaning toward him and hoping that he'd do the same. Hoping that the hand-holding and the I-like-you weren't simple friendliness.

And that bit of worry evaporated when he leaned forward, our mouths a hairbreadth apart, and whispered, "Best compliment ever," before his lips landed on mine, filling me with a happiness I hadn't even dared to imagine would find me. "He's watching us," Ben said when we parted.

"Who?" I said, worried.

"The troll." He pointed under the overpass, and in the deep shadows the torso of a giant rose from the ground.

"Whew," I said. "So glad. Worried it was that psycho killer."

~

IT WAS LATE WHEN THOMPSON, Ben, and I walked into the hotel lobby. "Well, thanks for seeing me back," I said.

"Let's not do that," Ben said, renewing his grasp on

Thompson's leash and looking at me straight in the eye. His dimple wasn't anywhere to be seen.

"Do what?"

"The thing were we pretend that this day didn't happen. We're not doing that."

"Okay, but I'm going back to Kansas City in the morning."

"And you may end up here. And if you do, I'd like to hang out again. And if you don't, we can keep in touch."

"Ben," I teased, drawing out the sound of his name into multiple syllables and batting my eyelashes at him. "Are you asking me to be your pen pal?"

"Yeah," he said, huffing out a little laugh and lacing our fingers together again. "Let's start with that." The smile was back on his face. "It's been a great day, Ali."

"It has."

He leaned in toward me again, not demanding, but inviting me, inviting me to be here with him in this goodbye that I hoped wasn't a goodbye.

Back in my hotel room, I found Jess lounging in bed, watching a movie. "You're alive," she said clicking the TV off and sitting up.

"Yeah," I said, feeling bad for ditching her for a whole day. "I'm sorry."

"I'm not. So it was a date?"

I nodded and tried to keep my smile reasonable and not the million-watt version that was trying to light up my face. "Yeah, it was a date." I set my purse down and took off my shoes.

"Oh Ali, that's great. And I won't tell anyone. But if anyone asks, you were exhausted and crashed out and ordered room service and that's why you missed dinner with everyone."

"I didn't know we were doing a big family dinner. You should have told me. I would have come."

"Executive decision. You needed your date more than you needed a dinner where Becca threw a roll at Charlie and then Charlie took the lid off his cup and poured milk all over the floor."

"That sounds less than awesome."

"It wasn't their finest moment. Made me glad that mine are older. Heads up though. Patrick wasn't exactly thrilled about you being MIA."

"He'll get over it. I'm going to go get cleaned up."

By the time I'd showered the long day off me, brushed my teeth, and put on my pajamas, Jess had turned off the lights. I carefully navigated in the darkened hotel room, trying to find my bed without tripping over anything.

"Time for my bedtime story." Her voice wasn't drowsy or sleepy. She was very much awake.

"Okay?" I asked, crawling under the covers of my own soft hotel bed.

"Last night it was Alice and Elliott. Tonight, I want Ali and Ben."

"I don't know what to say about it."

"You spent over eight hours with him and you don't know what to say? That's ridiculous. Spill."

"We clicked, I guess."

"You two turned a quick coffee into a whole day. You definitely clicked. Now tell me about him."

And I did. I told her about his cute dimple, and his glasses, and that he was funny in a way that made me laugh, and how he was a data whiz, and about Thompson, and how he'd given me a tour of the city.

"He give you a tour of his place?"

"Jess!" I lobbed a pillow at her bed. "I just met him!"

"Sorry. I couldn't help it." She giggled.

"What's next?"

"If I get the Seattle job, we'll see each other again. If I don't, we'll keep in touch. He's a cool guy."

"And you're a cool girl, Ali. Really. He'd have to be stupid not to like you."

∾

WAITING at the gate for my flight home the next morning, I opened my text thread with Jess and saved Ben's number that he'd sent to her from my phone.

Me: *Hey. It's Ali.*

Ben: *Hey. At the airport?*

Me: *Yeah.*

Ben: *Next time you come, I'll make good on the mystery soda machine.*

Me: *Fingers crossed on the job offer then.*

Ben: *Got other options in the pipeline?*

Me: *Orlando is a definite possibility.*

Ben: *That's moving in the wrong direction.*

Me: *Right direction is toward Seattle?*

Ben: *Right direction is to Seattle.*

Me: *Gotta get an offer first.*

Ben: *You'll get it.*

Me: *Fingers crossed.*

Ben: *Fair warning. I'll be charming and try to convince you to take it.*

Me: *Fair warning. I'm not moving across the country for you.*

Ben: *Don't expect you to.*

Me: *Note: I didn't say I wouldn't move for Thompson.*

Me: *About to take off now.*

Ben: *All the ladies love Thompson. Text me when you get home.*

Ben: *You home?*

Me: *Yes. Busy week ahead. You?*

Ben: *More of the same. But tomorrow is sushi day in the cafeteria.*

Me: *Sushi! Your cafeteria is nicer than mine.*

Ben: *Welcome to tech. They throw us bones so we don't jump ship.*

Me: *And sushi is the way to do that?*

Ben: *The sushi chef at work is really good. He makes sushi for me that gets creative and feeds me while keeping my carbs in check.*

Me: *You have a personal sushi chef at work? I should have stayed in computers.*

Ben: *Not my personal sushi chef, and Hisao is a good guy.*

Ali: *Favorite vacation. Beach or mountains?*

Ben: *Why pick? Seattle has both.*

Ben: *Books or movies?*

Ali: *Books.*

Ben: *I can go either way.*

Ali: *Books always. My grandmother was a librarian. I've been a reader since I was five.*

Ben: *What are you reading now?*

Ali: *A murder mystery thriller. Do you read at all?*

Ben: *Mainly biographies.*

Ali: *You should write a biography of Elliott.*

Ben: *He's a fascinating guy. Found out that he testified before Congress about giving the Philippines their independence.*

Ali: *What side was he on?*

Ben: *Don't know yet. The records aren't online. I have to physically go to one of like three libraries in the country to get access.*

Ali: *He had an amazing life. No doubt.*

Ben: *Alice's wasn't too shabby either.*

Ali: *Not in the least.*

～

Ben: *The cafeteria had this killer tuna sashimi today. Yellowfin.*

Ali: *I had a protein bar between procedures.*

Ben: *You should have stuck with computers.*

Ali: *Nah. I helped a little boy get bilateral hearing.*

Ben: *I helped a company increase its share price. You win. Even accounting for the protein bar. No doubt.*

～

Ali: *Recruiter said it's down to me and another candidate. Fingers crossed.*

Ben: *You've got this.*

THIRTY-SIX

ALI

arch

"You're going to take it, right?"

Caroline stared me down over a margarita the size of her head, a celebration for surviving Bess's first birthday party.

After a few phone calls with the recruiter and folks at the hospital, I had gotten an offer letter in my email yesterday afternoon. "Yeah. I am," I said, biting my lower lip and nodding, amazed at my confidence in making this decision. It was the right move for me. It was an amazing move for me. And while I thought I might hem and haw over the decision, when I got the offer, I knew I'd take it. No hesitation or regret.

"Well, then," she said, nodding toward my equally huge

drink and hefting hers into the air. "I wish you every success."

We clinked glasses, trying our best not to spill our drinks and failing miserably. I grabbed some napkins to mop up our disaster while Caroline looked around in a mad panic before laughing.

"Okay, don't laugh at me, but I was just looking for the diaper bag to get some baby wipes to help clean up and had a bit of anxiety that I'd lost the diaper bag."

"Lost it and the baby."

"Not a baby anymore," she said, pulling a sad face.

"Big girl Bess," I agreed.

"I'm going to miss you. It's been nice having you home."

"Well, I'm not leaving tomorrow. You've got me until the end of May. And you can come visit me in Seattle anytime. Bring Bess and Stu. Or leave them at home."

"I'll leave them at home. Girls' weekend."

"Many of them." We toasted our glasses again in a promise.

"So you've told Ben?"

"Not yet."

"Why?"

"Because I don't want to move *for* him. I don't want him to think that I'm doing this for *him*. I'm doing this for *me*."

"And the possibility of him is part of that."

"Yeah," I said with a shrug, not denying that Ben was a part of the equation. But how big a part of the equation I wasn't sure. I ate some chips and salsa while Caroline sipped her drink and waited for me to talk more. "Here's the thing," I said with a big exhale, wiping my hands on a napkin. "I don't want to look back in twenty years and wish that I'd explored this with him. I don't want to have a file on a computer somewhere of all of our text messages and emails and let a big 'what if' haunt me."

"I get it. You don't want to be Alice with her box of love letters."

"Exactly. I'm not Alice. I'm Ali and I don't want that ship to sail without me."

~

WHEN I GOT home from dinner with Caroline, I texted Ben.

Ali: *Got the offer.*

Ben: *Awesome! Congrats!*

Ali: *Yeah, I'm pumped.*

Ben: *Happy for you.*

Ali: *I can't wait to get an annual pass.*

Ben: *Pass to what?*

Ali: *Disney World!*

Ben: *Oh, so Orlando. That's awesome.*

Ali: *Kidding. Seattle.*

Before I could text again my phone rang and lit up with *Ben Copley* bold across the screen.

I swiped it to answer and chirped a hello at him.

"You got the job!"

"I got the job!" I laughed at his excitement. In my mind I saw his face lit up in happiness.

"And you're taking it? You're joking about Orlando, right?"

"Yes. I'm joking. Yes. Absolutely I'm taking it. I'm

moving to Seattle. I got the offer yesterday and thought about it and I'm doing it."

"When do you start?"

"June."

"That's months away," he said, his voice getting serious, and I knew the dimple was gone.

"It is. And Ben," I said, sighing, wondering how I could tell him that this decision was mine. That it wasn't because of him, but also that it wasn't not because of him.

"You're not moving for me. Loud and clear. And, this sounds harsh and I don't mean it that way, but I don't want you to move for me."

"But I'm still moving in with you, right? Thompson is going to dig my hundred-gallon saltwater fish tank." The line filled with silence and I worried that he hadn't gotten my terrible attempt at a joke and that I'd ruined everything that was building between us by pushing too hard, too soon. "Kidding. I was kidding." I began to backpedal. "It was a bad joke. I guess I should wait until we have a second date and you tell me you're a serial killer before I joke like that."

"Well, I hate to spoil the surprise, but I'm not a serial killer. And we're not there yet, Ali, but that doesn't mean that we won't get there. But you'll come up to apartment hunt, right?"

"Yeah."

"So a second date? Mystery soda machine and maybe we can take a ferry to one of the islands and let Thompson run on a beach?"

"Sounds like a weekend."

"Let me know when and where and I'm there. And

without being creepy, I may have a few leads on places for you to rent."

"Not in your neighborhood?"

"I live near the troll in Fremont, which conveniently isn't far from the hospital, but I was looking more in Green Lake for you. Great trail around the lake to walk dogs and it's an easy bus to the hospital and to Fremont. I hope that's okay."

"More than okay."

THIRTY-SEVEN

ALI

M*ay*

TWO DATES. We'd had two in-person, face-to-face, real world dates. And countless emails and texts and calls and video chats. After I said yes to the job in Seattle, I'd gone up for a long weekend to scout apartments and walk my favorite dog and hang out with the man with the dimple and glasses who made me laugh. And now we were going to spend five days driving across the country. My things were being shipped and I could have shipped my car too, but when I'd floated the idea to Ben about him and Thompson coming with me on a road trip, I was nervous and played it off as a joke, because showing your cards is always scary. Two real dates and I was asking him to spend a week with me in my car? It was impetuous for me, but as I thought about the idea, I kept seeing us on the road together, exploring greasy diners and cheesy roadside attractions, and I screwed up my nerves and asked a week before I was supposed to leave KC.

"That sounds cool, but I don't drive, Ali," he said, his voice a simple statement, like my invitation might have been for us to go to the moon.

And it made me want to go on a road trip with him even more, to go on this little adventure with him because it wasn't something that either one of us would do alone. "In an emergency you can, right?" I urged him to agree.

"Yeah," he huffed, and I smiled, happy that he was going to say yes.

"We're good, then. You navigate and feed me caffeine and I'll pilot the ship."

And that's how I came to be standing just outside the security checkpoint with a poster clutched in my slightly sweaty hands. I was nervous. Because here I was, not only showing my cards, but pretty much offering up my heart on a silver platter.

"You should take a sign to the airport with you," Caroline had said a few hours earlier. We were out for one final lunch before my big move in the morning. My things, including what felt like half of a house that Grammie had given me, were on a truck bound for Seattle, and I was down to a suitcase and the overstuffed trunk of my car, with the box of Elliott's letters tucked safely inside.

"A sign?"

"Yeah, a funny sign for when you pick up Ben at the airport. Like the signs chauffeurs have, but the more ridiculous the better. It's a thing that's going around the internet. I picked up Stu from his business trip last month with a sign that said *Hello, Lover Boy.*"

"You did not." I'd been slightly mortified on behalf of her reserved husband.

"Okay, maybe I only thought about it, but it would be funny. You should do something."

"I don't know if that's Ben's style."

"He took you to see a wall of used chewing gum and a giant troll statue, so my money is on him being as goofy as you can be when you're not being a doctor. Come on, what was his nickname? Duke Ben?"

"Baron," I said, letting the idea of a silly sign at baggage claim roll around in my head. "Yeah. Baron Ben von Copley and Lord Thompson of Labrador."

Now, rocking my weight from foot to foot on the airport's floor, I looked down at the sign in my hands, the capital letters appearing upside down to me, and I decided to toss it in the trash. It was stupid and silly and if we were actually a couple—

"Countess Alice of Kansas!" At the sound of Ben's voice, my head popped up and my eyes immediately found him in the crowd. My heart settled in my chest, solid and warm.

"Ben!" I hurried over to him, not giving any thought to my sign or the people around us, and not even bothering to glance at Thompson. My favorite man with the glasses and the dimple was here.

The nerves I had were replaced with a sense of relief, of rightness, as he wrapped me up in a hug and whispered against my ear. "I missed you."

WITH THOMPSON in the back seat, we pulled up in the driveway of my parents' house for my farewell party.

"Last chance to back out."

"Nah," he said, swapping out his sunglasses for his regular glasses. "We're good. But I'm holding a marker for when we have to go to my parents' place."

"How bad can it be?" I said with a half-smile.

"Well, last time I was at their house, I realized my mom is an under-the-roll toilet paper person."

"Good thing you emailed me back rather than your mom, then." I stuck my tongue out at him and he laughed, the crinkles at the corners of his eyes letting me know that his joy was real.

"Absolutely," he said, his dimple falling away as he jutted his chin toward the front door where my big brother stood, giving my car an unimpressed stare. "Let's go do this."

~

AS THE PARTY WOUND DOWN, I left Ben hanging out with Stu and went into the kitchen to get another slice of Tippin's pie, and it didn't escape my attention that Patrick followed me in.

"Yes, Patrick," I said over my shoulder, while deciding to go all in and add a scotcharoo to my plate along with the generous wedge of coconut cream. I didn't know the next time I'd have a chance to enjoy my favorite Missouri treats and I was going to have seconds and perhaps thirds.

"I don't like the idea of you driving across the country with someone you met on the internet. I mean, he seems fine, but you never know."

I set the pie server down before turning to face him. "He's a good guy."

"Who you met on the internet."

"No, I met him through email. It's not like I was prowling dating sites or personal ads."

"I don't like this. I don't like you doing this."

"Noted. If it goes poorly, make sure to put a nice picture of me on the milk cartons."

"Ali…" He sighed in frustration.

"Patrick…" I answered, owning my bratty baby sister role.

"But you're still going to do this?"

"I am."

"He's got a serious medical condition."

"He's got diabetes. He's a grown-up, and I'm a doctor."

"Ali, it's serious. He's got a service dog."

"Thompson is amazing," I said, warning him to back down.

"No doubt," he said, holding his hands up in surrender.

"And I trust Ben to make good decisions about his own life."

"And he might be a cool guy. I just met him. I don't know him. All I know is that no one knows him, and that he's got a pretty serious medical condition, and you're going to spend a week in a car with him and his dog, driving across the country? What if something happens?"

"What if we have a great time? What if we decide to run away and join the circus or get matching tattoos?"

"Don't make me into the bad guy here."

"You're not the bad guy. And Ben's not a bad guy either."

"Hey," said Ben, stepping into the kitchen with us. "Did I do something?"

"Nope," my brother and I said in unison before Patrick turned on his heel and left Ben and me alone.

"Okay, well, that's good to know. I was looking for you and another Diet Coke."

"I'll get you one." I set my overfilled dessert plate down on the counter and reached into the fridge for a can, and awareness washed over me with the cool air. "Um, so, I have a sweet tooth," I said, full of guilt because I was enjoying something right in front of him that he couldn't eat.

"Not a deal breaker," he said, taking the can from me.

I looked at the coconut cream pie and square of peanut-butter-butterscotch-and-chocolate goodness and then back at him. "Sorry."

"Really," he said, popping open the soda can. "I mean, I don't run around apologizing how awesome it is to get to have Thompson with me everywhere, so you don't need to apologize for getting to enjoy sweets."

I looked at him carefully, trying to figure out if the comment was loaded with secondary meaning or if I should take it for face value.

"Really, Ali. I was diagnosed when I was nine. If people eating pie bothered me, I'd be a pretty miserable person. Enjoy the pie and don't sweat it."

"Sure?"

He picked up the plate and handed it to me. "Enjoy it. And later you'll tell me why your brother doesn't like me."

∿

WITH KC in my rearview mirror, I drove north with Ben next to me, and his yellow lab in the back seat. Because here we were, here I was, making a decision and going for it. Not regretting it. Not wondering what could happen, what might happen, but enjoying what we had while we had it. And I hoped we had it for a very long time, but I knew it was still fresh and new, so doubt lingered at the edges of my thoughts.

The Corn Palace, the Badlands, Wall Drug—I kept waiting for the shoe to drop as we watched the country fly by outside our windows. At each destination he took pictures of us and texted them to me so that I could send them to my sister and brother, supposedly as additional proof of life, but I knew better because the lock screen on his phone was me and Thompson walking the beach on Vashon Island. He'd taken it without me knowing it on my apartment search weekend. He was taking pictures of our trip for himself. And I liked that he was as happy to be with me as I was to be with him.

Mount Rushmore, Crazy Horse, and when we hit Wyoming, I was still holding my breath at times, waiting for us to find a deal breaker.

"Bagels or toast?" he asked as we crawled through the parking lot after watching Old Faithful.

"What about toasted bagels?"

"Bzzzz," he said. "Cheater. That's a foul. You must pick."

"Bagels," I said with a laugh because being with him just wasn't good, it was easy. "Are baked goods going to be a deal killer?"

"I'm reserving judgment as we work through this crushed ice versus ice cubes dispute."

"No room for dispute. Crushed ice is so much better because it's crunchy."

"It melts too fast. Is crushed ice what you and Patrick were arguing about?"

When we'd swapped childhood stories along the drive, I'd focused on me and Jess, pushing Patrick to the edges of the conversation. I'd tried to avoid this conversation and did the best I could to forget that Ben had walked in on my big brother in full big brother mode.

"Typical big brother stuff. He thinks you're some stranger on the internet and I've been lured to a chat room of doom where you'll kidnap me or something."

"The big hole that I dug in my basement works better for kidnapping you than a chat room."

"I totally agree. And how you lower a basket down with my food is super clever. Really, though, he's never been a fan of anyone I've dated—" My eyes went wide as the word escaped from my mouth and I was thankful I had my sunglasses on to hide behind. Whatever Ben and I were, we hadn't gotten around to slapping a label on it.

"Oh, I get that. My sister hated my ex-wife, but she likes you."

I kept my eyes on the road, but felt my forehead crinkle up in confusion.

"Your sister?"

"Yeah, she's glad that I have a girlfriend who isn't my ex-wife. But my parents also don't like the internet thing, so I've downplayed that."

"But it's not weird," I insisted. "Millions of people make friends and even end up with people they met online."

"I agree. Is it weirder to start talking to a stranger in a

bar or because the cosmos aligned so that you meet the descendant of a woman your great-grandfather fell in love with over a hundred years ago?"

"Bar. I hate small talk."

"Exactly."

"So it's the way we met? I've been texting your sister proof of life pictures, but I can loop in Patrick, if that makes everyone happier."

"It wouldn't make me happier. And he and I have been texting, so he knows I'm alive."

"You didn't answer my question, Ali," he said, the humor gone from his voice. "Did I do something to upset him?"

"Other than breathe?"

"Other than breathe or be divorced," he said with a nod. "Can't help either of them and I don't plan on stopping breathing any time soon."

"That's good to hear," I said with a smile, the ease of being with him letting me talk freely. "Patrick worries about me. I'm not delicate or breakable or anything like that, but despite our age gap and the boy-girl thing, we've always been close. He looks out for me. I can't tell him to stop. Well, that's not entirely true. I've told him a million times, but that's the way he is."

"And I worry him," said Ben.

"You're an unknown," I said, taking a moment before deciding to tell Ben about Patrick's other concern, which, like the breathing thing, he couldn't do much about. "He's worried that your health—" I could sense Ben's body tensing. Thompson shoved his head over the center console to check on Ben and then went back to lying down in the back seat. "It doesn't bother me. Your diabetes. It doesn't bother me at all."

"It *should* bother you, Ali. It's a hassle."

"No, it shouldn't. Hear me out. I know some things can't be fixed, but I do know some can be made better and that we can live even with the less-than-perfect parts. And if you'd tell a little boy that he's somehow worth less because he was born with a hearing deficiency, then we've got a problem that we won't ever be able to get past. Because that's not right in any sense. You're not worth less because you need insulin and Thompson. You're not worth less because you wear those sexy Clark Kent glasses. And I'm not worth less because—"

"Ali…" His voice was calm and he took my right hand in his. "I get it. I get what you're saying."

"Because I'm ten pounds overweight and have a crazy sweet tooth?" I said, finishing my rant with a joke, hoping to show him how much I cared for him. I glanced over at him, pulling my eyes away from the dimple carved in his cheek and forcing them back on the road in front of us.

"I was going to go with 'amazing,' but take your pick," he said.

As we drove, we talked more, talked about things that I'd only talked about with my sister after she and I had shared a bottle of wine, and we settled back into being us. Being comfortable and happy and right. We wound through the park roads until we found a picnic area to enjoy the lunch we'd bought from a grocery store that morning.

"I know we don't really know each other, but I feel like I've known you forever," he said, snapping closed the lid of the now empty plastic salad container.

"I know. I'm glad to find someone who doesn't mind my stinky salt and vinegar potato chips," I said, smiling and grabbing a few more chips from the bag I'd bought.

"It's the strangest thing, and I don't think it's the chips, and I hope I'm not reading this thing between us wrong."

"You're not reading it wrong on my end," I assured him, feeling so relieved at finally being able to talk about the connection between us.

"Think it's genetics?" He laughed, taking a swig from his water bottle before capping it.

"What's genetics?" I asked, lost at his comment.

"That something in our makeup got us to this place. That Kellers and—what was Alice's maiden name?"

"Hirshhorn." I balled up the wax paper that had held my turkey sandwich and began to pack up our things.

"Yeah, that Kellers and Hirshhorns have some sort of genetic affinity for each other? Because I've never been a believer in fate or destiny or anything like that."

I stilled my hands and looked at him. I really looked at him. I looked at the man in front of me in the bright spring sunshine, his eyes hidden behind sunglasses, wearing a T-shirt that had *terrific* spelled out in a spider web, his dimple letting me know he was truly happy, and I knew I could do this. I knew that we would do this. That we were in this place together.

"Me either," I confessed. "It's always been work."

"Yeah. The same. And I keep thinking about you and how this hasn't been work. It's like the opposite of work. It's easy. Wait, that's the wrong word. Easy sounds bad."

"No, it's not. This is easy."

"Good. I'm glad. And you probably don't want to hear about my ex-wife, but that was work from the day we met. I chased her and—oh, this isn't going well and I need to shut up."

"It's going fine. Keep going." Because I wanted to hear this from him. I wanted the confidence of hearing him say that we were in the same space. That this wasn't my wild imagination. That this was real.

"Anyway, it was work."

"I get that. I do."

"I'm not scared of work, and I know you aren't either, Madame Surgeon, but it's nice not to have to work so damn hard."

By the time we stood on the rim of the park's canyon in the fading daylight, I couldn't remember my life without him in it.

~

"WELCOME TO COEUR D'ALENE," he said from the passenger seat the next day.

"You've been here before?" I asked, surprised, because other than Yellowstone, the rest of the trip had been new to both of us.

"Maybe in another lifetime or alternate universe or maybe it's my first time." I looked over and he was tapping away on his phone. "I think this is near where Elliott got on the train when he met Alice. Take the next exit. There's a park near the lake and maybe we can let Thompson roam a bit." He called out directions and the lake appeared before us. Deep blue and sparkling in the afternoon.

"This has been a great trip," I said, picking up a smooth flat stone and skipping it across the surface of the lake as Ben and Thompson waded in the water.

"Four days and you're just now accepting that we're having fun?" he teased, that dimple I loved saying hello. "We always have fun."

"That we do. And we've got all of tomorrow too," I said, a little sad that our road trip was coming to an end and the real world was rushing toward us.

"Sure about that?"

"Yeah, I mean, unless you've got an idea about somewhere else to explore," I called to him. "No doubt the movers can hold my stuff for the right price. I've still got a week until I'm due at work and I don't know when I'll get my next vacation."

He stretched out a hand to me, inviting me in the water, and I stepped to join him, lacing our fingers together, the cool water a contrast to the bone-deep warmth I felt in his presence.

"Ali, I've finally got one that is a deal breaker," he said. Inches from me, he dropped his voice to a whisper. "Now or forever?"

"Both," I said, and under the bright sun, we kissed with Thompson splashing in the water around our feet.

THIRTY-EIGHT

ELLIOTT

J *uly 1937*

HE WALKS the waking streets of New York. From the steps of the Sherry-Netherland, he wouldn't know of the crisis. No visible breadlines on the Upper East Side. Summer is here in the city and as stifling as the locals think it is, it's not Singapore. His meetings don't begin until the afternoon, so he strolls through the park. The three weeks of travel since they'd left home have him discombobulated. He skirts the edge of the lake, the city all around, reciting all of the stops between here and home—London, Paris, Brindisi, Athens, Alexandria, Cairo, Gaza, Baghdad, Basra, Kuwait, Bahrain, Sharjah, Gwadar, Karachi, Jodhpur, Delhi, Cawnpore, Allahabad, Calcutta, Akgats, Rangoon, Bangkok and Alor Setar.

The walking clears his head and he begins to look for breakfast. Ten years ago was the last time he'd made this trek around the world, and then it was to be promoted to run the Asia division. Now he is back, this time to talk of war and alliances and plans to steady the company's future amid quickly shifting winds. A Japanese embargo is likely, but there is no doubt that even if the company ignored Japan, Japan would be paying keen attention to the company's oil wells and production facilities throughout the region.

He finds a narrow sidewalk café, and places his order with the server. He feels still as the world wakes up in a hurry around him. He removes his glasses and places them on the table, closing his eyes and turning his face toward the sun. The weeks of travel have made him dull and gray. The life in his limbs slowly returns as he basks in the sunshine. He's pulled from his languor as he feels eyes upon him. He opens his own eyes and returns his glasses to rest on the bridge of his nose.

He looks and there she is. On the other side of the hedge that separates the café from the entrance to a hotel. His breath catches in his chest. His heart seizes. The travel must have exhausted him more than he thought. *Alice*. In New York. Not a dozen feet from him. He blinks slowly to right himself, to gather his wits.

No, it is her.

The blue eyes that still appear in his dreams. The face he studied every night before he fell asleep for years is now softer with age.

It is absolutely his Alice.

He pushes to a stand and his napkin falls unnoticed from his lap to the ground. The only thing in the world he sees is her. He opens his mouth to speak, but he cannot find words. His mouth is dry and he's half convinced that this is some dream, some exhaustion-induced hallucination.

"Alice, sweetheart." She turns away from Elliott and toward a man, tall and neatly dressed with a head full of gray hair. "The concierge is going to get us tickets to *Babes in Arms* for this evening, if he can. If not, it will be tomorrow."

Elliott knows in an instant. *Her husband.* Of course, it's her husband. Did Elliott ever know his name? He can't recall, but the hurt at her choosing another—time didn't heal that wound entirely. And while it's far from fresh and gaping, it remains a tender pink scar.

Her profile is to him and he's back on that train, studying her in secret. Somewhere in Idaho, in an observation car. Fifteen years ago? Twenty? Twenty-five? A lifetime ago and yesterday at the same time.

He shakes his head, a wide smile pinching his cheeks, and he takes a half step toward her when he is stopped by her blue eyes focused on him. A sweet smile on the lips that he has longed to kiss, and her right hand raised to her chest in surprise, which she double taps, and a few words mouthed at him. He tries to decipher the unsaid words. He recognizes his own name on her lips.

"Elliott. Always."

He takes another step to her, now urgently needing to speak with her, to hold her, to kiss her, to burn down his entire world if it means that he can be with her again. She slightly shakes her head, takes her husband's arm and disappears down the bustling sidewalk.

"Your ice water and coffee, sir," says the waiter. "Is everything fine?"

"Yes," replies Elliott after a beat, retaking his seat. "All is well."

His family is with him this trip. He and Pearl will settle their boys into schools in New Hampshire, before retracing their path around the world. They will stay in Paris this time. For a week. See the sights. It will be his first real visit. They will attend the opera and stroll along the banks of the Seine at twilight, and then he will tell Alice all about it in the letters that he still writes her in his heart.

AUTHOR'S NOTE

On September 1, 1915, Erwin F. K. stepped aboard a train bound for Seattle, Washington, and settled in the observation car. He noticed a woman select a magazine from a stand and was taken by her. That evening, there was a mix-up with their Pullman berths and Erwin met my great-grandmother.

Five days later, he sailed for the Philippines and she remained in Seattle.

Over four long years and throughout the tumult of the First World War, he wrote her over forty letters. The last letter is postmarked a few months before my great-grandmother married my great-grandfather. And, although I wouldn't be here if Erwin had married my great-grandmother, my heart broke for Erwin when I read that letter.

I first found the box of Erwin's letters one summer when I was in high school. I spent a lazy day lying on the shag carpeting of my grandparents' living room floor, reading every last word Erwin wrote and imagining his life.

My grandmother explained they were letters that her mother had kept and she couldn't get rid of them, but she'd never read them herself.

While cleaning out the house after my grandmother's passing, my mother found the box of letters, and the letters came to live with me. They were the one thing I'd wanted from the house. Though, like Ali in the book, I got a lot more things from my grandmother's house, including the dresser with a secret drawer that makes an appearance in the story.

Genealogy doesn't contain Erwin's letters. Instead, I used Erwin and his letters as a jumping-off point for creating Elliott, and Elliott's letters to Alice.

But how do I know that Erwin met my great-grandmother on September 1, 1915 on a train bound for Seattle?

Luckily, on August 29, 1916, when they'd been separated a year, Erwin wrote a letter reminiscing about how they'd met. Borrowing details from Erwin's letters and expanding upon them and changing them has been a joy. I truly wish I'd been able to meet him.

One day I'd love to share Erwin's letters with his descendants. I'd also love to share the photographs that he sent to my great-grandmother. I've tried my own hand at genealogical research, and I haven't been able to locate Erwin's living descendants, but I'm not giving up.

Regardless of whether I ever find his family, Erwin will continue to live in my imagination, and I'll continue to treasure his letters.

I hope you enjoyed *Genealogy*, and that it warms your heart and inspires you to learn about the people in your life and those who came before you. Please consider leaving a review where you purchased this book.

XO - Mae

www.maewood.com

Mae@Maewood.com

DISCUSSION GUIDE

Suggested questions for a book club discussion or to think through on your own after reading *Genealogy*.

A printable version of this discussion guide is available at www.maewood.com

1. Elliott and Alice are kept apart by forces outside of their control and the fact that communication and travel in the early 20th century were too onerous to allow for long-distance love. Is their tragic love story a product of its time, or could modern couples similarly find themselves torn apart—despite cell phones, social media, intercontinental flights, and the like? What would a modern equivalent look like?

2. Is it possible to fall in love as quickly as Elliott and Alice did? Was their connection truly a lifelong love, or the

kind of passion that would have fizzled if they had been able to stay together?

3. How do you think Elliott and Pearl's marriage played out? Do you think she knew she wasn't the love of his life? Do you think Elliott told Pearl about Alice?

4. Ben's life seems to parallel Alice's in some significant ways. Like Alice, he lands in Seattle even though it is not his home town. In addition, they both have a health issue about which they feel self-conscious. Considering the parallels between Alice and Ben, do you think that Ali is Ben's Elliott or his Fred?

5. Grammie states that she does not want to know what was in the letters between her mother and Elliott. Would you feel the same way upon finding love letters between one of your parents and a previous lover?

6. How was Fred able to be so sanguine about Alice's love for Elliott? Do you think he would have been upset if he'd seen Alice mouth "Always" to Elliott when they catch a glimpse of each other in New York? What does Fred's acceptance of Alice's past with Elliott tell you about his love?

7. Why did Ali think that she and Scott belonged together? What did the letters teach her about relationships that she didn't know before the start of the novel?

8. What is the importance of female friendship in the book? How do Caroline and Frankie help keep Ali and

Alice grounded and how do they encourage them to dream?

9. If you were to name a child after a family member, what name would you pick and why?

10. If you were Alice, would you have made the decision to marry Fred or would you have continued to wait with the knowledge that you might never see Elliott again?

11. The author told the historical portions of the book in present tense and the contemporary chapters in past tense. How did this impact your understanding of the story? Why do you think the author made this decision?

12. Have you researched the life of any of your ancestors? Did you learn anything interesting or surprising? If you were to deeply research the life of one of your ancestors, whose life would you like to discover more about?

Discussion Guide prepared with the assistance of Emily Guy Birken, avid reader, book club enthusiast, and author of *The Five Years Before You Retire* and *End Financial Stress Now*.

ACKNOWLEDGMENTS

I always compare writing a novel to running a marathon. And even though I've only run 10K runs, I think the analogy holds well. Both writing novels and running marathons require working long hours before or after work, pushing yourself through darkness, perseverance through pain, and ignoring that little voice in your head that keeps asking if you should stop. *Genealogy* took me over two years to write.

For those who run with me - Lucy Score, Kate Canterbary, Claire Kingsley, Eli Carter, Melanie Moreland, B. Cranford, Hilaria Alexander, Zeia Jameson, Anne Conley, Maria Luis, Pippa Grant, Kathryn Nolan, Dylan Allen, Tess Woods (no relation, but I wish!), Karin Enders, my Manuscript Minxes, my Indie AFers, my Renegade Writers. Thank you for training with me on those long, pre-dawn runs.

For those who coached me - Julia Ganis, Becca Hensley

Mysoor, Emily, Kim, my first readers, and my beta readers. Thank you for believing in this book.

For those who kept me nourished, body and soul - My husband, my parents, my children, and my dog (who leant his name to a character in this book). Thank you for believing in me.

For those who cheer along the route, giving me support when I'm a hot, sweaty mess and unsure if I can take another step - The members of my reader group, Jess, Dawn, Mila, Karen, Stephanie, Sam, Meggie, Kenysha, Tasha, Natasha, the Jaimes, the Julies, Aerin, Deedy, Misty, Holly, Jodi, Joyce, Melanie, Michelle, Sarah, Erin, Peggy, Josie, Caitlyn, Cameron, Maggie, Taylor, Chloe, Greer, Valerie, Rebecca, Judy, Lori, Deidre, Kim, Beth, Jay, John, Joe, Em, Shantel, Lori, and everyone else. Thank you for wanting this book.

For Candy, who read my first book and then emailed me to ask if I'd write another. Thank you for the push. It was the first encouragement from a stranger I'd gotten and it meant the world to me.

For you who are reading these words — Thank you for taking a chance on *Genealogy*. I hope it exceeded your expectations.

ALSO BY MAE WOOD

Genealogy is Mae Wood's fifth novel. Her earlier books are
steamy, contemporary romances set in Memphis, Tennessee.

THIS TIME IS DIFFERENT

Life can change in a flash.

Marriage and a baby wasn't Amy Forsythe's college plan. After a
shotgun marriage glued together by her son, she's convinced
that love isn't meant for her. Now nearing forty and single for
the first time since her senior prom, her friends are pushing her
to date. Her teenager isn't thrilled by the idea and neither
is Amy.

Silver fox Thomas Popov isn't looking for The One. He found
her decades ago. And fell apart when she died. At fifty-three
with a new job, a new city, and an empty nest, he's focused on
climbing the corporate ladder.

When a softball accident lands Thomas in Amy's dental chair,
sparks fly.

Lightning doesn't strike twice. But love might.
This time is different.

Read *This Time Is Different* http://amzn.to/2y8RDuw

PLUS ONE

If you can stand the heat, there's a hot single dad in the kitchen.

At not-quite forty, Bert's going to be dining alone.

His restaurant's wine rep has a few ideas on how he might sate all of his appetites.

He hasn't been buying what she's been selling, but she's only in Memphis for a few months before moving back home to California.

Besides, it's not like he's going to fall in love for the first time in his life or anything crazy like that, right?

Read *Plus One* http://amzn.to/2vZVN6S

Learn about all of Mae's books at
https://www.maewood.com/books

ABOUT THE AUTHOR

Professional sassypants and novelist, Mae Wood has been a bookworm her entire life. She loves cheeses, complicated crafts that she'll start but never complete, and puns.

A while ago Mae decided that she needed to give up the fear that she couldn't write "great literature" and write what she wants to read. And she wants romance. And laughter. And real life.

So, what do you want to know about her? Drop her an email, ask questions, and she'll respond.

Keep in touch by signing up for her newsletter at
www.maewood.com

MaeWoodWrites@gmail.com

 facebook.com/authormaewood

instagram.com/maewoodwrites

pinterest.com/maewoodwrites

goodreads.com/MaeWood

bookbub.com/authors/mae-wood

CPSIA information can be obtained
at www.ICGtesting.com
Printed in the USA
LVHW090234071118
596278LV00001B/149/P